# Son of No One

# Son of No One

## SHERRILYN KENYON

St. Martin's Press
*New York*

SON OF NO ONE. Copyright © 2014 by Sherrilyn Kenyon. All rights reserved. Printed in the United States of America. For information, address St. Martin's Press, 175 Fifth Avenue, New York, N.Y. 10010.

www.stmartins.com

The Library of Congress Cataloging-in-Publication Data is available upon request.

ISBN 978-1-250-02991-1 (hardcover)
ISBN 978-1-250-02992-8 (e-book)

St. Martin's Press books may be purchased for educational, business, or promotional use. For information on bulk purchases, please contact Macmillan Corporate and Premium Sales Department at 1-800-221-7945, extension 5442, or write specialmarkets@macmillan.com.

First Edition: September 2014

10  9  8  7  6  5  4  3  2  1

*To my own special Welshman who's shared most
of his life with me. Love you more, every day.
And to the three boys who mean the entire
world to us both, and who proudly sport
Welsh names no one can spell or pronounce.
Love you all. Thank you for being the
best part of my life.*

# SON OF NO ONE

# PROLOGUE

*1045 AD*
*Wessex, England*

"No!" Cadegan shouted as he found himself trapped inside a dark, grayish hell. Furious at the betrayal, he tried to break the looking glass that served as his window into the human world he'd just been violently sucked out of.

Forever.

"Leucious! You can't do this to me! I'm your brother!"

But the words had no effect on the cold heart of the bastard half demon who stared at the glass without mercy or pity. And when those bright blue-green eyes locked with his, Cadegan knew for a fact that Leucious heard him.

And didn't care.

For centuries, Cadegan had given everything he had for Leucious. He'd served him loyally and with complete trust. Only to be damned without the benefit of a doubt. No questions asked.

Just misassumptions made against him, over an action he'd been forced to take to protect himself.

His beautiful features stern, Leucious splayed his hand on the glass that separated them. "God have mercy on you, little brother."

Still bleeding profusely from his wounds that Leucious hadn't even acknowledged, Cadegan snatched the conical helm from his head and slammed it against the glass. It made no impact whatsoever.

A single tear slid down Leucious's cheek. He wiped it away with an angry hand before he covered the glass with a black cloth. And consigned him to hell.

"Leucious!" Cadegan tried again. He kicked at the glass. His chain mail and spurs jingled, but again the glass held fast.

"Thorn!" he tried one last time to reach the brother who'd betrayed him. "Thorn! Come back!"

It was no use. Like everyone else in his life, and against his own promises that this would never happen, Leucious had abandoned him.

*"For crimes against Our Lord, for breach of my trust, I condemn you to the shadowed lands of your mother. No more are you to walk this earth as a living being. You will spend eternity remembering what you've done, and regretting your actions. You are no longer one of us. For that, you are sentenced and banished from the world of man. Forevermore."*

Leucious's words haunted him as Cadegan gnashed his teeth.

"I will escape this hell one day, brother. And when I do, yours is the heart I will claim first. A life for a life. Blood for blood! If it takes me a thousand years, I will be free and you will pay for this. So vows Cadwgwn Maboddimun! Your death, Leucious. My life! I swear it!"

# 1

New Orleans, Louisiana
September 18, 2014

"You know, Selena, there's a fine line between important to me, and dead to me. And you're currently stomping all over it."

Standing in the hallway, next to a stack of boxes, Selena Laurens laughed at her cousin's surly tone. "That's all right, Jo-Jo. Just remember with our Cajun-Romani blood, even if I'm dead to you, in either realm, you'll still be able to hear me. I will haunt you forever."

Josette Landry cringed at a childhood nickname that had always made her feel like a yappy Pomeranian. Normally, she'd correct Selena's usage, but at this point, she was too tired and soul-sick to bother. "Look, the only thing I want to summon right now is a trip to Baskin-Robbins. So unless you've got a quart of creamy goodness in your purse, stop talking and start driving." Jo gently tugged Selena toward the door and ignored the bells that jingled from the hem of Selena's silver and purple broomstick skirt. A self-proclaimed fortune-teller, her cousin bought into the weirdness of their gypsy heritage lock, stock, and both flaming barrels.

Jo paused as she swept a glance from the top of Selena's long, curly brown hair, white peasant blouse, and loud, statement moon necklace to her Birkenstock sandals.

Take that back. Selena didn't buy into it, she rolled around in the bad stereotype like a happy piglet in a mud factory.

Selena snorted. "Drowning your problems in Rock 'n Pop Swirl sherbet isn't going to solve anything."

"Forget sherbet. This day calls for Strawberry Cheesecake with fudge sauce . . . triple scoops. Now mush!"

"You'll hate yourself in the morning."

"I hate myself right now. At least let me hate my life with

the happy memory of yummy, frozen happiness in my bulging belly."

"Fine," Selena groused. "I'll even pay for it."

"Of course you will." Jo pulled her tattered messenger bag over her shoulder. "I'm broke."

Selena snorted again as she dug her huge, fluffy key ring out of her hippie wicker handbag. "You're not right, are you?"

"I'm genetically linked to your branch of the family. Of course I'm not all right. I'll *never* be all right."

Shaking her head, Selena waited while Jo locked her apartment door, though why she bothered, she had no idea. The only thing of value was her three dogs. And if the burglars were toting Beggin' Strips, they'd happily abandon her without a fight. Evil drooling canine snots.

Jo caught a glimpse of the boxes she'd been packing through the window and winced. If her lifelong run of bad luck didn't change soon, she would be out on the street and she'd be forced to turn her beloved dogs over to a shelter.

Or worse, her older sister.

How could it have come to this? This was not supposed to be her life. She'd never been irresponsible. While other kids went out drinking and partying, she'd stayed home and studied hard. Graduated at the top of her class. She'd scrimped and saved, and had lost her entire nest egg on lawyer fees when she'd divorced her husband for refusing to work. The reason being that if Barry Riggio was working, he wouldn't have time to screw other women in their bed, while Jo slaved away at two jobs to support them!

Yeah. She'd never felt more betrayed or hurt. *I won't ever trust another man again.*

And if that wasn't bad enough, corporate downsizing had cost her her day job, and she'd lost her night job six weeks ago after the factory had burned down from a freak electrical fire.

Overwhelmed by the failure of her life and ambitions, Jo turned toward the street and headed for the curb where Selena's Jeep was parked. If only Selena's husband and his law firm handled divorces, it might have saved her something. But Bill's specialty was corporate and criminal law, not family law. And while his attorney friend had given her a discounted rate, it'd still taken every dime of her savings to offload the cheating freeloader.

"What am I going to do, Lainie?"

Selena opened the car door for her. "Breathe, honey. This too shall pass. In the meantime I can—"

"I will *not* take a loan from you. Ever!"

"Will you take a job?"

Jo waited until Selena got into the Jeep on the other side before she responded. "I can't read tea leaves or palms. And if you put me in your store, be warned, I'm not sure I can leash my sarcasm."

"Yeah, I know you and retail are a bad combination. Your uncle Jacob is still railing at family get-togethers about the one *day* you spent working in his garage."

"Don't be so melodramatic . . . I only worked there for two hours before Aunt Paulina gave me the heave-ho."

Selena burst out laughing. "My point exactly. Anyway, as I value my customer base and respect them highly, I have no intention of putting *you* behind a counter where you'll single-handedly drive my business into the gutter. What I have for you, Ms. Snark 'Ems, is to do what you do best. Work as a camerawoman."

Jo perked up immediately. "Oh? Really?"

Selena nodded as she navigated through traffic. "There's only one small catch."

"Ah, gah, I knew it! It's for a porn site, isn't it?"

"No!" Selena screwed her face up, then appeared to consider it. "Although, knowing you, you'd probably prefer the porn over this assignment."

A sick feeling settled in Jo's stomach as she realized it had to be something paranormal, and dumber than dumb's widow's doorknob. "What?"

"I have some friends . . ."

"No! I've met your friends. I'd rather work at Tabitha's triple-X-rated store, sorting glittered pasties and edible thongs."

"I can arrange that, too. Just remember, you have to learn the difference between K-Y and—"

"Stop! Right there! I don't want to know about your sister's depravity. I'm still scarred from the story she told of finding someone's dentures in the back thong drawer."

"You're such a prude."

"Me and Amanda. The sole bastions of nonlunacy in a long line of certifiable nutsos."

Selena paused at a light to glare at her. "Do you want me to tell you about the job or not?"

"Fine," Jo conceded reluctantly. "I'll listen, and at least I can jump out of the car from here and walk back."

Selena snorted. "My friends are trying to get their own cable show."

Jo suddenly regretted her snottiness. "That actually sounds promising. What kind of show?"

"*Hell's Calling. The Women of Demonology and Possession.*"

"Hello, detour back to the No-way-in-hell-will-I-do-this exit ramp."

"Fine." Selena turned left. "Just out of curiosity, I know it's been almost five months, but have you told your parents yet about the divorce, and your foreclosure notice?"

"I hate you, Selena."

"No, you don't. You love me with the passion of a thousand paparazzi after an Emma Stone exclusive."

Jo blew her cousin a raspberry. "You keep believing those lies."

"Not lies. I'm psychic. I *know*."

Amused and disgusted, Jo rolled her eyes. As much as she hated to admit it, Selena was right. She loved and adored her quacky older cousin more than anything. Lunacy and all. "How much does this job pay? And when would they want me to start?"

"If they could find a reliable, unflappable cameraperson, they'd start tomorrow. But everyone they've brought onsite has fled screaming in fifteen minutes or less."

Wow, that was impressive. Even for Selena's group of *special* weirdos. "Are they that hard to work with?"

"No. They're actually quite lovely. . . . The place they're investigating is *that* haunted."

This time, Jo gave in and burst out laughing. "You're not serious?"

"Swear it."

"And where are they investigating? The LaLaurie mansion?"

Selena shook her head. "Karma's house."

It figured. In their long familial line of peculiar characters and those willing to believe in flying fairies, alien possessions, and Santa Claus, Karma Devereaux was Queen Lunatica . . . the woman had even nicknamed her own son E.T. and the kid's real name was Ian.

"Lainie, if I roll my eyes any farther back in my head, I'll probably swallow them."

Selena reached over and playfully Gibbs-slapped her.

"Hey!"

"You needed it. Besides, that cynicism will serve us well. We need someone who doesn't spook onsite with the camera."

"Yes, well, having survived many a sleepover and family reunion with you bunch of loons, I'm immune to *most* anything. Aunt Xilla not included."

"Good. I'll call everyone and tell them to be at Karma's by eleven tomorrow. Will that work for you?"

"Maybe." Jo narrowed her gaze on Selena as she pulled up to Baskin-Robbins. "You still haven't told me how much I'll make for this misbegotten journey to the Armpit of Hades, AKA Karma's."

"Three hundred and fifty a day, plus meals."

Jo gaped. "You're joshing me."

"Nope. That's what we've had to go up to, to entice anyone to the job. But we have yet to pay anyone more than twenty bucks for their fifteen-minute appearance, and most have told us to keep our money because they're afraid it's cursed or haunted, too."

Jo scoffed at the paranoia. "What a bunch of superstitious pansies. . . ." But that might be a good thing for her. "You think I can get four hundred a day?"

"At this point? Probably." Selena reached for her phone. "I'll text Mama Lisa and find out."

"All right. You get me that, and you have a fearless photographer, camerawoman, gofer, janitor . . . whatever."

"Would you be willing to spend the night there, too?"

"No," Jo said emphatically.

Selena looked up from the phone with an arched brow. "I thought you weren't afraid."

"Not afraid of ghosts or demons. I'm terrified of Karma. No offense, your sister's crazy."

"Yes, she is. Honestly, she scares me, too." Selena's smile widened. "Mama Lisa agrees to your price. She said that if you'll actually make it through three days of filming, there's a thousand-dollar bonus for you."

Jo was almost ecstatic. Until the reality fairy came and slapped her. Suddenly terrified, she started searching the sky above them.

"What's that look mean?" Selena asked as she, too, searched the heavens.

"Things are going too good." She slid her gaze back to her cousin. "I'm waiting for lightning to strike me."

"Don't be ridiculous. It's a perfectly sunny day."

"Yeah, and hell's just a hot tub. I'm telling you, Lainie, something real bad's going to happen. I know it."

'Cause from the moment of her first breath, she'd been cursed. And nothing *ever* worked out for her.

Hey, Ma?"

Karma Devereaux sighed heavily as she heard her son's call from the hallway upstairs. She stepped out of her living room to look up at the landing. "I'm a little busy, Boo. What do you need?"

As her twelve-year-old leaned over the balustrade to look down at her, his dark curls were a mess around his head as if he'd been out in a wind. Something strange, since it'd been a warm day with little breeze. "You know this freaky-creepy weird vase up here that has that moon rune writing on it? The one you told me to never touch?"

The blood left her face. "You didn't touch it, did you?"

"Nope. But Rug made another break for freedom and when I cornered him in the room I'm not supposed to be in, I saw it on the floor, broken. And I swear to all that is holy, neither me nor the hamster did it. It looks like it's been done."

Terrified for her son, Karma ran up the stairs as fast as she could. "Did you touch *any*thing?"

E.T. held up the hamster cuddled in his hands. "Just Rug."

"Put him in his cage." She waited for her son to leave before she entered the room cautiously. Dread consumed her, and as soon as she saw the broken vase, she knew why. That hadn't fallen on the floor and broken by accident.

Something had caused it to *shatter*.

And that explained why there'd been so much activity in her house lately. Why everyone new ran screaming for the door.

One of the oldest, deadliest beings in the universe had been set loose.

Sick to her stomach, she pulled her phone from her pocket and dialed the number of last resort.

Zeke answered on the first ring. "Pest Control by Zeke Jacobson. What's eating your soul today?"

"You're really not funny."

He ignored her droll tone. "Karma? That you?"

"Yeah. We got a problem, buddy, and I need the cavalry."

"What'd you do now?"

"I swear I didn't do this. I'm really not sure how this happened, but . . . Valac escaped."

"Please tell me that when you say that, you mean he's slamming at your doors and wants out to play. Not that he's out, out, as in out."

"He gone. High-tailed. Skedaddled. I didn't even know he'd broken loose. No idea when he took off."

"Was he summoned?"

She toed at the vase. "Yeah," she breathed. "But how did they get to him past my protection?"

"No idea. But they had to be strong and fierce in their own right. Given that, I've got to call out the heavy artillery."

"You *are* the heavy artillery, Zeke. Isn't that the whole point of a Necrodemian? You kill the big evil."

"Yes and no. There are roughly one hundred known demons who are beyond our abilities to battle and kill. Those who have origins so powerful and old that they have been sealed away and are supposed to stay there. For this level of demon, we need nuclear-devastation capabilities. Only one of his ilk can battle him and put him back in his bottle without dying in the process."

"Wait. You're not proposing we summon a stronger, more *evil* demon to capture him?"

Zeke was about to draw Thorn into a horrific mess. More than anyone, Karma knew what a bad idea that was. The last thing Thorn needed was temptation. Everyday, he was slipping toward the realm of his father, she could feel it every time they talked. But Zeke was right. What choice did they have?

"Yeah, we don't call the Hellchasers out often. They're like rabid dogs, and we're usually fighting them as well as the gruesomes. However, it's the only option in this case. Unless you want Valac free to roam, and I don't think that's a good idea, especially with Halloween coming. Just hang tight, and I'll be there as soon as I can."

Karma hung up the phone as she scanned the room where she warehoused and cleansed some of the scariest relics and items in the paranormal realm. She'd never wanted to keep Valac, but when her sister Tiyana had died, she'd inherited his guardianship. Tiyana had made her promise that should anything happen to her, Karma wouldn't entrust his container to anyone else. Not for any reason.

Now . . .

*Please don't let this be the worst mistake of my life.*

# 2

Jo had just finished packing her gear into her rusted-out 1964 Ford Falcon that used to be red, but now was more primer gray than anything else, when her cell phone began ringing. Answering it, she went to the driver's side and tossed her purse in.

"Hey, coz. Quick change of plans. We're not meeting at Karma's. Rather, we got an emergency call in for the Gardette-LePretre Mansion on Dauphine."

"You've got to be kidding me. That weird old place where the sultan and his harem were slaughtered?"

"That's the one. See you there . . . oh, and the man's paying us through the nose. Your bonus just had a baby! Mazel tov!"

Hoping this wasn't an additional sign of a pending Apocalypse, Jo hung up and got into the car. Well, she'd always had a morbid fascination about the place that was only a couple of blocks from her family's Voodoo store, Erzulie's. When they'd been kids, their aunt Kalila had regaled them with scary stories about that old mansion and the horrors that had taken place there almost two hundred years ago.

Yeah.

But she couldn't quite suppress the sadness at the thought of driving past the store where her cousin Tiyana had died. Since that horrible night, she'd done her best to avoid the entire street. She could only imagine how much worse it had to be for Selena and her sisters, especially Tabitha, who now owned it.

Out of all the mixed nuts in the Devereaux bowl, Tiyana had been one of Jo's favorites. Though she'd never believed in any of what her father called their otherworldly crap, Jo used to stop by and nab the special oils and soaps that T and their aunt Ana made for Erzulie's.

*Don't think about it.*

It was hard not to. The one lesson Jo had learned was just how fast life changed. One minute you were walking along in a little cocoon of copasetic numbness. And the next . . . bam! Your world went skidding off the rails, leaving your heart in little bloody chunks on the sidewalk, that made you wonder how you'd ever be able to put it back together again.

It really ought to be illegal for life to do that without *any* warning.

Disgusted, she turned the ignition key. Her car sputtered to life with a death rattle and a great belch of black smoke that fanned out for a full block. Yeah, it was embarrassing, but she had to give the old Falcon credit. At age fifty, it had more life in it than she did at present.

Pushing everything out of her mind except the Prince song on the radio, she headed over to Dauphine, where Selena and Karma were already waiting, along with four women she'd never met before.

Jo pulled up behind Selena's Jeep and parked on the street. After an extremely long and humiliating round of yeah-I-turned-my-car-off-and-it's-still-running,–don't-know-if-it'll-ever-stop-so-bite-my-heinie-and-be-glad-it's-not-you, she got out and gathered her bags. As she neared the others, she couldn't help noticing the expressions on everyone's face that said they had a bet going to see how long she'd last.

Sidling up to Selena, she grinned. "Put me down for eight."

"Eight what?"

"How long I'll last before I run screaming for home."

Karma laughed.

The rest looked confused.

With a dismissive snort, Selena gestured toward the petite blonde on her right. "Jo, meet our fearless leader and primary exorcist, Mama Lisa. She's the one who does the *Voices Carry* Internet radio show on Wednesday nights."

Jo knew the show well. It was the only one Karma listened to that she could stand.

Holding her hand out, Jo inclined her head to the woman with friendly eyes and a beautiful smile. "Nice to meet you."

"You, too."

Next, Selena indicated the two brown-haired women who looked enough alike to be related. "Sister Jordan and her real sister, Sarah."

They exchanged pleasantries.

"And last, but never least, Mistress Mercy."

Plump and adorable, she flashed a set of deep dimples. "Hi, Jo. Hope you don't scare easily. We've got a doozy today."

Jo winked at her. "Looking forward to it."

"You're not scared?" Lisa asked doubtfully.

"You've met Karma, right? Imagine sharing summer bathrooms and beds with her. She's a pig. Nothing scares me more than her midnight bathtub rituals."

They all laughed. Even Karma.

"All right, Ms. Unflappable." Karma grabbed the bag from Jo's shoulder. "Get ready for scary!" She made a fake bwa-ha-ha laugh as she left.

Jo passed a less-than-impressed stare at Selena. "I feel like I'm stuck at the lake house with her again . . . help me."

Shaking her head, Selena grabbed the tripod and carried it in. Jo followed them, but hesitated in the foyer. Not because she was scared, but because it was absolutely lovely. While the outside of the house was classical Greek Revival, complete with ornate wrought-iron balcony—the whole nine yards—the inside was completely modern and contemporary.

Polished woods. Ceiling fans. Beautiful coffered ceilings. Exquisite.

Jo tried not to gape in awe. "I thought this was apartments."

Selena set the tripod down. "It was. A year ago August, it was bought and converted to a single home. Nine bedrooms, ten baths. Over seven thousand square feet of utter evil."

"Doesn't look evil. Looks really nice."

"Thank you."

Jo turned at the sound of the man's deep voice. Dressed in a green golf shirt, he was middle-aged and held the air of a man in charge.

"Cal," Lisa said in greeting. "Thanks for letting us do this."

"No, thank *you* for coming. After last week, my wife has refused to return. She's already calling to have the place re-listed. Wish she'd done that before the last remodeling bill. But what can you do? Cheaper than divorce lawyers, I guess."

Selena pulled out a spiral-bound vinyl notebook that had cute little monsters on the cover, and a feathered flamingo pen. So much for looking professional. "What exactly's been going on?"

"Honestly, nothing at first. We were here for almost a year with no occurrences whatsoever. Like everyone else, we thought the stories about the place being haunted were bogus. And then . . ."

Selena looked up. "What?"

"We came in one night from dinner out and there was a strange odor. I can't even describe how foul it was. We thought maybe a sewer line had backed up or something."

Lisa paused next to the hall console table. "Something was out of place right here." She waved her hand over the bowl of marble balls.

Cal nodded. "Someone had put a single red rose there."

"There was a scream upstairs," Jordan whispered, as she repeated whatever she thought had happened. "Your wife ran back to the car to call the police while you went to the fourth floor to investigate it." She looked back at him. "But you found nothing. The room was completely empty."

Scowling, he nodded again. "How do you know that?"

"They're very sensitive." Karma turned back to Jo. "Shouldn't you be filming this?"

"Sorry." Jo put her camera bag on the ground and pulled out the Digital Camcorder. Steadying it on her shoulder, she turned it on, then frowned as she flicked at the switch. "How odd."

"What?" Selena asked.

"I took the battery off the charger right before I came over and it's empty now." Jo changed it out, only to learn that both backups were dead, too.

Selena made a note. "Everyone, quick. Check your phones."

One by one, they reported the same thing. "Completely drained."

"Oooo," Karma breathed. "We have activity already." With the eagerness of a kid at Christmas, she looked back at Cal. "Have you seen an apparition?"

"A light-haired man. Young."

"Where?"

"Upstairs. Antique hall mirror that's now in a closet. It came with the house. I took it off the wall after my wife started having nightmares about it, a month ago."

"Let's see it and . . ." Lisa's voice trailed off as she opened a door on her left and wandered into the bedroom there. She drew up short.

As did the others.

One by one, they each turned to stare at the owner.

"You really like antiques, huh?" Selena asked.

He shrugged. "I'm a historian. They're artifacts I collect. Mostly from eBay, and friends who are anthropologists and archaeologists."

Karma turned to Selena. "What's the time period?"

"Babylonian. Lot of Babylonian."

Cal nodded. "Akkadia and Sumer are my primary focus. Is that a problem?"

Karma shook her head. "You know Dr. Parthenopaeus?"

"Tory? Yeah. I've known her for years."

"What about Dr. Julian Alexander?" Selena asked.

"Him, too."

"Should we call them?" Karma whispered to her sister.

"I'm not sure. Yet. Let's look around a little more." Selena tucked her pen into her notebook. "Show us this mirror."

Jo followed the others as they headed up the stairs. She was trying not to be psyched out by it all, but the thing with the batteries was really strange. Over and over, she tried to think of a logical reason for it.

She couldn't. Nothing should cause a total discharge of power. Of *all* items.

That was peculiar.

Cal led them into another bedroom and opened a walk-in closet door.

"You feel that?" Jordan shivered.

Her sister nodded. "There's something here with us."

"Sheets," Jo said. "Pottery. Lots and lots of rugs and art."

They passed her an irritated glare that said her bonus might be shrinking.

Cal and Lisa brought the mirror out. Over seven feet tall, it was an impressive antique that reminded her of hundreds of such that she'd seen in the antique stores that lined Royal Street. For whatever reason, Jo had always been fascinated by mirrors, especially old ones. So much so, that she'd lined her whole room in them as a girl. Something that apparently ran in her blood, since her mother had confessed to her that she'd been the same way as a girl.

"So how many years of bad luck if you break that?" Jo was trying to lighten the mood.

All it did was tick off her companions.

"Pretend to be serious," Mercy said with an irritable glare. "We *are* professionals here."

Reminding herself that her bonus had a baby if she didn't blow this, Jo stepped back. "Sorry."

Bored out of her mind while they studied it and blocked it from her inspection, she glanced around the room, which had an awesome view of the St. Louis Cathedral down the street.

Without conscious thought, she moved to the window that reflected back into the room. She saw a shadow pass over it.

*Are you the one. . . .*

She turned at the whisper. No one was there. The others were still gathered around the mirror, comparing notes and speculating oddities.

Hmmm . . .

*Yeah, I'm losing it.*

They used to do this when she was a kid. They'd act all oooo and ahhh, especially around mirrors, and see things until they'd convinced her she saw them, too.

But she knew better.

The Devereauxes were the strangest of the strange. Starting with Aunt Rocky and moving through all nine of her wacked-out, freakfest daughters.

For that matter, Jo's mom wasn't exactly normal. The Floras had a long line of eccentric, yet mostly lovable quacks. Even their Romanichal grandmother had a vein in her foot that she swore only protruded whenever a flood was coming. You could bet the bank on it.

But one good thing about them—family picnics and reunions were *never* boring.

"You coming, Jo?"

She turned at Selena's question and realized that everyone had vacated the room while she stood daydreaming. "Right behind you."

As she followed them around, she had to admit there was something rather creepy about the place. Bright and pathologically clean, it was unsettling. Really, no one should have a house this immaculate while they were actually living in it.

Yeah, the house oozed oddity.

Her gaze went to Karma.

*And there it is. The source of all freakiness.* Jo bit back a laugh at the thought.

Ignoring them while they prattled about stuff she didn't know nor want to learn about, she drifted toward the back door that let out into a small courtyard. She froze as she came across the most incredible mural she'd ever seen. Made out of what appeared to be panels of antique mirrors that reflected into the house, they were covered with metal pieces, fashioned to look like 3-D trees, with the back door cut in the center of them. It gave the illusion of walking into a mystical orchard.

*I need this in my apartment. . . .*

"Beautiful, isn't it?"

She turned at the sound of Cal's voice. "Yes, it is. Was it here when you bought the house?"

"No. A friend of my wife's is an artist. He does a lot of the murals you see in these older homes."

"I can see why." She smiled at him. "You have the most amazing home. I know you and your wife are very proud."

At the same time he opened his mouth to speak, Lisa called for his attention. He left her to attend them.

Alone, Jo moved closer to the metal trees to study the artistry. That took more patience than she'd ever had. But the artist in her was greatly intrigued by it.

As she gently fingered the enameled edges, her gaze went to the old, stained mirrors that had been meticulously joined together and placed for effect. Yeah, she definitely wanted to do this with some of the ones she'd collected over the years.

A shadow light moved behind a pane.

Scowling, she turned to see if someone was behind her.

The room was empty.

*Don't be stupid. And don't let them in your head. Not unless you plan to charge them rent. You could use the money.*

Laughing at her thoughts, she went to the door, intending to investigate the courtyard where the renter of the property was said to have been buried alive during the massacre that had taken place in the home.

But as she started through the door, she tripped on the

edge of the rug. Jo reached out to catch herself against the wall. Only instead of touching the mirrored panels, she went through them.

Completely.

# 3

Jo froze as she found herself in the strangest place she'd ever seen. Creepy Fairy Forest—complete with twisted trees that looked like they should come alive and try to eat her head.

*Now ain't this a bitch. . . . I've fallen into TV Land and I can't get up.*

And from the looks of it, it was a missing episode of *The Addams Family.*

Maybe *The Munsters.*

Definitely, definitely one of the two. Turning a slow circle, she saw nothing but an unending darkness. No color whatsoever. Even her skin was a pale, icky gray. So much for her Eastern European skin tone.

Weird.

*This is why Technicolor took over movies. . . .*

A chill wind howled around her, stirring her hair and raising goose bumps on her skin. Wrapping her arms around her body, she stumbled forward, through the night, seeking a way home.

"Selena! Karma!" She paused to listen for them, and heard nothing but the wind. "This isn't funny! I swear, Karma, Jo's the bitch here! Not you! I will get you back for this! You have to sleep sometime!"

*C'mon, Jo. Wake up.*

*Just a stupid dream.*

Yet, as the seconds turned into minutes and nothing changed, she began to get worried. Scared, even.

All of a sudden, she heard the sound of feet running not too far away. "Lainie? Over here! And bring a flashlight!"

The sound slowed, then turned in her direction.

Relieved, she let out an elongated breath. Until she saw the source of the sound.

*Oh hell no. . . .*

They were the rotting refugees from one of those scary

zombie movies her cousin Tabitha went to bed watching every night.

Terrified, Jo turned and ran as fast as she could. But as her luck would have it, these weren't the slow-moving *Walking Dead* zombies. Oh no . . .

She got the lottery-winning *Resident Evil* super zombies, with steroids and Olympic training. One launched itself at her as it tried to bite her. Jo ducked and twisted before she ran in the opposite direction. Frantic, she looked for a weapon, but all she could see was fog and dark, and dark's first cousin.

Useless!

*Next time I have this dream, I want night-vision goggles and a machete!* Not to mention a couple of hot bodyguards.

And in all those awful, horrific movies Tabby had forced on her, the one thing Jo had always hated most was the screaming idiot girl who ran helplessly, usually in heels, and didn't even try to save herself.

But what the hell? There was nothing else to do.

Letting out a blood-curdling holler, she ran, and slammed straight into a hard, unforgiving tree that appeared out of nowhere.

Or so she thought. The black tree wrapped two arms around her and pulled her behind it before it twisted and drew a sword so fast, it took her a minute to process what he was doing. The sound of scraping metal sent an even bigger chill over her.

Her gaze could barely follow as the extremely tall man cut through those things as they sought to kill him and nab her. Man, they were trained. But nothing compared to the guy. He twirled and parried and thrust like some macabre ballerina.

It was obvious he'd been up against them more than once.

Even though it took several minutes, he fought them off with absurd skill and precision.

After they finally lay scattered in the fog around them, he turned slowly to study her. In the lightless ick, she couldn't make out any detail of his body. At all. Swathed in black on black from head to toe, he reminded her of a killer monk.

Sheathing his sword, he spoke to her in a language she'd never heard before.

When she didn't respond, he grabbed her arm and growled out more gibberish.

She shoved at him. "Dude, don't have Babelfish here. No Rosetta Stone. I don't even know what continent *that* comes from."

"Human?" His deep baritone froze her. Ooo, sexy-sounding voice double-wrapped in a gorgeous accent. Nice and soothing, unlike the fierce grip he kept on her arm.

"After my first pot of coffee. Most days. Yeah, I'm human."

She tried to pry his hand off her. "Have you had your caffeine? Daily enema?"

His grip tightened on her biceps as he pulled her away from the bodies.

"Hey! Tall, irritating, and scary, not your bimbo." She popped at his mail-covered hand. "Want to take it easy on the merch? You break it, you buy it, and it ain't cheap. I've got three dogs to support, you know? Beggin' Strips are costly. And Maisey's addicted to the expensive buttered microwave popcorn. And the store brand just won't do."

Cadegan had no idea what the woman was saying. While he understood most of the words she used, others left him as baffled as her sudden appearance in his realm. And her sentences were absolute nonsense.

By her clothes, he knew she was from the current human world. But why was she *here*?

How had she gotten here? While some of the others who called this hell home could come and go, they were sorcerers, Adoni, or other nether dwellers. Humans didn't have the liberty to venture here without aid.

And whenever a human was sent here for him, he could smell the touch of a demon on them from leagues away.

She was different. While there was something familiar about her, she bore no scent of anything, save humanity.

Kindness.

It was what drew the twisted graylings to her and made them attack. Innocence was the most precious and prized commodity in this hell realm. And it was one that never lasted for long before they converted the innocent.

Or killed them.

Cadegan froze as he heard more graylings and sidhe running for them. Worse than that, it sounded like they had MODs with them. The Minions of Death would give anything for a bite of her pristine human flesh. And they would devour her just to hear her screaming for mercy.

"Stay." He left her to engage the dark, twisted beings who preyed on anyone dumb enough to be out in the Nachtmore Forest at this hour.

*Duw!* There were a lot of them who'd detected her, and they seemed to be spawning more by the heartbeat. He ducked a grayling sword before a MOD charged him.

The woman moved forward, toward the fray.

Distracted, he felt the bite of the creature he was fighting. Cursing, he beat it back and killed it an instant before she started running again.

"Halt!"

She froze and held her arms up, away from her sides. "Don't shoot!"

Why would she think that? "I have no bow or crossbow, lass. They be useless against them, anyways."

"Okie-dokie, then." She turned to face him.

Cadegan's breath caught as he finally took in her sassy features. Tall and thin, she lacked the curves he'd once preferred on a woman's body. But her face was that of a dark, innocent angel. Her silky black hair and dark eyes reminded him of home. Worse, he held a sudden desire to touch her long tresses to see if they were as silky soft as they appeared. To inhale them for her sweet scent.

*Canolbwyntio!* This had to be a trap of some sort. That was all that awaited those damned to this never-realm of madness. Neither the human world nor Camelot nor Avalon, this was Terre Derrière le Voile—the dark hole between those worlds where his brother had sent him to wait out eternity. Forever able to see the color-filled realms he could no longer reach or visit, no matter how much power he wielded.

*Leave her to them, then, and go.*

It was the sanest thing to do. But then he'd gone insane centuries ago.

Now . . .

Like the ones out to claim her, he wanted her with him. For a bit. If for nothing else, just to ease the loneliness that was his sole companion.

Was a few minutes of conversation really too much to ask?

*Damn it to Lucifer's bloody hell.*

And damn him as well.

Before he could stop himself, Cadegan held his hand out to her. "Follow with, lass, and I shall see thee to safety."

Jo hesitated as she tried to make sense of his singsongy words. "Who are you?"

"Cadegan."

Man, that was one seriously thick accent on that boy. And it was an odd one, to boot. A peculiar cross that landed somewhere between an Irish or Scottish brogue and thick English. Yet it was nothing like she'd ever heard before. "Cah-who?"

He slowed it down for her. "CUH-doo-gun."

"Cadegan." She cringed, hoping she didn't insult him with her mispronunciation. If she did, he didn't correct her for it. "Mine's easy. I'm Jo."

"Jo. We must to do now. I've hit them sick, but we can't stay. There will be more. There always is."

This was worse than trying to understand her Romanichal grandmother when she got onto one of her serious Angloromani kicks. "Are you trying to help me?"

"Aye."

"All right, but I have a shoe, buddy, and I'm not afraid to use it."

Cadegan had no idea what that meant, but it sounded vaguely like a threat. If they had more time, he'd laugh at the thought of such a skinny woman thinking she could do him harm. Or any woman or man, for that matter. But this wasn't the time. They had to get away before something pinched her from him.

She finally placed her delicate hand into his, and he cursed the fact he wore the gauntlets that kept him from feeling her skin on his. He'd been without a human touch for so long that he couldn't remember the sensation at all. Not that he'd ever known much.

Still . . . everyone yearned for some degree of physical contact.

Even the cursed and damned.

He pulled her back toward the dugout that had served as his home since Leucious had imprisoned him here. It wasn't much. A hutch, really. Yet it was clean and serviceable. Best of all, it could be locked down and sealed to keep the others out, long enough for him to sleep or eat, anyway.

With his powers, he opened the stone doorway and allowed her to enter his home first. "Sorry it's such a *daever*."

"Diaper?"

"Diaper?" he repeated, not comprehending her term any more than she understood his. "Hovel," he tried again.

Jo smiled as she finally got his meaning. "Same thing."

"Ah."

Frowning, she watched as he spread his hand out and a massively huge rock rolled over the opening they'd stepped through. The moment it was in place, ten sconces lit themselves around her, showing her the hobbit hole he lived in. The floor beneath her feet was made of high-polished hardwood planks, while twisted saplings appeared to hold up a curved hand-plastered ceiling over their heads. They also supported a small, raised, second-floor loft where a modest bed was set on a small platform that appeared to have drawers in it, and a washstand. All in all, the place reminded her of an earthen studio apartment. Probably around a few hundred square feet in total.

There was a hearth to her left with a small black cauldron and percolator in it. Two more pots and a Dutch oven hung from mantel hooks. The walls were bare, except for a collection of impressive swords, spears, and axes. And more shields than she'd ever seen in her life. It was only then that she realized she could see color inside here. Unlike the outside that had been in pure black and white.

"Would you be craving for a dibble, lass?"

She returned her gaze to him, then gasped as she realized how much larger he was than she'd assumed. *Holy snikes!* He had to be well over six feet, with massively broad shoulders. Dressed in a black monk-styled robe and cloak, complete with a rope belt, he was mountainous. He pulled off a pair of chain mail gloves and tucked them into his belt.

When she didn't respond, he lowered the robe's cowl to finally show her his face. Her breath caught as she saw eyes so blue, like a clear Caribbean sea, they were electrifying. Unnatural. His dark blond hair was cut way too short. Fierce military style. And while his blond whiskers were a bit long, as if he hadn't shaved for a few weeks, they weren't a full beard, nor were they unkempt. It was a sexy mess that added an extremely rugged quality to an otherwise beautifully perfect masculine face.

"Did you hear me, lass? Would you be craving for a dibble?"

If a dibble was a warm Cadegan in her bed, then heck yeah. Sign her up and spam her e-mail! She'd take *that* and then some.

"I'm not quite sure what you're asking me."

A slow, teasing grin spread across his handsome face, making him all the more appealing and delectable. "Food. Drink. Be you craving a . . . bite?"

Disappointment made her pout. Not the offer she was looking for. She shook her head. "I'm good. Thanks, though."

He inclined his head before he removed his cloak with a flourish and hung it up on a peg in the wall. Turning back toward her, he hesitated. His unexpected bashfulness was sweetly charming and made him seem almost real.

"So Cade . . . you're tall, sexy, swanky, live in a hobbit hole. Anything else I need to know about you? Like is there a Mrs. Giant-Hobbit you share your abode with?"

He didn't answer, as he appeared to be struggling with comprehension. Instead, he dropped his gaze to her hand. A hunger she couldn't fathom darkened his eyes. "May I?" he asked hesitantly.

"What?"

Approaching her slowly, he reached for her arm as if he expected her to evaporate. With an unimaginable tenderness, he took her hand into his and closed his eyes as if savoring the feel of it. He bit his bottom lip in the hottest expression she'd ever seen on a man's face, and cupped her hand between his. His breathing ragged, he led her hand to his cheek and held her knuckles to his skin as if she were a sacred relic. He actually trembled as he mumbled in that melodic language she couldn't even begin to decipher.

A part of her was terrified by his actions. Was he totally nuts? But he wasn't threatening her. Rather, he acted as if he hadn't been around another person in a really long time.

"Are you all right?"

He inhaled her skin an instant before he released her and stepped back. "Sorry, lass. I didn't mean to frighten you."

"No problem. I've been on much creepier dates than this. Embarrassing, too, and that was while I was actually awake for them . . . with witnesses I knew."

He smiled at that, then went to a handmade cupboard where he poured himself a goblet of wine. Just as he started to take a drink, something slammed into the stone he'd rolled into place as a door.

Gasping in fear, Jo sidled up to him.

Cadegan handed her the goblet. "Set your nerves, lass. Have a dab. I promise you, they'll not get in here. And never through me."

She thanked him and took the wine while whatever was outside did its best to make him out a liar. "Can I ask you something?"

He poured himself another goblet. "Aye."

"What language are you speaking?"

"English, I be thinking." The way he said it sounded more like Ang-lish.

"Aren't *you* English?"

Rage flashed so heatedly in his eyes that she stepped back immediately.

"Sorry, Cade. I didn't mean to insult you."

A tic beat in his jaw before he downed the contents of his goblet in one gulp and poured another. "I'm *Brythoniaid*."

"That is absolutely beautiful. No idea where it is or why my brain is coughing this up, but okay. I must have been cruising Wikipedia entries again." She clanked her metal goblet against his. "Here's to Bri . . . whatever it is you just said."

Cadegan laughed at her words, then froze as the sound

shocked him. Honestly, he couldn't remember the last time he'd laughed. At anything. It sounded so strange to his ears.

She was charming him to a frightful level.

And she made him ache for things he knew could never be his. "You might know me as Cymry or . . . Welsh."

"Ah! Now *that* I do know. Explains a lot, actually. . . . Awesome sauce." She finished off her wine and set her goblet on his small table. "I always wanted to hit the UK. Must be why my brain's conjuring this up during my coma state. Now that I think about it, you kind of remind me of the dude who plays the Arrow. . . . Yeah, I'm seeing the connection finally."

Cadegan snorted at her gibberish. "If I sound as *moithered* to you, lass, as you do unto me, I apologize to the cavern's depth for it."

"I think 'yeah' is the right answer to that. But it's okay. Comas aren't supposed to make sense. Right?"

He smirked at her question. "I hate to be the breeder of bad tidings for you, but you're not sleeping."

Jo tensed at that. It couldn't be right. *Please be lying to me.* "Pardon?"

He gestured around his cave. "This is as real as Bran's thorny horns."

"No. It's not." This being real made no more sense than anything he said to her.

Nodding, he set his goblet aside.

"I don't believe you. Prove it."

Cadegan had no idea how to do that without harming her, and for some reason, that was the last thing he wanted to do. He rather enjoyed her bantering nonsense, and liked the fact she didn't fear him.

"Well?" she taunted.

A devil grin curved his lips as he thought of a way to prove it and not hurt her. Before he could reconsider it or stop himself, he dipped his lips down to hers and kissed her deep. But he was wholly unprepared for the sensation of tasting her so intimately. For the sensations that kiss would ignite inside him.

Sucking his breath in sharply, he fisted his hand in her silken hair and explored her mouth with a forgotten hunger and longing that resurfaced with vengeful talons. His body came alive with a need so fierce, it challenged every bit of his will to restrain himself.

*Duw* give him strength.

Jo couldn't have been more stunned had the man slapped her. But as he held her so close to his lush, hard body while he boldly explored her mouth, she realized just how ripped he was. How incredibly masculine and hot. Wickedly warm, she wrapped her arms around him and held him close, aching for a body she was sure would feel incredible on top of hers.

If this was a dream, she didn't want to wake up. Not if he wouldn't be there with her.

When he finally pulled back, he stared down at her with a bitter ache that made her chest tighten.

"Do you believe me now, lass?"

Reaching up, she fingered his lips as his taste lingered with her. She loved the sensation of his whiskers teasing her flesh. "If I'm not unconscious, where am I?"

He winced before he released her and stepped back. "Hell."

"No." She looked around the stark, pitiful cave as those creatures still attempted to get in. "No," she repeated a little less certain this time. "No. It's not possible."

"Why not?"

" 'Cause . . . I didn't earn hell." Suddenly angry, she glared up at the ceiling. "What? You cheat on one stupid little eye test once in tenth grade because you don't want to wear glasses and look like a nerd, and you get banished to hell for it? Really?"

She glanced back at Cadegan. "Yeah, you're right. *That's* my crappy luck. I knew I should have cheated on my taxes. At least once! But no. I play by the rules, and get screwed. Always. Set your clock to it, folks." She nodded as she paced the small room. "I do believe you! I am in hell. How perfect is this?"

He snorted at her outburst. "You don't belong here. You're right about that. How did you get in, anyway?"

"I tripped on a rug and must have cracked my head on the sideboard and died. How spectacular is that?" She looked up at the ceiling again. "Thanks, Selena! You bitch! I couldn't even go out choking on a banana split. Nah, I go out stupidly and on a diet, no less. No fair! I should have had French toast, cake and ice cream, and not plain icky diet yogurt for breakfast. Where do I lodge a complaint?"

He laughed.

Until she popped him lightly on the belly. "It's not funny! My whole life has been nothing more than to serve as a cautionary tale for others. Unbelievable."

Rubbing his stomach, he stared at her in disbelief. No one had ever treated him so lightly before. "You're not dead, Jo. You're in Glastonbury Tor."

"Like the abbey?"

"In short, aye. This is Terre Derrière le Voile—a realm where things are sent to be forgotten."

"Yeah, but no one sent me here. I fell into it."

He scratched at his cheek as he considered her words. "Then you must have stumbled through a hidden access. It doesn't normally happen that way, but I've seen much stranger things than that occur here."

"Does that mean I can get back home?" she asked hopefully.

For reasons he didn't want to fathom, the thought of her

leaving hurt him deep inside. "Aye, lass. Providing we find your point of entry."

"Oh, that's easy. Go left at the darkness and keep walking until you go blind with it." She held her hand up when he started to speak. "I was being sarcastic." She frowned at him. "Did you fall in here, too?"

Cadegan wished. "Nay, lass. I was put here, quite intentionally."

Jo paused as she considered what he was saying. That didn't make any sense to her. How was he here by design? "For what?"

"It doesn't matter. It was a long time ago."

She raked a look over his monkish robe that could be ancient or modern. It was very similar to the ones Brother Anthony wore on Sundays for Mass. "How long exactly?"

He hesitated before he answered. "Since Edward the Confessor was king of England."

Selena would groan at her stupidity if she were here. But history had never been much of an interest for Jo. "So that was what? Fifteenth century or so?"

"I know naught of that, lass. But it was the year of Our Lord 1045 when I was cast into this hell."

Jo's head reeled at what he was saying. Was he serious? "For real?"

"Aye."

"Whoa . . . that's ancient."

He arched a brow at her whispered tone. "How ancient?"

"Thousand years of ancient."

Cadegan couldn't breathe as reality sank in and the blood washed from his face. He'd known from his glimpses through the glass that years had passed, and things had changed quite drastically. But this . . .

A *thousand* years.

A full millennia.

Bitter pain devoured his heart and choked him as he realized that Leucious had truly abandoned him. As stupid as it seemed now, a part of him had held out hope that his brother would forgive him and return to set him loose.

He hadn't.

Like everyone else, Leucious had turned his back on him and banished him from his thoughts like some dithering *cythral* sent to torment him.

*You make me flesh skitter! Dor, how could anyone ever love a monster like you?* Cadegan ground his teeth as he sought to silence the blind hatred that had haunted him through the centuries. The hatred that had driven him to destroy everything he'd ever held dear.

Everything he'd ever known.

"Are you all right?"

Nay. But unwilling to let Jo know the truth, he nodded

before he turned away and fought against the utter despair that shredded whatever was left of his wanged-out soul.

How could Leucious be so cold and unfeeling, after all the wounds Cadegan had taken for him?

After all the good Cadegan had done, it'd been a single act of entitled rage that had forever damned him.

By his own brother's hand.

How he wished Leucious were here. Just for one final heartbeat as he squeezed the life from him.

Jo watched in silence as the darkest sadness she'd ever beheld came over his features. She couldn't imagine what he'd been through.

*It's not real, Jo. He's not real. This is just a dream.*

*What if it's not?*

Yeah right, she sounded as crazy as the rest of her idiot family. Yet . . . this *felt* real. It sounded real and there was no way to deny how he'd tasted.

No dream had ever felt like this. Solid and complex. She could even smell the ashes in the hearth.

Reaching out, she brushed her hand against the coarse wool of his monkish robe. The rough fibers scraped her skin and she felt the texture of the chain mail he wore beneath it.

This *was* reality.

Somehow.

But one thing made her leery of fully accepting it. "If

you've been here for a thousand years, how do you understand me?"

He snorted as a glimmer of amusement returned to his eyes. "I don't, most of the time. Much of what you say is half soaked. But as to why I know this version of English, I can hear your world while I rustle about near the borders. Not to mention, I was born with an innate ability to pick up languages rapt fast."

"Really?"

He nodded as the hopeless sadness returned to his entire demeanor. "We need to be getting you on to yours, lass. Now, in a minute. But there's a fright bit of madness about. Best to wait till morning for it."

"Wow. It's like trying to decipher Shakespeare or Chaucer."

Tilting his head, he frowned at her. "Beg pardon?"

"You know? The famous writers?"

"You mean a scrivener?" He held his left hand up as if he was writing on something.

"Yeah. My bad. You totally predate them, don't you? And have no idea what I'm talking about. Jeez, what *don't* you predate?" Then she had another thought. Unlike her cousins, she wasn't a historian of any kind. Really didn't have much of a handle on any kind of historical timeline. "So were you a Crusader knight or something?"

"I'm not quite certain what you're asking me, lass."

"Your clothes and armor. Were you a monk? Knight? Sword boy?"

"I was a knight."

"To King Edward . . . no, wait, you hate the English. King of Wales? Not that I know the names of any, but king of Wales?"

He shook his head as he went to pull out a chair and cushion for her. Now that she looked about, she realized it was the only chair he had. "Would you care to sit a bit?"

"Where are you sitting?"

"Floor be good enough for the sorry likes of me."

"Your . . . hobbit hole. I feel bad taking the only chair."

Removing his sword and hanging it next to his cloak, Cadegan shrugged. "Suit yourself, then." He moved to sit on the floor with his back to the wall. He stretched one insanely long leg out and bent the other.

Since he wasn't using it, Jo took the chair after all. "So what do you do for fun here?"

"I don't understand your question."

"Fun. You know, that thing you enjoy doing?"

He frowned at her. "There is no fun here. Only survival."

"Yeah, but when you're holed up, like now. What do you do to pass the time?"

"Ah. Play *tafl, cross,* and *disiau.*"

She loved listening to his speech and thick accent, but

dang, it was giving her a migraine as she tried to make sense of it. "Really feel like we need a translator."

He laughed before he pushed himself up and moved to the small table where an old box was set. He pulled out a smaller box and a worn leather pouch. Jo peeked over his shoulder to see what else the larger box contained. It had hand-carved pieces similar to chessmen. And now that she was paying attention, she realized the entire table was grooved and gridded like a board for chess or checkers, with a beautiful Celtic design over it.

Without comment, Cadegan opened the small box that had wooden pieces marked with Roman numerals. The pouch contained a set of wooden dice that he handed to her.

She fingered them, amazed at their quality and age. "How long have you had these?"

"Brother Eurig made them for me when I was a nibbler . . . a lad."

"Brother Eurig? Was he a priest?"

"Monk."

Gaping, she cradled the worn dice in her hand as she struggled with reality again. "These are almost a thousand years old?"

"Thirteen hundred, more like. I was born in the year of Our Lord a score and seven hundred."

"720?"

He nodded.

"How old were you when he gave these to you?"

"Eight or so."

No flippin' way. She stared at the dice in awe, until his age dawned on her. "Wait . . . that means you were put here when you were what? Three hundred years old?"

"Aye. Thereabouts."

Trepidation filled her at that newest disclosure. *This can't be good.* People didn't live that long.

Not naturally.

She scowled at him. "Are you a vampire?"

"You've baffled me again, lass."

"What *are* you?"

Cadegan stepped back at the sudden fear he saw in her dark brown eyes. A panicked expression that hit him like a blow to his gut. It was ever the same. Everyone feared him. They always had. Even when he'd been a mere lad, the monks and priests had known he wasn't quite human and had treated him accordingly—like excrement that was best buried before it tainted those around it. But it'd been so long since he was around another that he'd forgotten how much it hurt to be so rejected.

*"You are an abomination to God! A cursed bastard! Unfit to be with your betters."*

He winced mentally at the memory of his commander.

He'd sworn to himself that he'd never again be so stupid. So desperate. That under no circumstance would he allow another into his world or heart.

It just wasn't worth the pain that invariably followed.

Though it wasn't in him while in a fight or battle, he knew it would be best to withdraw from this conflict before she attacked him. No good could come of it. Besides, he was used to solitude. There was no need in learning better now.

"Stay in safety, lass. I shall return come morning and show you the way home." He used his powers to pull his cloak and sword to him, and quickly left what little *cwtch* he had, taking only a brief pause to ensure she was secured inside so that nothing could reach her.

In the bleak darkness outside, he stood with his hand on the stone he used for a doorway, and sighed as old memories ripped through him. Only then, it'd been a petite blonde who'd stared up at him in terror as enemies had ransacked her home and conquered her people.

They would have slaughtered her and her family, too. But like a fool, he'd risked his own life to save theirs.

He rubbed at the scar on his chest and pushed the thought away. Like Æthla, the past was long gone.

There was nothing to be done about it, for sure. He'd made his thorny bed. And now he knew there would never be a reprieve for the useless likes of him. This was his eternal reality.

Bitter isolation and the harshest survival.

So be it.

But as he turned to walk through the twisted, gnarled forest where his enemies waited to battle him, he remembered the taste of a warm kiss from Jo, and the sensation of a soft hand in his.

*You could keep her here.*

There was no way for her to cross over without his assistance. She'd never make it back to the portal on her own.

But as he heard the shrill banshee cries and the sound of night predators searching for blood, he knew he couldn't do that to another.

He wasn't his brother.

And unlike *him,* she'd done nothing wrong. She'd said it herself. She didn't deserve to be sentenced to this hell.

Wishing himself mortal for the millionth time this day alone, Cadegan transformed to a small blackbird and flew to nest in a tree for the night.

With *a heavy* sigh, Jo returned the dice to the leather pouch and tucked them and the small box back into the larger one where Cadegan kept them stored. Her heart lurched at his paltry entertainment.

So much for Xbox. He'd probably kill to have something like that here.

As she closed the lid, she scowled at the sight of a bright red spot on top of the wood. It was fresh blood. Glancing around, she saw more spattered drops and a few smears, and realized that Cadegan must have been injured in his fight while he protected her.

Why hadn't he said anything about it?

And as she stood there, she saw images in her mind of Cadegan alone at the table, playing against his own shadow, for hours on end, as he faced the sparse earthen wall.

Night after night.

How did he stand it? The solitude alone had to be excruciating. No music. No TV.

No conversation.

In fact, she was able to search his entire place completely in less than half an hour. It was the tiniest of homes.

His cupboard held some dried meat and fruit. A few onions, small bowls of dried leeks and barley. Flagon of wine and mead. His old-styled pots were as meager and bare as the furnishings. A few skins on the floor.

Damn.

After climbing the narrow wooden ladder, she stood in

the small loft and stared at the twin-sized pallet that said he didn't entertain others in his bed. Ever. She was actually surprised the tiny thing fit him alone.

The thin mattress was made of straw and covered with a clean, worn linen bedsheet and furs. There was a larger old-fashioned trunk set next to it that contained another black robe like the one he'd worn, along with a leather-wrapped kit for mending his chain mail. A needle and thread. Two white linen tunics and three wool breeches. Three pairs of scratchy wool socks.

Dang, his life sucked. She'd never again complain about hers. It might have moments of supreme misery, but she always had her family around to make her laugh no matter how bad she felt.

Sitting on the bed, she heard a slight rattle. She glanced at the post and found an old wooden rosary, of all things, hung there.

"Guess you can't be a vampire and sleep with that."

As she leaned back against the headboard, she realized that it was an ancient shield of some sort. Celtic in design, yet she'd always assumed they used small round shields, like the ones hanging in his walls. This one reminded her more of a long Roman type. And it appeared to be made of solid gold.

"Shiny," she breathed, running her hand over the ornate engraving on its surface. In addition to the traditional Celtic scrollwork were harps and cauldrons. In the center circle was the image of an oak tree with what appeared to be ruby apples hanging from its branches.

It was the only thing of true value that he owned, and it seemed oddly out of place. And unlike the other weapons, this one didn't have a ding or scratch on it. It was as pristine as the day it'd been created.

Yeah, okay, in a hobbit hole of oddities, this was the strangest of all.

And none of it gave her the slightest hint as to what kind of creature Cadegan might be. Assuming this was real and not a coma or dream. What kind of creature lived for hundreds of years and didn't age? Carried a rosary, ate food, lacked fangs . . .

None of it made sense.

For the first time in her life, she wished she'd paid more attention to her family's insanity and interests. Those loons could probably not only read the rune writing on his stuff, but they'd know exactly who and what he was. Someone in her family had probably even written a book on his breed.

She pulled the rosary from the bedpost and wove it around her fingers. On the back of the cross, worn Latin words were etched. *Pax Vobiscum. . . . Peace be with you.*

Yeah, that was strangely fitting for the quiet man who'd

fought off her attackers with terrifying skill and ease. There was a peace to him that went against the violence she knew him capable of.

In that moment, she regretted chasing him away. But then that was what she did. Every man she'd ever been with had hit the door running. Some even screaming as they went.

Especially Barry.

In his defense, she'd been throwing flaming objects at him as she chased him out of her house. But that was another story.

Yet the saddest part? She didn't really miss her ex-husband. How could anyone be married for five years, after dating for two, and not cry over a divorce? She'd screamed plenty. Had even allowed Selena and Tabitha to make Voodoo dolls of him. And Karma to curse his penis.

But no tears. Not a single one.

What saddened her was the empty house. The vacant areas where his stuff had once been stored. She missed having a body around, especially at night.

*I'm broken.*

That was why she loved her dogs so much. They didn't judge her and find her lacking. They never criticized. Rather, they loved her, even when she wasn't worthy of it.

Of course, they'd love anyone with the opposable thumbs required to open and dispense Alpo and Kibbles.

Yeah. Not wanting to think about the truth in that, she moved back to the tiny washstand that stood beside his chest and washed her makeup off. With nothing else to do, she went to bed and hoped that in the morning, she'd wake up in her own world.

But sleep didn't come as she lay nestled in furs that held the rich, masculine scent of the most enigmatic creature she'd ever met. It made her wonder where he was sleeping tonight. Surely he wasn't out there with those creatures.

Was he?

*Why do you care?*

Jo glanced around the stark, torchlit room and wondered how many countless nights Cadegan had lain here. In solitary agony. And in that moment, she realized why she cared.

No one deserved this.

"Cadegan?" she whispered. "If you can hear me, I'm sorry if I hurt you. And if you *can* hear me, can you come back? I hate to be alone. Please, don't leave me like this."

A tear slid from the corner of her eye as the harshest reality of all bit her. Because she had such a humongous family, she'd never spent five minutes alone. It was the reason she had three dogs.

Her hell was isolation. She couldn't stand this feeling of being alone, with no one around.

As she wept silently, the shield began to glow and hum. Jo lifted her head to frown at it.

What the . . . ?

Deep in the gold, a blurry male face glimmered.

# 4

Terrified, Jo pushed herself away from the shield as the face became more defined and clear.

"Jo?"

She froze as she saw Cadegan's image there, staring at her. "What the hell? Cade, we really need to chat about the size of your iPhone, buddy. Are you overcompensating for something? Hmmm?"

The baffled expression on his face said that he was completely clueless.

She smiled at him. "Sorry. We use iPhones to chat with images like this. But they're only this big." She held her hand up to illustrate the size of it.

"Oh. I'd pondered that word before." He paused. "Have you a need, lass?"

She nodded before she could stop herself. "Can you come back here?"

Adorably sheepish, he materialized beside the bed. With a stern scowl, he brushed a knuckle against her wet cheek. "Are you injured?"

Jo took his hand in hers and held on tight as she pressed it against her cheek. "I don't like to be alone. I know it's weird at my age, but there you have it."

He offered her a kind smile. "It's not off. I more than ken your sadness at it."

Of course he did. He knew the misery much better than she did.

Dropping her gaze to his other hand, she finally saw the blood that was drying there. "You're hurt?"

Nonchalant about it, he shrugged. "A grayling got in a nip earlier."

"Grayling?"

"The knobby creatures what attacked you on your arrival. They be fast. Sometimes even faster than I."

Jo got up and went to the washstand to wet another cloth. "Let me see the wound."

He didn't move. "No worries. It'll heal, now, in a minute."

She wrinkled her nose. "You keep saying that phrase, but it doesn't make any logical sense. *Now, in a minute* is a serious oxymoron."

He snorted. "Fancy that, will you? Being criticized for me sentence by a woman I only understand every third word of."

Laughing, she tugged at his robe. "Off with it, bunky. I want to check that wound."

Cadegan hesitated before he obeyed. He pulled the robe over his head and folded it, then placed it on top of his holding chest.

She gave him an irritated smirk as she pinched at his mail tunic. "That was rather pointless, huh?"

With a half laugh, he untied then removed his chain mail and padded gambeson before he unlaced and rolled back the sleeve of his undertunic.

"Oh my God, you're like a Russian nesting doll. How many layers are you wearing?"

He shrugged at her shocked, teasing tone. "Just what I've always worn."

Rolling her eyes, she pushed the sleeve back until she had the raw, jagged wound exposed. She cringed at the sight of it. It had to hurt like the dickens. Yet he didn't react to it at all. That more than anything told her how miserable an existence he lived.

Jo hesitated as she saw the true depth of the bite, as well as the number of other scars on his forearm. Claw marks, bites, and other things she couldn't even begin to guess at. His flesh was riddled with them. The strangest, though, were the ones wrapped around his right forearm and fingers that appeared to be row after row of diamond-shaped scars. It reminded her of a press of some sort that had waffled his arm. Had he caught it in a wringer or some such?

She ran her fingers over the odd scarred pattern. "What's this from?"

His cheeks mottled with color before he glanced away. " 'Tis naught."

" 'Tis something. Why do they embarrass you?"

A tic started in his jaw. "They don't matter." He started to pull away.

Jo held him by her side. "Then why not tell me?"

He fisted his right hand and sighed before he finally gave in. "When I was a lad, Brother Owain used to pinch at the coffers for his gambling. When Father Bryce noticed the missing coin, he blamed me for it, as I was the one Brother Owain said was the last in the room with it all. The scars are left from me hazard over it."

Jo struggled to follow his words and understand the story. "Your brother did this to you?"

"Nay, I was an oblate."

She held his arm as she washed at the clotting blood. "I don't know that word."

"Me mother tossed me to the monks as soon as I was whelped. I was raised in the monastery, destined to take me vows."

Well, that explained the Benedictine robe he wore. "Did you?"

He shook his head. "Right before I was to make them, the king came and took me to battle."

That was a strange way to phrase it. Did he mean what it sounded like? "Kidnapped you?"

He snorted in bitter resentment. "He was king, lass. It was go willingly or die voluntarily."

She winced at the awful choice he'd been given. It had to have been hard to go from a monk's life to war with so little warning. Which begged another question, especially if he'd been given to the monastery as an infant. . . . "Did you even know how to fight?"

"Nay, but battle learned me quick."

She could just imagine. It was a wonder he hadn't been

slaughtered the first day, and it explained a lot about the sword skills she'd witnessed on her arrival. "How old were you?"

"Ten-and-four."

Her jaw dropped as she imagined a skinny little boy being dragged away from his home by armored knights to fight in a medieval battle. He must have been terrified. "You went to war at fourteen?" she asked incredulously.

"Aye." It was a simple statement of emotionless fact. But she knew better than that. There was no way a child could be put through those horrors and not be scarred inside from it all. It was unfathomable.

And what they'd done to him was unconscionable.

As she cleaned his wound and really saw the deep scars those battles had left him with, her heart broke for him.

She fingered the diamond-shaped ones that had started her down this brutal path. "So what you're saying is that you were tortured because one of the monks was stealing from the monastery in order to gamble, and blamed you for the theft?"

He sighed wearily. "We're all brought up under a tub from time to time."

"Meaning?"

"Sooner or later, all of us take the blame of another's ill actions."

Truer words . . .

But it didn't take away the internal agony such things left

behind. That sense of brutal betrayal. No one liked to be blamed for things they did, and to take the blame for something you didn't do was all the worse. Not to mention, Cadegan would have been younger than fourteen when they did that to him. How could a grown man allow a mere boy to suffer so for his crimes? She'd never understand such cruelty.

"I'm sorry, Cadegan."

He shrugged. "No worries. Could be worse. Could've lost me hand entirely. Damn near. Luckily, it just left me coggy-handed."

She frowned again at a term she'd never heard before. "Coggy-handed?"

"I primarily use me left hand, nowadays." He glanced past her shoulder to see his rosary on the bed where she'd left it. Without a word, he returned it to the bedpost.

"Was that yours at the monastery?"

Nodding, he rolled his sleeve back down and laced it closed. "I shall leave you to sleep."

As he started for the ladder, she caught his arm. "I really don't like to be alone. Can you stay in the loft with me?"

Cadegan glanced to the tiny bed before another rush of red stained his cheeks.

She wasn't immune to the thought herself, but her racing blood didn't go to her face. Rather, it went to a part of her body that made a demand she wasn't sure would be the smartest thing to do. Against reason, it begged for her to strip his clothes off and explore every vast inch of his hard body.

"Are you sure you want me up here with you, lass?"

"Please."

Averting his gaze from the bed and her, he moved to sit on the floor, by his shield. With his legs stretched out before him, he folded his arms over his chest, lowered his head, and closed his eyes as if he intended to sleep that way.

It was such a sweet, innocent, and unassuming action that it made her smile.

"Cade," she said in a chiding tone. "When I said stay in the loft, I meant share the bed with me."

His eyebrows shot north as he opened his eyes and locked gazes with her. "Beg pardon?"

"We're both adults, right? We can share the bed and nothing else. You stay on your corner of the cot. I stay on mine."

He actually pouted as he considered her proposal. After a few seconds, he nodded. "Very well, lass. If it pleases you."

She toed her shoes off before she returned to the bed and rolled to her side to make room for him.

Cadegan hesitated at the sight of her in his bed. He'd never really shared a bed with anyone before. At least not for anything more than a few carnal hours.

And it had never been *his* bed, but rather the woman's.

A smile toyed at the edges of his lips as he watched her

trying to get comfortable without a pillow. Since the austere abbot had considered any kind of comfort sinful, Cadegan had grown up without one. After he'd been conscripted to war, he'd had even fewer bodily comforts as they battled against the English.

He'd never given thought to it before this. Now . . . he manifested a pillow for her.

When he handed it to her, her entire face lit up. "Thank you!"

He gave a curt nod and watched as she promptly tucked it between her head and arm. She looked adorable like that. Preciously sweet, and much more tempting than she should be.

Trying not to focus on that untoward line of thought, he slid into bed beside her and gave her his back. He bent his arm under his head and closed his eyes to sleep, and not think about the warmth pressing up against his spine, or the gentle vanilla-almond scent that made his mouth water and his groin heavy.

He ground his teeth in an effort to squash his useless fantasies.

"Cade?" she whispered after a few minutes. "Are you still wearing your shoes?"

"Aye."

"Aren't you uncomfortable?"

"I don't understand your question."

Jo rolled over, colliding with him until she'd wiggled enough that she was now facing his rigid back. From the waist down, he still wore his chain mail. Even his spurs. "You always sleep in your armor?"

"Aye."

"Seriously?"

He didn't move or react to her shock even a bit. "Aye."

"Always?" she repeated.

"Aye," he said yet again in that ever-patient tone.

She lifted herself up to look down at him. He had his eyes closed, and but for the gentle rise and fall of his chest, she'd think him asleep already. "Does it not chafe?"

"I suppose. . . . Does it matter?"

Well, yeah.

It probably shouldn't, and yet she didn't like the thought of him in perpetual pain. "Do you ever take it off?"

"Aye, to bathe."

"But not to sleep?"

"Nay, lass." He sighed before he explained more fully. "Habit of the army. The Mercian's dodges were to come at us in the midst of the prime hour of the Sidhe court."

She scowled at his excuse. What the heck did he just say, anyway? "English, dude. Speak. English!"

He laughed at her feigned angry outburst. "We were oft

attacked in the midst of night, by our enemies. Therefore, we slept armed so as not to be caught bare-arsed in a fight."

Oh . . .

The harshness of his life washed over her. And before she even realized what she was doing, she reached out to brush her hand through his short, prickly hair. It was barely half an inch long. Her cousin Molly had longer leg hair than what was left on his head. But then, he had no one to grow or style it for.

From the looks of it, he'd sawed it off with one of his swords so that he wouldn't have to bother with it.

She had a bad feeling from his calm acceptance of this life that he'd never known anything else. And that made her wonder one thing. "Has anyone ever loved you?"

Cadegan swallowed hard as her question awoke bitter memories. Memories that led him back to one single truth. "Nay, lass. I've no understanding of that word."

Closing his eyes again, he savored the sensation of her gentle fingers brushing against his scalp. No one had ever touched him like this.

Like he mattered to them.

Much of it he'd written off as his being reserved. He was a bit much for most. Too tall. Too intense. Too scary. Too demonic.

Too scarred.

In his monastic youth, he'd known nothing about women

and the pleasures they could provide a man. He'd only seen them at a great distance from his garden duties, whenever they might venture to the alm's door to beg for charity. It was as far as they were allowed into the monastery. And from that distance, they'd been indistinguishable from men.

Once his mother had birthed Cadegan in a monastery cell and abandoned him there, Father Bryce had strictly refused to allow any woman inside the gate. For any reason. And Cadegan had been forbidden to venture near any gate or door that led outside the stone monastery walls.

Cadegan hadn't even known what a female voice sounded like. Not until he'd been conscripted. Only then had he heard their shrill cries of pleasure, and seen how the soldiers frolicked with the tarts that followed after their troops, trading themselves for coin and scraps.

Afraid of embarrassing himself and being mocked for it, he'd withheld himself until he was nearly a score in age. He would have most likely gone longer had one of the trollops not plied him with drink one night after a brutal battle that had made him crave any distraction from the memories of it.

In the end, she'd taken his virginity and robbed his coin, and left him with a back burning from her scratches, a merciless headache, and four days of bitter hunger because he'd lacked the silver to purchase anything to eat. That had learned him as well as his first foray into battle to keep his wits about him at all times whenever a woman was nigh. They were as dangerous as the trained Mercian and Saxon knights out to spill good Cymry blood . . . and far more treacherous.

But as Jo's breath fell against his skin whilst she played in his hair, he felt himself being witched by her tender spell. His sense told him to remain at the ready where she was concerned.

It wasn't that easy. Not when his cock was so hard and aching. When his heart was weakening him with a longing for things he'd never known.

Right then, he'd gladly offer up his life for the lass if she'd just dance her fingers over a lower part of his body.

Jo frowned as she dropped her gaze to his neck and saw another awful scar peeking out from beneath his linen collar. She traced the raised, puckered flesh with her fingertip. "How did you get this?"

"No memories of it, in particular."

How could he not know? It had to have been a bad . . .

Her breath caught as she slipped the collar down to see a bit more of his back.

No. . . .

Biting her lip, she pulled the hem of his shirt up to expose his back that was completely disfigured by scars. "Dear Lord, Cade. What did they do to you?"

He pulled his shirt down and returned to his rigid pose. " 'Tis naught."

No wonder he hadn't reacted to the bite on his arm. Compared to that mess on his back, it was nothing, indeed.

He sighed again. "You should sleep whilst you're able. The cock's crow won't be long now. Then, I'll see you off to yours."

As gently as she could, Jo rolled him to his back so that she could see his face. His expression blank and unassuming, he stared up at her. But his eyes held so much agony and want that it made her heart break for him.

A thousand years of solitude.

"Did the graylings scar your back, too?"

He shook his head. "What does it matter?"

She glanced down to where his shirt parted over his chest, revealing even more damage. No wonder he kept himself wrapped up like a cloistered monk. He even had a deep scar over his heart as if someone had dealt him a killing blow. "What are you, Cadegan? Really? Why was this done to you?"

Swallowing hard, he looked away.

At first, she thought he'd dodge the question.

He didn't. Drawing the cloth together to keep her from seeing his scars, he licked his lips before he spoke in a low tone. "Me father is a demon prince who seduced me mother so that he could steal from her. Once she learned the truth of him, she had no use for me." He rubbed at the scar over his heart.

"When I refused to steal from me mother for me father, he sicced his legions upon me. They hunt me, even here." He swallowed hard as a single tear slid from the corner of his eye. "Even though I be demonspawn, I harbor no harm for you, lass." He started to rise.

Jo held him in place. "What are you doing?"

"Leaving before you toss me from the bed." His emotionless tone told her that it was what women had always done to him.

She cupped his cheek in her hand and forced him to meet her gaze. "I'm still not sure this isn't a dream or hallucination. And I've never done anything rash in my life. Even after I caught my husband in bed with another woman, it took me three days to react to it."

He arched a brow at that. "Three days?"

She nodded. "I live in a splendid place I like to call denial. And I don't like change."

"So what did you do?" he asked.

"First, I had my cousin Karma put a pox curse on his junk, then I divorced him."

"His junk?"

She dropped her gaze down to Cadegan's groin.

Laughing, he reached up to touch a lock of her hair. "He must have been a great fool to choose another over you."

"Says the man who has yet to meet my frightening family.

Then again, being demonspawn, you'd fit right in with them. Karma would probably try to add you to her collection. Selena would want to interview you, and my cousin Molly would try to have you hunt down something she misplaced."

He frowned at her teasing tone. "I don't scare you?"

"Nah. The only thing that really scares me is the sound of an unknown person coughing under my bed."

"Pardon?"

She wrinkled her nose at him. "My mom and her sister would take me, my sister, and brother and cousins to my aunt's lake house every summer. My cousins are a little rowdy and either Karma or Essie would hide under the bed and mess with you whenever you slept. Coughing under the bed was one of their kinder, gentler pranks. After about age three minutes, I got used to it. They kicked the pansy right out of me. Toughened me, like hand-beaten leather."

Amazed, Cadegan sank his hand in her hair. "You're unlike any woman I've ever met."

"Yeah, that's me. *'You'll never forget Josette.'* And it was never said as a compliment."

He cocked his head curiously. "Josette?"

"My full name. Jo's the nickname I use because Josette, or worse, Josie the Pussycat, was mocked so abysmally in my youth."

He wrapped a lock of her hair around his forefinger so

that he could rub it with his thumb. "It's a beautiful name. As is the woman who bears it."

Those words melted her. *Don't you dare. . . .*

*Don't even think it. . . .*

But it was too late. She wanted him with a ferocious hunger that wouldn't be denied.

*What if it's not a dream and he's really a demon?*

*Do you hear yourself? You're an idiot. He can't be a demon. You don't believe in those things. You're in a coma. Accept it and do this hot piece of cheese before he turns into something foul.*

Cadegan held his breath as he felt the change in her. As her eyes darkened with the same needful longing that possessed him. She dipped her head toward his.

Against all common sense, he took that kiss and returned it with everything he had. Unlike the last one, this was fierce and demanding. A kiss born of raw lust, and it ignited a ferocious hunger inside him.

She pulled back, nipping at his lips as she lifted his tunic and ran her hands over his chest. He groaned out loud at the sensation of being touched by another. And when she bent to lave his nipple, he cried out and trembled in pleasure.

Laughing, she tried to untie the laces on his chausses.

Until she pulled back with a curse. "What in the name of

chocolate? Are you hermetically sealed in this thing? Dude, this is so cruel."

His laughter joined hers as he reached down to undo them, then realized she'd knotted and snarled the laces to the point they were impossibly tangled. Growling, he yanked at them. "It's like a bloody damn chastity belt."

"Give me a knife and I'll cut them off."

He froze to gape at her. "You're mad, woman, if you think I'm letting you near me tenders with a knife. Have you lost ever bit of your better noggin?"

"I heard a definite *yes, Jo. You can indeed cut me out of these* in that garbled mess you mistakenly think is English."

She actually reached for one.

Aghast, and somewhat afraid, he quickly used his powers to strip off every stitch from his body. "Don't you dare, lass!"

She passed a beguiling grin of devilry at him. "Hah! I knew you could do that. All you needed was a little motivation."

Ach, she was precious to him. Smiling at her teasing ways, he kissed her gently as undefined and unknown emotions swirled inside him. He'd never laughed and been teased in bed like this.

Out of bed, either, for that matter.

It was a wonderful feeling.

Jo couldn't breathe as she savored the taste of him while his tongue danced with hers. The image of his naked body was branded in her mind. Even covered with scars, he was exquisite as he slowly unbuttoned her shirt.

Until he got to her bra and pulled back with a Welsh curse. "What the devil? How does this monstrosity work?"

She rubbed her nose against his. "No fun, is it? Trying to unwrap a present that's been super-glued together."

He narrowed his gaze playfully before her clothes vanished as quickly as his had.

Gasping, she pulled the sheet up to cover herself. "Yeah, okay. You got some wicked powers there, buddy. Careful with those."

His eyes dark, he didn't answer as he slowly lowered her hand so that he could reach to cup her breast. The warmth of his callused fingers sent chills over her. He returned to her lips before he laid her back on the bed and parted her thighs with his knees.

Biting her lip, she reached for the medallion he wore, cradling it in her hand so that she could see it. A little larger than a quarter, it held the image of a three-headed dragon clasping a shield in its claws. Something was written in runes across the shield. "What does this say?"

He glanced down and whispered against her skin as he nuzzled her neck, *"A ddioddefws a orfu."*

"Easy for you to say, Welshman. What does it actually mean?"

"He who suffers, triumphs."

She cupped his face in her hands as tears choked her. How apropos for him. No wonder he wore it. Wanting to soothe the pain she saw in his eyes, she wrapped her legs around his waist and cradled his entire body with hers.

Cadegan sucked his breath in sharply at the sensation of her naked skin on his. He'd forgotten just how soft a female's flesh could be, and hers was the softest he'd ever known. Scented with almonds and vanilla, she made his head spin, especially as she breathed in his ear and nibbled his lobe. It was all he could do not to come from the pleasure of it alone.

Biting his lip until it bled, he knew he was tilting against Goliath with a broken lance.

His breathing ragged, he met her dark gaze while he trailed his fingers over the curve of her smooth cheek. "I swear, Josette, I'll spend the rest of this night making amends to you. But I cannot withhold myself a moment longer." Unable to stand it, he slid himself deep inside her.

Jo moaned at how good he felt as he thrust himself against her hips. Thick and hard, he filled her completely. She'd forgotten just how good sex could be. Then again, no one had ever made love to her like this. Like she was the very air he needed to breathe. He kept his gaze locked with hers as he quickened his pace with a fierce growl.

She ran her hand over his scarred back until she cupped his hard, gorgeous rump.

Suddenly, he shuddered against her and cried out as he came, panting in her arms. He buried his face in the crook of her neck and held her as if she was the most precious gem in existence.

Jo started to pout, but then caught herself. Yes, it'd been a year for her, but that was absolutely nothing compared to his record.

For that, she'd cut the boy some slack. In a weird way, she was even a little flattered.

She rubbed her cheek against his as she ran the bottoms of her feet down the prickly hair on his legs. Closing her eyes, she savored the warmth of his body on hers. It was good just to be this close to someone again.

Bashful, Cadegan lifted his head to meet her gaze. He brushed the hair back from her face. "Sorry, lass. I know you deserve better than that from me. I promise you, I tried to stop it. But your sweet beauty overcame me faster than I could fight it."

She started to tell him it was okay when all of a sudden she felt something hard and deep inside her again.

*What the . . . ?*

It began to vibrate and radiate out in the most erotic sensation imaginable. Honestly, it felt like he was still inside her as he dipped his head to gently suckle at her breast. Frowning, she glanced around the room, wondering what the heck was going on.

A slow, insidious smile spread over Cadegan's face. "Like that, do you?"

Her breathing ragged, she stared at him. "Is that you?"

He nodded as he moved to her other breast so that he could lick and tease her all the more. "My powers are infinite, and right now, I can think of no better use for them than to put a smile on your lovely face."

That was a serious understatement of his abilities. His fingers teasing her, he kissed his way to her stomach as his powers continued to vibrate inside her.

Her body on fire, Jo cried out as unimaginable pleasure splintered through her entire being. Holy cow!

Slowly, methodically, Cadegan tasted and stroked every inch of her while he continued to use his powers to fill her.

When she finally came, it was the hottest, most amazing orgasm she'd ever experienced. She screamed out so loudly, it left her hoarse.

Yeah, he definitely made up for his earlier quick-draw release.

And then some.

Reeling and breathless, she draped herself over his body. "That was incredible."

"Mmm," he breathed against her hair as he carefully separated the folds of her body with his fingers while he began growing hard again. "Surely you didn't think I was done with you so soon?"

Jo couldn't respond as she slowly rode his fingers.

His smile widened. "Like that, too?"

She nodded.

"Good, 'cause I intend to fulfill my promise about the night."

And that he did. Over and over, until she was weak and spent, and sleeping like a baby in the circle of his muscular arms.

Completely satiated for the first time in his life, Cadegan played idly in Josette's dark hair as he listened to her soft, gentle snore, while she slumbered on top of him. He still couldn't believe this was real. That she'd shared her body with him so thoroughly, and now lay draped over him like the warmest blanket he'd ever known. For no real reason, other than she'd desired him.

He couldn't fathom it.

And in that moment, he wanted to keep her here in his arms. Nothing else would give him more pleasure. *You can't do that to her, and you know it.*

He ground his teeth as anger flogged his reason. Why couldn't he?

*You know why.*

It would be wrong. She didn't belong in this cold, drab world. Not when she had the bright, brilliant realm she called home, waiting for her.

Family and friends who would mourn her absence.

Yet in this quiet moment, he didn't want to do the right thing. He was so tired of being alone. Of being punished for a birth he'd never wanted. Begging for a death that was denied him.

Was it too much to ask that he be granted one person, just one, who could cherish his presence? Seek him out for warmth and companionship?

One person who could love him?

*"For your crimes, I curse you to eternity alone!"*

Cradling her head against him, he flinched at the angry voice that was never far from his thoughts.

Maybe this was his new hell. After all these centuries, he'd finally purged the memories of a woman's body from his heart and learned to live without longing.

Now, the memories were fresh, and far sweeter than they'd been before. Josette hadn't used him for protection. She hadn't lied to him and given him false hope.

She seemed to even like him.

His heart breaking, he glanced around the dingy walls that had been his home for countless centuries. This night with her had been a mistake. He should have let the graylings take her.

But from the moment he'd heard her scream and looked upon the face of an angel, he'd been sunk.

*Damn you all for this.*

There was nothing to be done for it. At least he'd had one night with her.

As with all things, he'd find a way through the pain. Learn to soldier on past it.

Lifting her hand, he laid her palm against his cheek and wished for things he couldn't have. Wished for impossible dreams.

Most of all, he wished upon her the life she deserved. A man who would cherish her. Children who would adore her. Peace, and eternal happiness.

Aye, a soul so kind and generous had earned that and more. As soon as she awoke, he'd take her home and set her free to live for both of them. In the realm of light.

But he knew the bitter truth of it. He'd spend the rest of her life watching her from this shadowed realm, wishing he could be with her in hers.

That would be his true hell. To see her, and never again touch her so intimately.

He winced at the future he didn't want to face.

*You win, Father . . . Leucious. I cede victory to you both. You've done what you set out to do.*

They'd finally broken him completely.

# 5

Jo sighed contentedly as she awoke to the most incredible sensation of warmth and security. She'd never known anything like this. She felt invincible. How stupid was that? She was buck naked and in a hole, yet she had the sensation that nothing bad could touch her. Ever.

Blinking her eyes open, she found herself still on top of Cadegan, who was sound sleep. He held on to her with one arm while the other was draped over his eyes.

Granted, the pallet wasn't all that comfortable, but his body was a different story. She fit perfectly against him. As if the contours of her body had been made solely for his. Smiling at the thought, she ran her fingertip over his nipple, skimming the small dark blond hairs that surrounded it, and admired the way the torchlight played across his tawny skin and muscles. Only the sight of his myriad of scars dampened her mood.

So *much* needless pain.

She fingered his medallion that was warm from his body's heat, and wondered how he'd gotten it. Had it been a gift from someone? He didn't seem the kind of man who'd buy something like this for himself.

*He who suffers, triumphs.*

Yeah, it sounded like something one of the monks from his childhood would have given him to encourage him, and to remind him that things could get better. Yet, for him, they never had. And that made her ache for him that he was kept chained here, like an animal in the zoo.

How he found the strength to get up every day and soldier on with nothing to look forward to astounded her. How could he do that, for a thousand years? There were days when she didn't want to get out of bed.

Today being one of them, but that was for a whole other happy reason.

As she placed the medallion back on his chest, she saw that he was now awake and watching her from beneath his arm.

"Good morning, sunshine," she teased.

He offered her a sexy half grin. "Morning, *caru*."

Rage infused her. So much for feeling bad for the jerk! *You asshole!* "It's Jo! Not Karen. Oh my God, I can't believe you don't remember my name!"

When she started to pull away, he held her immobile with a strength that was now terrifying as she realized how easily he could hurt her if he chose to.

"I remember your name, Josette. How could I ever forget it? *Caru* isn't another woman's name. It means *love* . . . it was meant as an endearment. Never an insult to you."

Suddenly, she felt like an idiot for overreacting. *Damn you, Barry, for that.* "Oh. I'm sorry."

He brushed his hand through the tangles in her hair. " 'Tis I who am sorry for the man who hurt you so much that you think another would not remember the touch, face, and name of the goddess Aphrodite after a night she's spent in his arms. How could I ever confuse you with another when you are the most beautiful woman I've ever seen?"

Tears blurred her vision at his sincere words. No one had ever spoken such poetry to her. "Only you have ever made me feel beautiful," she confessed. For that matter, he was the only one who'd ever made her feel safe and treasured. How stupid was that? She hadn't even known him a full day and yet there was no denying what she felt deep inside.

Damn it all, she was falling in love with a complete stranger.

He ran his hand along the edge of her jaw, raising chills over her arms. "Then you've never met a real man, Josette. Only great fools."

Smiling, she fingered his lips. As she tried to rise up to kiss him, he caught her against his body.

"Careful with me goods, love. There are a few things down there I'd like to keep attached for a while longer."

Laughing, she kissed his cheek. "I'd hate to deprive you." Jo glanced around the room as she realized something very important was missing. "Um . . . out of curiosity, where might one go to do some business?"

The frown on his face said that he had no clue what she meant.

"Bathroom, Cade. I need one. And not *now, in a minute.* Now as in *now.*"

"Ah."

Clothes appeared instantly on their bodies. One moment they were nestled in bed and in the next, she found herself outside, near a small brook in the forest.

As Cadegan started away from her, she grabbed his arm. "Where are you going?"

He arched a brow at her question. "I assumed you'd want some privacy for your *business*."

"Yeah, but where's the bathroom?"

He gestured at a copse of trees.

"Seriously?"

"Aye. It's all we have."

Ew! It was as bad as going camping with Uncle Tom and Essie and Tiyana. Nature sucked when it came to bathroom breaks. "You don't have any TP?"

"TP?"

"Toilet paper, for the love of God and his saints, man. Cottonelle. Scott. Quilted Northern. Angel Soft? *Any* of that ring a bell with you?"

He dared to laugh at her outrage. Something that made her want to choke him. With a devilish grin, he held his hand out and a roll of modern convenience appeared instantly. "Will this do, lass?"

"Yes! Thank you." Grabbing the roll, she headed for shrubbery. And if a knight who said *Ni* appeared, she planned on screaming.

Loudly. And with great passion and fearless embarrassment.

Once she'd finished, she made her way back to where

Cadegan waited with a small bowl of gray, seeded berries. He was chewing on what appeared to be a stick of some kind.

"What is that?" she asked, gesturing to what had to be a most unappetizing breakfast as he literally gnawed on it, like a dog with rawhide.

He swallowed before he answered. "Merlin Root."

"Is it good?"

He screwed his face up. "Not even a trifle." He held the bowl out to her. "These are much better for the tongue, but there weren't many to be had, as they mostly bloom at night, so I saved them for you."

Hesitating, she picked one of the grayish round berries from the bowl. "Why is there no color here?" Even their skin was back to being gray.

" 'Tis said that when the great Penmerlin Aquila pulled Avalon and Camelot out of the human realm to protect the race of man from the fey queen's army, part of Morgen's court ran to the abbey, thinking they'd be safe from her powers. As they did so, it pulled the Merlin's magick here and damned the unfortunate occupants to dwell in the shadows for all time."

Was he talking about *the* Morgen and Merlin the Magician? "Camelot? Like King Arthur and Lancelot?"

He nodded as she took a bite and found the berry to be quite tasty in spite of its unappetizing color.

Jo turned around to see the area with new eyes as she

digested his tidbit. So this was the Glastonbury Tor she'd heard her cousins talking and arguing about. Wow. Not what she expected, by a long shot. "Were you one of Arthur's knights?"

Offended, Cadegan snorted. "I'm not *that* old, lass. Arthur died long before I drew me first breath."

"Oh, sorry." She picked up another berry. "But you have to admit, you are older than older's older cousin."

Cadegan didn't want to cede any such truth. Ignoring her sarcasm, he sucked his breath in as he saw the juices from the berry on her lips. Before he could stop himself, he lifted her chin and kissed it from them. His heart pounding with needful longing, he breathed her in, wishing he could stay right here, in her arms, for eternity.

But alas, he needed to be sending her on her way. And sooner rather than later. Every second she was here, especially in the open, she was a threat to his life.

She lifted her hand to offer him a berry. "Can I ask you something?"

He almost declined taking her food. But before he could stop himself, he ate it from her hand, and allowed her to tame him when no one ever had before. Normally, he'd lop the appendage off anyone foolish enough to attempt such where he was concerned. Yet he didn't mind such intimacies with her. Rather, he craved them. "Of course, lass."

Frowning, she stared up at him. "How do you stand it

here? Really? How can you tolerate the unending silence and not go bat-shit crazy?"

Bat-shit crazy? He snorted at the hilarious term. "That's never been the part what bothered me."

She was aghast. "How can it not?"

He shrugged. "I reckon it has to do with growing up at Cymara Clas."

"Growing up where?"

"Cymara Clas . . ." He paused as he searched for the English translation for it. "Um . . . *clas* . . . cloister?" At her nod, he continued. "The monks there had all taken vows of silence, so I never heard human language until the king came, forced us to open our gates for his men, and took me away."

Jo swallowed her berry. It was a solid minute before the full weight of his simple statement hit her with a harsh reality. "Are you telling me that they took you to war, and you couldn't even understand or communicate with them?"

"Aye."

Her mind boggled as she tried to make sense of everything he'd told her. "But you knew the monks' names? How?"

He moved his hands in graceful gestures to explain it to her.

"Sign language? The monks spoke to you in signs?"

"Aye. Likewise, I think in pictures and not with words, even now."

She took his scarred right hand into hers as another awful

thought occurred to her. "And when they hurt you for the theft you didn't do, you couldn't sign, could you?"

He tossed a random stone across the small brook as they walked through the forest. "Not for nigh about a year."

Total silence. No way to speak and tell anyone anything. No way to ask for help . . .

Unshed tears for him tightened her chest. "Cadegan, how did you stand it?"

He furrowed his brow as if he didn't comprehend why she was indignant on his behalf. "It's all I knew, lass. You don't miss what you don't know. 'Tis the same as asking a fish if it grieves for not flying." He scratched at his cheek. "In a peculiar way, I find the silence and solitude here comforting. When I'm allowed it."

"Then what is it about this place that bothers you? If *that's* not the most irritating part?"

He picked up more stones. "Being stalked and hunted. Me worst fear is being taken for torture and never finding a way to escape it."

Again, her jaw dropped. Was he implying what it sounded like? "How often does that happen?"

"So far, never. I've always eventually found a way out whenever they take me."

He totally missed her point. "How often do they capture you?"

Screwing his face up, Cadegan paused as if he had to seriously consider the number. "'Tis not as oft now as it once was."

"Meaning?"

"I'm better at fighting them off these days, lass."

Dear Lord, it was exactly what it'd sounded like. It was so commonplace that he didn't even flinch or hesitate to speak about it. "Cadegan . . . we've got to get you out of here. How do we break the spell?"

He laughed bitterly. "There's no spell locking me here to be broken. Me brother sent me to the one realm he knew I could never leave from."

"Your brother? You mean another monk?"

His eyes sad, he shook his head as he tossed the stones into the water. "Me half brother, Leucious. Once after I'd been wounded in war, he came and offered me to ride in his army, to fight others of our kind. I agreed, with reservations I should have heeded."

"Then why did he put you here?"

Cadegan sighed. "'Tis a long story that matters naught."

She hated how he defaulted to that on things that mattered most of all. It was as if he thought that if he downplayed them enough, they wouldn't hurt so much. But that wasn't how it worked. The only way to ease the pain was to work through it with someone who cared. Someone who would pick you up when you fell, without hesitation, and not judge you for your past.

Jo had always had her family for that.

Cadegan had never had a single soul.

"Is your brother your only family?" she asked.

"Nay. Both me parents are still alive, and they have other children aplenty."

"Can't they get you out of here?"

He laughed bitterly. "Lass, as soon as me mother squeezed me from her body, she tossed me to the monks and never looked back. Me father sired me only to use me against her, which is why she wants nothing to do with me. I can't fault her there. Me siblings have their own lives that have never been a part of mine. And after what Leucious did, I realized I'm better off without any of them. Truth be told, I'd much rather be with meself than those who can't be trusted."

How could someone have so large a family and not a single member of it defend them? Love them? She couldn't fathom his circumstances any more than he could fathom hers.

"I refuse to believe you're stuck here."

He smiled sadly. "It matters naught."

"Cade! Stop saying that! Of course it matters. How can it not?"

He paused to give her an intense, sincere stare. "I've been here for a thousand years, lass. What do you propose I do in your world? Where would I live? How could I work? I barely understand half of what *you* say. You speak of things that are far beyond my ken."

Indignant and furious, she raked him with a scathing glare. "Oh fine, throw logic and sense at me, why don't you? What kind of asshole are you to argue with reason, huh?"

"And the taste to the pudding is that . . . what are you saying, lass? It makes no sense to me."

Honestly, she didn't know what her point was, either. She could barely take care of herself. She'd been a failure in everything she'd ever tried to do.

But there was one truth she couldn't deny. She pulled him to a stop and placed her hand to his cheek. "You break my heart, sweetie. It hurts me to see you banished here in this glum, forsaken hell."

He held her hand to his face as if trying to burn the sensation of being touched into his memory. "I am relegated."

"You shouldn't have to be relegated to this! No one should."

He cupped her hand in his before he kissed the back of her knuckles. "Nothing changes, love. Ever. Hope is a fickle vixen sent to torment us with discontent. And I am done with her, and her empty promises, and wishes unfulfilled."

His anguished gaze tore her apart. "A thousand years." He enunciated each word with harsh bitterness. "I would rather you flay me skin from me bones, than flog me heart with things that cannot be. Take your useless hope back to your world with you. I only pray she's far kinder to you than she's ever been to me."

Suddenly, a loud screech sounded.

Cringing at the nerve-shattering decibel level, Jo covered her ears.

Cadegan scanned the drab gray sky over their heads. "Time's passed, love. You've got to go." There was a panicked undertone to his voice.

"What is *that*?"

He pressed his forehead against hers. "Enemies who want what I will never give to them. I took an oath to Brother Eurig, and I will not break it." His brow furrowed, he placed the backs of his fingers to her cheekbone. "They've taken everything from me, lass. I won't let them take you, too."

He teleported them from the brook to someplace deep in a gnarled forest. While it was lighter now than it'd been last night, it was still dark gray and colorless. But there was something strangely shiny between two small trees to her right. It reminded her of a sideways pond that reflected light back at them.

Cadegan nudged her toward it. "You needs go through. You'll be with yours, then."

An intense pain racked her at the thought of abandoning

him here. In spite of what he said, she knew he was lonely in his isolation. He'd been too grateful for her touch for it to be otherwise.

"Come with me! We'll figure everything out together."

Agony darkened his gaze as he cupped her cheek in his gloved hand. "I can't, lass. No matter how much I wish it."

The screeching came closer.

"You have to go, Josette."

Tears filled her eyes. She couldn't make herself go through the gate. Not without him. "Cade—"

He silenced her protest with a kiss. "On with you, now. Live for us both."

Jo heard Selena and Karma calling frantically for her from the other side of the shimmering image. She looked back at Cadegan. "Are you sure you can't follow me?"

He placed his hand on the shimmering portal to show her that for him, it was a solid, impenetrable wall. "Nay, lass. I am damned here. Now go while you're able. And break the glass once you're clear of it."

The screeching was almost on top of them now. He unsheathed his sword and moved to protect her.

"Can I come back to visit you?"

Cadegan clenched his teeth at a question that tore him asunder. There was nothing that would give him greater pleasure. But alas, it couldn't be. " 'Tis too dangerous. For us both."

"Jo! Where are you! Don't make me call your mama! I mean it, girl! I will do it!"

She ignored Karma's angry tone on the other side of the mirror. "Cadegan . . ."

He said something in Welsh before he pushed her forward.

Like he'd done a moment ago, she slammed into a wall. "Stop!" she snarled as he continued to push her. "I can't go through it, either!"

Cadegan froze as he realized that she was trapped here, too. Nay. It wasn't possible!

Rage gripped him as he assaulted the portal with every bit of the fury he kept bottled inside himself.

Jo gasped as she saw a side of Cadegan that terrified her. He was out of control as he beat against the portal and shouted in Welsh. At least, that's what she assumed it was.

All of a sudden, the screeching was on them. And as she saw what made that sound, her stomach slid to her feet. Dark and twisted, they definitely weren't human.

"Cadegan?" She reached out to pat his shoulder. "What are those?"

He turned and let loose another string of curses. "Stay behind me." With the same skill he'd used the night before, he fought them until they were dead or fleeing.

By the time it was over, he was covered in bright red

blood—the only color that was evident in whatever possessed this land.

He wiped at his face. "Come, lass." He held his hand out to her.

No longer sure if she should be with him, she placed her hand in his and allowed him to return them to his hobbit hole.

He flung his sword down before he teleported to the washstand to clean himself. He'd barely left her side before the banging returned to his door.

Terrified that they might yet get inside, she climbed the ladder as fast as she could. "I'm so confused. Why did you fight them when you could have just brought us back here with your powers?"

He let out the bitterest laugh she'd ever heard. "Fancy that being the same as milking a bull, love. Bring you nothing save pain." He toweled himself off before he faced her. "If I open the ether to travel, they can follow. The door would then be useless. I have to have a certain range before it's safe to use those powers."

Oh . . . that made sense.

"What were those things, anyway?"

"Graylings." He ran the towel through his short hair. "They were once fey creatures who ran afoul of Morgen and she cursed them to those twisted forms."

He scowled fiercely at her. "I don't understand why you couldn't go. It should have been no problem for you to leave." Pulling her against his chest, he held her there. "I promise I'll see you home, Josette."

"I know you will."

He stepped away from her. "I'll be back. Now, in a minute."

"Where are you going?"

"To see about freeing you."

Even though she knew it was useless if he chose to use his powers, she blocked his way. "I'm not letting you go alone."

"Josette," he said in a chiding tone. "You've no idea the dangers waiting to devour your soul. You, with where I'm headed, might as well be a bleeding, three-legged stag in a kennel of ravenous hounds."

"Very descriptive and probably apropos. But—"

"No buts. Please. Let me do this."

A horrible feeling settled in her gut. Yet she knew that she had no real choice.

Stepping back, she nodded. "Godspeed you."


Karma *paused as* she heard Jo's voice off in the distance. "Josie Jo!"

There was still no answer.

"Hey, Karma!" Selena called from downstairs. "I need you."

She ran down the stairs as fast as she could, to find her sister in the dining room. Alone. "What is it?"

Selena handed her Jo's phone. "It was by the door."

How weird was that? Jo never let go of her phone voluntarily. "Did she go out the back?"

Selena shook her head slowly before she motioned for Karma to follow her out, into the small courtyard. "We have a problem."

"Yeah, no shit. We've lost Jo, and our mothers *will* kill us if we don't find her in one happy piece."

"Well, there is that. But no. Listen to me . . . I *saw* her."

"Where?"

Selena glanced to the house before she spoke in a whisper. "In the mirrors. She was with a man dressed like a medieval crusader."

The blood washed from her face. "What?"

"She's in another dimension, K."

Karma cursed. "What do we do?"

Selena wasn't really sure. But they couldn't leave their cousin trapped in some mirror realm. "I don't know. You call Zeke and tell him to meet us here and I'll call Ash. Maybe one of them will know where she is and how to get her out."

"I'm on it." She entered the house, and started for the stairs until she realized Selena wasn't following her. Rather, she was standing just inside the mirrored doorway. "What are you doing?"

"Staying here in the dining room, in case she finds her way home." Selena glanced about as an awful chill went down her spine. "I have a bad feeling about this."

Karma nodded. "Me, too. There's something truly evil here. And honestly, I'm not sure we'll ever see our Jo-Jo again."

# 6

"Well, well. Has someone awakened the dragon? Put a dagger through Morgen le Fey's blackened chest cavity? Surely some kind of unnatural event must have occurred for the son of Paimon, an infernal prince, to be standing so foolishly before me."

His arms folded across his chest as he stood defiantly in front of the shadow king's throne, Cadegan arched a brow at Brenin Gwyn ap Nudd's sarcasm.

"I know naught of what you speak, me liege. There's no infernal prince here. I am simply Cadegan Maboddimun."

A name that had been given to him on his birth by Father Bryce and recorded in the monastery's roll. A name that proclaimed to the world that he was Cadegan Son of No One— a bastard child, as motherless as he was fatherless.

But the shadow fey king gave him no reprieve. "So you say. Your father, however, has such a price upon your head that I can't imagine what madness has brought you to *my* door."

"I have need of your services."

The nebulous sharoc king passed an incredulous look to one of the sycophants who stood to his right. Shadowy and cold, light passed easily through sharoc bodies. Most were so transparent, they were virtually invisible and easily overlooked by the unwary or those ignorant of their existence.

These were the slimiest of the fey folk. Miscreants, with a foul cruel streak in them, most served Morgen directly as spies who hoped to curry her favor. In truth, he'd rather deal with an Adoni or grayling than Gwyn's people.

But desperation rode its victim with spurs. And the bastard had them dug deep into Cadegan's haunches this day.

"Hell has indeed frozen over." Gwyn rose from his throne and floated down his dais until he hovered before Cadegan.

Cocking his shadowy head, he narrowed his black eyes. "Name this service you seek, prince of perdition."

Cadegan forced himself not to react to the insult, or to show any emotion whatsoever. "A dragon key to the world of man."

"You wish to leave our pleasant company so soon?"

He'd hardly call a thousand years *soon*. But why quibble over a few centuries, one way or another. "What can I say, me liege? The constant sunshine here is blinding. Surely more than me weak eyes can take."

Gwyn laughed. "You're a cheeky one. Especially since you're here to beg favor. . . ." He tsked. "A dragon key. Now that, indeed, requires a special payment."

All dear things did. "Your price?"

Stroking his bearded chin, the king clicked his tongue in thought. "Before I name it, I must know why *now*."

Cadegan remained completely stoic before him. "Why now, what?"

"Why would you, son of Paimon, seek release from our hallowed realm after all this time?"

"Does it matter?"

"If you want a key, it does. Especially since I know *you* can't use it."

Damn him for that. Cadegan had hoped to keep that tidbit out of their negotiation.

His sycophant slithered up to the king to whisper in his ear. Gwyn listened quietly.

Laughing, he narrowed his gaze on Cadegan as the other sharoc slinked back to the shadows. "So it's a woman, then, is it?"

"I know naught what you speak."

Gwyn laughed even harder. "Of course you don't. Ergo, you crave a key to open a doorway you can't use. I think you can see why your logic baffles me?"

Cadegan sighed in feigned resignation. "I'd hoped to avoid visiting my uncle and ingratiating myself to him." For multitudinous reasons. "But as you leave me no choice . . ." He started to leave.

"Wait!"

He turned to look back at Gwyn. "Aye, me liege?"

"We don't have a key. Being shadowborn, we don't need them to pass in and out of the realms. And as you know, those who own them have a very nasty tendency to keep them well guarded, and to rip the wings and skin off anyone dumb enough to try and take them."

"Then why are you wasting me time here?"

"Because I can make you one, but it will require you to gather certain things that will benefit us both."

"Such as?"

"Short list, really. A dragon's claw. A stone from Emrys

Merlin. The lion's heart. A bit of hair from the White Stag. Some of Arthur's blood . . . lastly, we'll need the blood and sweat of a waremerlin."

That was one hell of a list. The only thing missing was a body part, rolling naked over flaming coals, and having a hot poker shoved into an uncomfortable exit-only orifice.

"Anything else?" Cadegan asked.

"To assemble the medallion? Nay. But there's still the payment to discuss."

"I'm listening."

"You and your woman's to stay here, in Castle Galar, while you gather the items and bring them to me. If you fail to return by fey vespers, with at least one item for the day, your woman spends the night with me . . . in my bed."

He felt his temper break at the mere thought. "She's not a trophy to be bartered."

"So, you admit to having a woman, eh? Fascinating."

Cadegan cursed himself for the slip. He'd alerted the bastard to much more than just confirming Jo's presence in their realm. His enemy now knew Cadegan's weakness.

Lamb's bullocks, not one of his more intelligent moves.

Sadly, not one of his least intelligent, either.

And now that Gwyn knew, Cadegan had a much bigger concern. "How do I know she'll be unmolested whilst she's here?"

"Word upon my crown. If any touch her during the light hours, I'll cede my throne to you, and the bullocks of the offender."

Cadegan snorted. "They touch her and I'll be taking more than just their bullocks. Aye, to the farm on that." Still not sure if he should do this, he tried to think of a better way.

Honestly, there wasn't one. Gwyn was the least of the devils in this place, and the only one who could provide a key for Josette, without immense bloodshed.

"So what's it to be, demonspawn?" Gwyn asked.

"Is that all you'll be taking from me?"

"Aye and nay. When this is done and the key is proven to work, I'll be handing you over to your father for payment. And you won't fight me or mine on it. You'll go peacefully to his loving arms."

For a full minute, Cadegan couldn't breathe at the severity of the price. Did Gwyn have any idea what he was asking?

*"When next I see your face, dog, you'll learn well why every hellborn demon fears me! And you'll pay for every ounce of demon blood you've spilled in service to that bastard I should have drowned at birth. I will dine on your worthless entrails!"*

It was a promise he knew his father would well deliver on. Cadegan's death wouldn't be easy and it wouldn't be soon.

His father would take his time, making sure Cadegan regretted every breath that kept him alive.

*What difference does it make?* Really? Compared to how he lived, it was just a change in scenery and wardrobe.

*Keep lying to yourself, lad.*

*There's a* big *difference.* But as he saw an image in his mind of Josette asleep in his arms, and heard the memory of her laughter, he knew he was more than willing to see this done.

For her.

She was worth his wretched life.

Cadegan slid his gaze to the shadow that was watching them in silence. "Agreed."

As he started to leave, Gwyn called out to him. "There's one more thing you should know."

Cadegan cursed silently. He should have known it wouldn't be as easy as it sounded. "That is?"

"The autumnal equinox occurs in three days. After that, the key will be useless to her. She'll be trapped here, forever."

A human in a land that preyed upon them, with predators who would tear each other apart to get to her. Never mind what they'd do to her.

Closing his eyes, he winced. There was no way to back out now.

He knew from experience that no one in Avalon would allow him entry or speak to him in any way.

Not even Varian duFey.

Because of the taint and stench of his father's blood, they refused to trust him.

He was the only chance Josette had. And Gwyn was the only possible exit available to them.

If he failed in this, he would make sure to kill her himself.

It would be the kindest thing he could do.

# 7

"So that's Castle Galar." Jo repeated the name
Cadegan had said to her earlier, wishing she
could roll her *r*s the same effortless way he did.
His medieval Welsh accent was the sexiest thing
she'd ever heard. And she had a sneaking suspicion that he could give her an orgasm by simply
whispering nonsense in her ear. She would kill
to hear him in an actual conversation with it.

It had to be incredible.

As they neared the castle, she slowed, partly in admiration . . . partly in stark, cold terror. While it was beautiful, the entire castle floated in the air. That would be scary enough, but while it had a stone bridge leading to it, there were two rickety hanging wooden bridges at the beginning and end of the stone one. Was he serious? No one in their right mind would walk over that thing that swung so high above a ground she couldn't even see.

Eyes wide, she stared at the single tower that rose up high into the heavens, and the spiral staircase that wrapped around the outside of it, leading to a smaller tower that vaguely reminded her of the Statue of Liberty torch jutting out from its side. No doubt, that was where the castle's overlord made his chambers.

Yeah, it was fitting for this fey land of drab scariness.

"Galar. The name has a beautiful ring to it."

Cadegan snorted at her words. "*Galar* means 'sorrow,' love. And the place is aptly named."

Oh . . .

"How screwed up is your language that something so pretty is a crappy thing, huh? You might as well be French. No matter what you say, it always sounds like a compliment."

He frowned at her. "French? What is French?"

"You know . . . you get in your boat and journey across that large watery thing called the English Channel, and hit the big blob of land on the continent south of England? Them people what live there are the French."

"Ah. Normans, Franks, and Gauls." He wrinkled his nose at her. "For what it's worth, love, not fond of them either."

"Is there anyone you do like?"

The humor faded from his eyes as they started across the drawbridge. He leaned down to whisper in her ear. "You."

That simple statement sent a hot chill over her and it made her long to take a bite of him. But he'd warned her thoroughly to keep her emotions concealed.

Even so, she couldn't help teasing him. "For the record, Cade? I'm part French."

He let out a light harrumph at that. "Then I reckon I like the Franks better than I thought."

"I should hope you do."

Once again, all humor fled his face as he jerked his head toward a shadow. Before she could ask about it, he manifested a ball of fire and threw it against the ancient stone wall.

The shadow yelped and scurried away.

Cadegan continued to toss fire at it until it was well out of their sight.

As they neared the portcullis, Jo was aghast at what he'd done for no apparent reason. "What was that action? Some kind of weird Fire Tourette syndrome?"

He gave her a pained expression of total confusion before

he spoke. "It was a sharoc, spying on us. They're shadow fey. You have to keep up your guard. They're very treacherous beasties."

"Ah. Hence the fire enema. Got it."

"Fire enema?"

She patted him gently on the cheek as he knocked on the gate. "Flames exploding on the rear of your trousers."

Before he could answer, the doors disintegrated to show a huge gray man with black eyes and gray flesh. He raked an unflattering look up and down Cadegan before using a more curious one with her. "Well, aren't you prompt?"

Jo drew up short as a man lifted himself off the wall in front of them.

By the sudden rigidity of Cadegan's body, she knew this was more foe than friend.

"No time to waste." Cadegan put himself between them. "Josette, meet Brenin Gwyn ap Nudd."

Now it was her turn to be baffled. "Which name does he go by?"

His gaze unwavering from the newcomer, Cadegan kept his hand on her arm. "Forgive me. *Brenin* means king. His name is Gwyn, son of Nudd. But for safety's sake, just refer to him as Your Majesty. And avoid him whenever you can."

The king tsked at him. "Still cheeky."

"And you're still annoying me, me liege."

Stepping back, the king made room for another shadowed male to join them. "Gage will show you to your new rooms." He narrowed his gaze on Cadegan. "And the sands are falling quick for you, boy. We begin today. You've not much time to vespers. Shouldn't you be about it?"

"I hate you," Cadegan snarled.

The king turned an evil, sinister grin to Jo. "You'll hate me even more if you miss your deadline. Oh, and I might ought to have said this to you earlier. But there's a specific order to how the items must be acquired. You needs steal the dragon's claw first."

The look on Cadegan's face said the king was lucky to still be in one piece. His eyes telegraphing loathing and fury, he turned toward her. "I'll have to leave you now, Josette. But I'll return as soon as I'm able."

When he started away, she grabbed his biceps. "Whoa, wait a sec. Why can't I go with?"

"With what?"

"With you, silly."

He glanced back to the king. "I think that would be a most prudent action, actually."

Gwyn narrowed his gaze before his smile turned cruel. "Fine. I shall allow it." He moved faster than she could blink and placed a small brass band on her arm.

Cadegan cursed. "You bastard!"

Unperturbed, the king gave him a cruel smile. "To ensure your return."

"What?" Jo asked, pulling at the band. "What is this?"

Gwyn answered for Cadegan. "If he fails to return through the portcullis by the designated time, without using his magick, you'll be missing one hand, lass. Maybe more, depending on my mood."

Her eyes bulged. "You know, Cade, I think I can cool my heels here."

" 'Tis too late."

The king nodded. "You set the terms yourselves." A bell rang out. "Look, you have an hour to return here with a dragon's claw. Good luck with that." Gwyn vanished.

Breaking out into a string of furious Welsh, Cadegan took her hand and ran with her back to the bridge. Once he was out from the castle, he used his powers to return them to the forest.

"Question."

"Aye, lass."

"You're not allowed to use your powers inside the castle grounds, are you?"

"Nay. 'Tis forbidden, and any violation is punished severely. It's why Gwyn never ventures from his home. He's a coward that way."

She held her arm up to show him the band. "Is that why

he wanted to make sure we came back? So he doesn't have to leave his home to come looking for us?"

He nodded as he walked cautiously through the woods. "Most likely."

Jo hated to be commanded by anything. Especially magick. So much for not believing in it. "So what's this errand we're on, anyway?"

"I must have a dragon's claw."

Not what she was expecting to hear. And honestly, it made her a little nervous. "So there be dragons in these woods?"

"Just one. Well . . . there are many mandrakes, but only one true dragon that I know of. And Gwyn said dragon claw, not mandrake claw. So I'm assuming he wants a claw from the one, true dragon."

Fascinating disclosure that left her wondering one thing. "What's the difference between a dragon and a mandrake?"

"Mandrakes are fey-born creatures. They be shapeshifting bastards who can take the form of either man or draig."

"Draig?"

"Dragon. And they're all currently enslaved to Morgen and live in and around Camelot. But the one . . . he's the last of his breed here. And he slumbers in yon den." He jerked his chin toward the looming mountain before them.

"Cool. I'll distract him. You knock him on the head and we'll be right out. Did you bring a pair of giant dragon-sized nail clippers?"

He gave her an adorably baffled scowl. Damn, he was the sexiest thing she'd ever met. "Sarcasm?"

She laughed at his question. "What was your first clue? The words or the tone of my voice?"

He smirked at her as he surveyed the area, and carefully led them forward without making a comment on her additional playful barb.

As they drew closer to the mountain, she began to see the number of human bones littered on the ground. And that brought the danger home with a terrifying reality.

They could die doing this.

"Um, Cade?"

"Aye, lass."

"How big is this dragon, anyway?"

He paused to consider it. "I've only seen him from a distance. When he's flying in the sky, hunting for prey. But from nip to tail, I'd say about twenty-five to thirty feet."

"Nip?"

"Mouth."

"That's a big-ass dragon. Does he breathe fire?"

"I know naught, but would assume it."

Great. A giant, fire-breathing dragon. Just what she'd put on her Christmas list.

Never.

Suddenly, Jo realized they weren't entirely alone in the woods. Trying not to panic or be an alarmist, she reached out quietly and put her hand on Cadegan's arm. "What would his range be on that fire?"

"No idea, lass, why?"

She held him by her side. "Because I'm looking at him and he doesn't appear happy that he has guests."

Cadegan froze as her words hit him. The blood drained from his face as he turned to see the dragon crouched low, watching them.

"Nice, draggy, draggy," Josette breathed in a singsongy tone. "You don't want to eat the nice people. Do you?" She shook her head. "No, you don't. We're not even snack size."

His jaw dropped. Was she out of her gourd? "What are you doing, lass?"

"Shh," she snapped. "I'm being a dragon whisperer."

He was even more aghast at her words. "A what?"

"Dragon whisperer." She slid her gaze to Cadegan. "I'm assuming that if you fight him, it's going to be a bloody mess. Right?"

"Probably."

"Could result in both our guts and entrails flying?"

"Most likely."

She patted his arm kindly. "Then let's try this my way first. Shall we?"

He snorted at her offer. "I'm not sure I like your way, Josette. It seems even more dangerous than mine."

She winked at him. "Not sure I like my way, either. Just promise me that if he starts to eat me, you'll flash us out of here."

"I shall do me best."

"Cool, now shush and let me do something galactically stupid."

Amused and horrified, Cadegan held his breath as he watched her bravely and slowly make her way toward the dragon. He wanted to stop her, but she was right. Battle wouldn't get them anywhere except wounded for him and probably dead for her.

While he'd fought and won against many mandrakes, he'd never come up against this beast before. He had no idea what, if any, its weaknesses would be. And it was a massive yellowish-orange beast with black-tinged wings and a spiny head.

He didn't even know how fast it moved. As he'd told her, he'd only seen it off in the distance, and always in flight. Never on the ground.

Jo stopped before she reached the nose of the creature.

Swallowing her fear, she knew she had to do this, even though what she really wanted to do was run screaming in the other direction.

"Hi, Mr. Dragon. How are you today? Feeling in a good mood, aren't you? Yes. Yes, you are. You don't want to eat people, do you? No. No, people taste icky. They're sinew and gross. No eat people." She shook her head to emphasize her words. "You're gonna be a sweetie, aren't you?" This time she nodded.

Maybe it was wishful thinking on her part, but the dragon seemed to be scowling at her as if he understood her words yet was baffled by her context. It was an expression she saw often on Cadegan's face.

She took a step forward.

The dragon actually inched back. He made a strange, rumbling sound. Not quite a growl.

"Shh, it's okay, Mr. Dragon. We're not going to hurt you. No. We like dragons. I used to draw you all the time when I was a kid. I did. I had a whole collection of dragon toys. 'Cause you're a cutie, you are."

It cocked its head.

Jo drew up short as she realized one of its wings was on the ground at a weird angle. "You got a boo-boo, Mr. Dragon?"

Cadegan drew closer to her. "Its wing's broken." He started to unsheathe his sword.

The dragon turned on him with a hiss.

"No!" she said to both of them. "Cade, keep your sword down."

"Why? Now's the time to strike."

She shook her head. "I think he understands me."

The dragon turned its head back toward her.

"You do, don't you?"

He appeared to nod.

She inched closer and closer, until she was able to reach out and touch the gray scales around his nose. Treating him like a dog, she allowed him to smell her skin. "See, I mean you no harm, little big dragon."

He didn't move as he eyed her warily. As if he was as suspicious of her as she was of him.

She moved her hand slowly to pet his head, near his ear. "It's okay." She cradled its massive head against her chest and stroked his dry, leathery skin. Then she looked over at Cadegan. "See? He's harmless."

"I wouldn't go that far. But I can understand his motivation. I'd be quiet too for a chance to rest me head on your breasts."

She blushed.

The dragon growled at him.

"Now, boys," she teased. "Play nice."

The dragon settled down and closed its eyes while she continued to soothe it.

She placed a kiss to its ear. "We just need a claw from the dragon, right? We don't have to hurt him for that, do we?"

"Depends on how fiercely he fights us for it."

The dragon growled again as if he knew exactly what Cadegan was saying.

Jo stroked his ear. "Can you heal him?"

Cadegan hesitated. "I can, but am thinking a healed dragon might eat us."

*If you heal me, I won't hurt you.*

Jo went completely still at the unknown male voice in her head. "Was that you?" she asked Cadegan.

He shook his head slowly. "That you?" he asked the dragon.

*Illarion, and yes.*

Still, Cadegan wasn't sold on it. "Can we trust you?"

The dragon glared at him. *If I wanted to harm you, demon, you'd both be in flames right now.*

"All right, then." Cadegan moved to the broken wing. "Stand back, lass. This might hurt him and I don't want him to harm you in turn."

*You'd best do as he says. Stand near the cave.*

Jo tapped the dragon on his nose. "Don't hurt Cadegan, either. I'll be very put out with you."

"And I won't be fond of you, either," Cadegan groused.

Illarion snorted as Cadegan moved to his injured wing and Jo sought cover.

As she started away, Cadegan stopped her. He pulled his good-luck medallion over his head and kissed it as a monk would a holy relic, before he placed it around her neck. "Never take it off and it will protect you always."

"Thank you, sweetie." She kissed his cheek and wished him luck.

Once she was out of the line of fire, literally, Cadegan touched the wing.

The dragon grimaced in pain.

"What did you do?" Cadegan asked him.

*Fell. Now are you fixing it, or am I having Welsh Rarebit for dinner?*

His snipe was as impressive as it was stupid. "Ooo, you're a bit bold, aren't you?" Cadegan summoned his powers. "Brace yourself. This will burn."

*Do it.*

Using his powers, Cadegan knitted the bones and sinew back into place. To the dragon's credit, he made no sound or movement at all. Not until it was done.

Then he lifted his wing to test its movement.

Cadegan had to brace himself from the stiff breeze of it.

"Can I come out?" Josette called.

"Aye, love. He's all better now."

Jo watched as Illarion lifted himself up to his impressive height and sat back on his haunches to watch them with his eerie yellow eyes.

*Thank you.*

Cadegan inclined his head to him. "No worries."

Jo smiled at them until her dragon became an incredibly tall man. Eyes wide, she jumped to stand behind Cadegan, who didn't react to it at all, except to put his hand on the hilt of his sword.

No longer a scaly reptile with wings, Illarion was seventy-eight inches of sex on a stick. Even more muscular than Cadegan, he had long, dark brown hair with auburn highlights, and silvery blue eyes.

"Why's he in color?" she whispered to Cadegan.

"Not really sure," he responded over his shoulder as he kept his eyes locked on Illarion.

*Neither Morgen's nor Merlin's magick works on me.*

Cadegan arched a brow. "Really?"

Illarion nodded as he tested his arm to make sure it was fully healed.

"I'm confused." Jo kept herself behind Cadegan. Just in case. "I thought mandrakes were the shapeshifters and not the real dragons?"

Cadegan shrugged.

Illarion offered her a patient smile. *In my true and natural form, I'm a dragon—born from an egg, as all my kith before me. But, because of the magick of a Greek king centuries ago, my kith have the ability to turn themselves into humans, under certain circumstances.*

"Did you know that?" Jo asked Cadegan.

He shook his head before Illarion continued. *At one time, there were many races and species of dragons. We walked the human realm, and fought many battles against each other. But between our wars, and the hatred of both your species, all dracokyn have been pushed to extinction or the brink of it.*

*What few of us remain are either enslaved, such as the mandrakes, or, like me, they're in hiding.*

Cadegan narrowed his gaze on Illarion. "What is your species?"

*I'm a Katagari Drakos. As far as I know, I'm the last of my breed.*

"And you can't speak, even in human form?" Jo asked.

He pointed to a place on his neck where it looked like someone had stabbed him in the throat. *While I was enslaved as a hatchling, humans tried to remove my ability to make fire. But the flames don't come from my throat, only through it.*

She cringed at the horrible scar. "I'm so sorry, Illarion."

Placing his hand over his heart, he bowed kindly to her. *Now what is this about a dragon's claw that you need?*

"It's needed for a sharoc potion."

Illarion scowled at Cadegan. *Since when do they make potions?*

"I'm hoping now."

"Hang on," Jo interrupted them. "If the magick here doesn't work on you, Illarion, can you leave this realm?"

His eyes dark with sadness, he shook his head. *As a dragon, I'm too large for the portal, and whenever I attempt to go through as a man, I'm transformed back to a dragon and am stuck. It's humiliating. I once spent two days with my ass hanging out while I tried to get my head back through the portal.*

Jo pressed her lips together to keep from laughing at the image in her head.

"Then how did you get here?" Cadegan asked.

*I was brought here against my will to battle Morgen's mandrakes by a Greek sorceress who'd been bribed by her.* He jerked his head to a stack of bones that had been pinned to the side of his cave in a particularly painful array. *Needless to say, I wasn't very happy about it. Neither was she, in the end.*

"I'm surprised you didn't befriend the mandrakes."

He snorted at Jo's comment. *Dracokyn are very territorial, my lady. We don't play well with others. 'Tis why there are so few of us left. I'd rather die alone than den down with my enemies.*

"You remind me of someone else I know." She glanced pointedly to Cadegan, then, impulsively, she hugged Illarion. "Again, I'm very sorry for what they did to you."

The expression on his face reminded her of Cadegan. As if he couldn't fathom compassion from another person. He passed an uncomfortable glance toward Cadegan, who didn't appear pleased that she was hugging another male.

Not wanting him to be jealous, she moved from Illarion to Cadegan and kissed his cheek. "Don't look like that, sweetie. We don't need to find out if dragon meat tastes like chicken."

*What?*

Cadegan snorted. "She does that a lot. I only understand about half of what she says. It's part of her charm." He looked up at the sky. "And we be needing a claw quick. We're almost out of time."

*You trust the sharoc?*

"Not really."

*Smart man. And when they said claw, what exact words did they use?*

Cadegan paused to think. "A dragon's claw. A stone from Emrys Merlin. The lion's heart. A bit of hair from the White Stag. Arthur's blood, and the blood and sweat of a waremerlin."

Illarion let out a silent whistle. *Quite a list you have there.*

"Aye, believe me, I know."

*And it's not a list so much as it is a riddle.*

Cadegan arched his brow. "How so?"

*A stone from Emrys Merlin would be a goylestone, not a rock. Arthur's blood is a flower that blooms on the other side of the Tor, and a dragon's claw isn't a fingernail.*

Cadegan growled low in his throat. "That dodgy bastard. I should have known it was a trick."

*Aye. I'm sure the others are every bit the riddle. But I don't know them. I only know those three because the goyle-stones are what the mandrakes feed on. It's easy to set a trap for them when they go to eat. The Adoni use Arthur's blood for healing, and I know exactly what my claw is.*

"And that is?"

*One of the most sacred of objects to a dragon. It's almost the same as asking you for a testicle.*

Cadegan actually blushed. "Watch your language before me lady!"

Unabashed, Illarion smiled at her. *Forgive me, my lady.* He turned toward Cadegan. *Why do you need this potion?*

"Me lady can't get through the portal without a key. Gwyn ap Nudd says he can make one for her."

*At what cost?*

"It's for me to pay. Later."

Illarion winced as if he understood how harsh the payment would be. *For what you've done for me this day, I will loan my claw to you, but you have to take me with you and return it once this is done. Understood?*

"You have me word."

*Word of a demon.* Illarion shook his head as if he couldn't believe how stupid he was being.

"He's good for it," Jo said without hesitation. "You won't regret trusting him."

Cadegan froze as she gave him the most precious gift of his life and she didn't even realize she'd done it.

She trusted him. Had faith that he wasn't the bastard demon everyone else thought him to be. For that alone, he could love this woman. But she gave him so much more.

And that was why he was willing to trade his life and comfort for her freedom.

Illarion hesitated before he unlaced the leather cuff from his arm. It appeared to have a metal baby dragon sitting on top of it. He handed it reverently to Cadegan.

"How's that a claw?" Jo asked.

Illarion pulled down the bar the dragon was holding on to, until it made a sound like it was locking into place. When it did, two sharp spikes shot out and a third shot from the dragon's head.

"Holy crap! What is *that?*"

Illarion smiled at her shocked question. *A dragon's claw. They are given to each Katagari Drakos once he or she comes of age, to protect us should we ever be locked by magick into a human's form.*

"Your weaker state."

He inclined his head to Cadegan. *As I said, my people were hunted to the brink of extinction.*

Respecting its sacredness, Cadegan held it with the same reverence. "I shall guard it with me life, and make sure it's returned to you as pristine as it's been received."

Jo frowned while Cadegan wrapped it in a cloth to protect it. "I have a weird question. Why would the sharoc need that? What purpose could it serve for a potion?"

*She's right. They had no way of knowing I would simply give it to you when normally, I'd kill before allowing another to take it.*

Cadegan sighed as he stored the claw. "Believe me, I've already thought of that. The purpose, obviously, was to get one of us killed. Maybe both."

*And to have you fail your quest.*

"Aye, to be sure. There is no other reason for this assignment." Cadegan winked at them.

"Now, what say we go and ruin Gwyn's day?"

Gwyn ap Nudd hit the wall behind him so hard, he was surprised his back wasn't broken.

"You fool! What were you thinking?"

Gwyn wiped at the blood on his lips as he faced the giant, demon overlord in front of him. Fire rippled over his skin as his wings spanned out, making him even more terrifying than normal. And that was saying a lot, since his normal demeanor would make the stoutest heart piss its pants.

For centuries, Paimon had offered unimaginable riches, and even magick, in exchange for the capture of his son. Given that, it seemed reasonable that the bastard held no love for the child.

It was *so* painful to be wrong.

Gwyn's hand shook as he lowered it from his face. "I thought you'd be happy. Now you'll have him."

Paimon rolled off unintelligible demonic curses. "His soul will not come to me. Not that I give a damn for it." But luckily, Cadegan didn't know that. "It's his living body I need!" He grabbed Gwyn by the throat. "If he's dead, he can't wield his shield. It's worthless then! Only one of his blood can command it!"

Oh, that stunk.

"Forgive me, my lord. I didn't know that."

Paimon flung him across the room. "Of course you didn't. Moron! And you better pray with everything you have that he survives this suicide venture you've put him on. In addition to your precious Morgen, Valac is now after him. If that bastard takes him . . ."

Gwyn arched his brow. "Why do so many dark forces seek him?"

"That's not for you to know! Your job is to return him to me, alive and breathing. Or you'll wish I'd have killed you this day." Paimon vanished instantly.

Gwyn licked at the blood on his lips as his mind swirled with the disclosure. While Cadegan had always been hotly sought after by their dark mistress and other demons, it'd never been this intense. Something strange had happened, and recently. And he needed to find out what.

One thing was certain, until he knew what was going on, he planned to keep his own eye on Cadegan. Mayhap the beast could help him, too.

No matter what, he'd have to move very cautiously. Cadegan was a cagey, skilled warrior, who'd disemboweled anyone foolish enough to attack him.

This would require skill and more magick, and an audacious affront Cadegan wouldn't see coming.

And the use of the one and only weakness the cold-blooded demonspawn possessed.

# 8

Not that Cadegan had any doubt that Gwyn had wanted him dead, but the look of shock on his face as they walked through the portcullis on time confirmed it for sure.

The fey king stared at him in disbelief. "You barely made it in time."

"I would say that I'm sorry to disappoint. But I'm not."

Ignoring the sarcasm, the king narrowed his eyes on Cadegan. "So where's the claw?"

Cadegan pulled it out and carefully unwrapped it. When Gwyn reached for it, he moved back and shook his head. "This be only a loan." He indicated Illarion with a jerk of his head. "The dragon wants it back when you're finished, and I promised him we would do so."

Gwyn paled as he realized who and what Illarion was. "How is this possible?"

Cadegan passed a grin to Josette. "It's amazing what a dragon whisperer can do." He handed the claw back to Illarion. "Now if you don't be minding, we're all a bit wanged-out from our adventure, and we wouldn't mind seeing to those rooms you promised us."

"Very well." Gwyn snapped his fingers.

A shadow servant peeled itself off the wall. Without a word, it showed them to rooms. But Cadegan refused his.

"I'll sleep on the floor outside your room, lass. Just to make sure no one bothers you."

Jo bit her lip at his precious protectiveness. She adored how honorable and noble he was. "You could just sleep in the room with me. Be easier to protect me that way."

His cheeks mottled in that adorable way they did every time something embarrassed him. "Are you sure about that?"

Nodding, she pulled him into the room with her.

Cadegan paused to look back at Illarion with an arched brow.

*I'll be back in the morning. Not sure I want to be sleeping in this place.*

"I feel your sentiments, brother. Had I a choice, I'd go with you."

*I'll see you two in the morning.*

Cadegan held his arm out to Illarion. "Thank you."

Illarion had the same reservation in his eyes Cadegan had whenever someone showed him any compassion or kindness. As if he was waiting for it to be a cruel trick.

Finally, he shook Cadegan's arm, then turned to leave them.

Cadegan narrowed his gaze on the shadow that had led them in. "That'll be all now."

It vanished instantly.

He closed the door and locked it. Not that it really mattered. There was no way to keep the shadow fey out, especially when you were on their home territory.

Jo didn't miss Cadegan's unease as he locked the windows. "What's wrong?"

"I've many enemies, Josette. I don't trust them to not find me here."

"Why do they want you so badly?"

"Me mother is the guardian for an object of immense power. One me father would do anything to possess. But even if he had it, he couldn't use it. You have to be born of me mother's blood to wield it."

"Then why not get one of your siblings for it? You said you had a lot, right?"

He laughed bitterly. "Me mother's a goddess, lass. Ergo, me siblings through her are all full-blooded gods as well. I'm only part, and that makes me the only one me father can control. It's why he seduced her."

"Can't you overpower your father?"

"It's not that simple. Me father's not the typical demon. He's one of the oldest and strongest. With three hundred legions under his command. I am but one. There's no way to fight through that number to reach him and be alive when I get there. They'd overrun and gut me before I got near him. And if I die, he owns me. Forever."

And that was Cadegan's worst fear. To be trapped for torture, with no way out. Now it really made sense. "I'm sorry, Cade."

"Nothing to be sorry for. 'Tis what it is. None can help what parents them." He double-checked the door and windows. "It wouldn't be so bad if me father hadn't put such a price on me head. Anyone who delivers me to him will have riches unimaginable and a lesser demon to control."

"Ouch."

He nodded. "Ouch, indeed." Taking her hand, he sat down on the bed and pulled her to sit beside him. "But I don't want to talk about them. Tell me of your parents, Josette. Witch me with your happy stories."

His humble request choked her. Biting her lip, she couldn't help admiring the beauty that was her demon protector. "I don't know what to say. My mother's a bit off. She's part Romanichal."

"And that is?"

"Gypsy."

Scowling in an adorable way, he scratched at his ear. "I've still no idea."

She laughed. "I don't know how else to describe them. They're Eastern European by way of Greece, and migrated to France and England before heading to America. It's a very special culture, and I'm proud to be a part of it, but it's distinctive and unlike anything else you've ever encountered. My father's a typical Cajun-Creole with roots that run deep into the Louisiana swamps."

Smiling, he stretched out on the bed to listen.

"You have no idea what any of that is, do you?"

He gave her a charming, warm grin. "Not a bit. But I hear the love in your voice when you speak of them, and that's what I pine for. Tell me more of your mixed family heritage."

She curled up beside him, wishing he'd take his armor off so that she could feel closer to him. "My aunt Marie, who lives for genealogy, swears that my father's family is actually Welsh in origin and that we have Druid blood in us. But that would have been centuries ago . . . maybe even before *you* were born."

Cadegan laughed at her swiping at his age as he listened to her stories about her cousins and their lunacy as they sought ghosts and goblins, and how they'd sell their souls to spend a night in a fey castle.

She was so normal, and it made him wonder what it would have been like to have a family such as hers.

As a boy, he used to dream of what the world would be like outside the monastery walls. Brother Eurig would oft take him to task for his idle thoughts.

*Pray you never know the misery and horrors of the lay world, boy. Be grateful you're here with us, toiling for Our Lord.*

Yet his curiosity was never far away. It was why he'd volunteer to ring the monastery bell to call the others to prayer.

In the bell tower, Cadegan could see out to the lush, rich world that seemed to stretch endlessly in all directions. There he would dream of normality. Of living an adventure, where every day brought him new, exciting things to see and do, instead of the same drab walls, and boring routine of prayer, chores, and more prayer.

All that had changed in an instant when the Powys king, Elisedd ap Gwylog, had brought his army through their gates for refuge from the Mercians who were in pursuit of them. The Mercian king, Æthelbald, had been new to his throne and eager to prove himself against both the Cymry, Saxons, and his own Mercian people.

Though he had his eyes on being named the *bretwalda*—king of all Britain—the best Æthelbald had achieved, before his own bodyguards had slaughtered him, was to rule the English land south of the Humber.

Senseless bastard.

Æthelbald's campaign and that of Elisedd had caused Cadegan to be ripped from his home, and thrust into a bloody war at an age when lads should be in their mothers' arms, not knee-deep in fields soaked with entrails. He'd learned fast how right Brother Eurig had been to take him to task for wishing to leave the monastic life.

All Cadegan had wanted then was to go back to what he'd known, what he'd so foolishly spurned. It'd taken him three years before his army passed the quiet hill where the monastery had been built.

Joy had raced through his veins as he rode hell-bent to see the brothers and embrace them.

The moment he'd topped the hill and seen what remained, his heart had shattered. Within days of his conscription, Æthelbald had led his soldiers to the monastery and laid waste to it in retaliation for the aid they'd been forced to give to Elisedd and his troops. The monks had been brutally slaughtered and the monastery savagely burned to the ground.

Only ashes remained, along with the husk of the bell tower where Cadegan had once climbed to summon the monks for prayer hours.

The furious anger over that injustice was what had unleashed the demon in him. A demon he'd turned loose on the Mercians and Saxons and anyone who got in his way. Blind with hatred, he'd lost himself to war.

Until the day he'd met Æthla.

She had given him back his soul. Or so he'd stupidly thought. Lies, deceptions, ruthlessness.

Hatred.

It was all a demon like him deserved.

"Are you listening to me?"

He brushed his hand through Josette's soft, dark hair. "Aye, love. I've heard every word of it. And I'm sorry you're aggravated that your cousin Amanda abandoned you to be the only normal one in your clan. She should never have sided with her twin for the paranormal against you."

She smiled sweetly at him. "You *were* listening." She leaned down to kiss his lips.

Cadegan wanted to run from the tender feelings she stirred in his heart. They terrified him.

Was it all deceit again? Could she, like Æthla, only be preying on his loneliness? Æthla had deceived him so completely. He'd vowed to never allow anyone else to ever do that to him again.

In all the pain of his life, nothing had cut more than Æthla's confession that she hated him . . . that she had always hated him.

*You're a monster! I live only for the day when I hear news that you've been gutted in battle!*

"Cade? What's wrong?"

His breathing ragged, he tried to put down the past. But it wouldn't go. And the last thing he wanted was to be left shattered again. "You're lying to me, aren't you?"

Indignation darkened her eyes as she pulled back from him. "Pardon?"

Hissing, he rolled from the bed and paced the room. "*Dwr!* I know better than this. I'm not a fool, Josette. I won't let you play me as one."

Jo stamped her anger down, even though she wanted to insult him back. Badly. Having been handed her heart on a platter by Barry's betrayal, she understood his fear. His inability to trust.

But she'd done nothing to make him mistrust her.

"Why do you think I'm lying to you?"

"Because I'm not human. You know I'm not human. You've been railing against your crazy family and their beliefs. Yet, here I am. The epitome of everything you hate about them."

Tears choked her as she realized what she'd inadvertently done by railing against their paranormal obsessions. "None of that was directed at you, sweetie."

"How can it not be?"

"Because . . . I vent. It's my pressure valve. But I don't mean it. I don't hate my family. And I definitely don't hate *you*." She left the bed to cup his face in her hands. "You are not a monster."

For the first time, she saw tears gathering in his eyes.

"I don't want these feelings you give me, Josette. Take them and go."

"What feelings?"

He pressed her hand to his heart and held it there while his gaze searched hers. "You make me dream again. Hope. And I cannot allow myself to feel either. Every time I have . . ." Clenching his teeth, he looked away.

Jo did her best to understand the fear and anger she saw in his eyes. It ignited her own fury that he'd been hurt so badly by others that he was now incapable of accepting her heart. "What?"

"It matters naught." He tried to pull away.

Jo held him in front of her. "It matters all. *You* matter most."

He shook his head. "I don't believe you. I can't."

"Why?"

When he looked at her with that anguished, celestial gaze, she saw every bit of his scarred soul. "Because you will have to abandon me, too. And I'm done with it. I'm tired of being left behind."

Jo pulled him into her arms and held him close. "Then I will stay with you."

"You can't do that. You have to return to your family, and your life."

She snorted. "My life is a disaster, Cadegan. The divorce bankrupted me. I'm losing my house. I had to beg a job off my cousins. Right now, the only thing in my life, other than my dogs, that makes me want to get out of bed in the morning is *you*. Well, not entirely. I'd actually prefer to stay naked in the bed with you forever, but you know what I mean."

"Nay, Josette, I don't. The last time a woman plied me with such sentiment, she carved out me heart and fed it to me until I choked on it."

"And my husband told me I was the only woman in the world he'd ever love or want. Then I find him in bed with not one, but *two* bimbos. Notice, I'm not holding his assholishness against *you*."

"We can't stay together, lass. You know that."

"I refuse to believe it. I was put here for a reason. Right?"

"Aye. To torment me more."

She popped him lightly on the stomach. "Stop that! I am not going to give up on you, Cadegan. Not without a fight."

His eyes darkened with agony, he shook his head. "I am Cadegan Maboddimun . . . son of no one. Wanted by none. Conceived for evil intent. I entered this world alone and that is how I was destined to stay in it. I will not ask you to sacrifice yourself for me."

He broke her heart in so many ways. It didn't make sense. She didn't know him at all and yet he owned a part of her that no one had ever claimed.

All she wanted was to save him. To pull him to safety and keep him far away from all the ones who were out to cause him harm. It was so unfair that a man so decent was locked in here, while the world she knew was filled with utter assholes.

"That's the thing about love, Cade. You don't have to ask for anything."

He laughed bitterly at her words. "You don't love me, lass. You can't."

How she wished feelings were that easy to control. That she could magically take away hurt and grief, and tell her heart who she wanted it to beat for. And have it listen to her.

Unfortunately, the little bastard didn't work that way. It did what it wanted to, regardless of feelings and intent. Regardless of common sense and wishes.

She nuzzled his shoulder. "Then I'm falling head over heels for someone who looks an awful lot like you, buddy. Same eyes. Same lips. Same irritating tendency to look at me like I'm crazy. He even has a last name that sounds like he's lisping when he says it."

Cadegan laughed. "The things you come up with, lass. You are a real star-turn, aren't you?"

"Like a wombat in a cornfield."

He scowled at her. "Beg pardon?"

"You're not the only one who can throw together random words that make no sense and use them in a sentence like they do."

Cadegan laughed out loud at her silly nonsense. How could she make him laugh when he felt like utter shite? Make him want to be inside her when he should be running away as fast as his feet could carry him?

Unable to sort through the myriad of conflicting emotions she stirred inside him, he buried his hand in her dark tresses and fisted it. Then he did the one thing he wanted to do most.

He kissed her until his head spun with her sweet scent.

Jo was completely unprepared for the intensity of his kiss. For the hunger he made her feel. Wanting to show him just how much he meant to her, she pulled at his robe. "Take your clothes off, Cadegan. I want to feel your skin on mine."

She'd barely finished the sentence before they were both naked and he was inside her.

Sucking her breath in sharply, she groaned aloud as he held her while he thrust against her hips. "We really need to talk about foreplay, sweetie."

He paused to stare down at her. "You want more people for this?"

"No!" She laughed at his assumption. "Foreplay is the petting that leads up to this. Not that *this* isn't incredible, but a little pre-petting goes a long way."

"Sorry. I always thought women wanted it over with as quickly as possible."

"Why would you think that?"

" 'Tis what they've always said to me. 'Hurry and be done with you.' Once they have their fancy, they're ready to leave."

She cupped his cheek in her hand and stared into his beautiful eyes that betrayed all the hurt that had been ruthlessly served to him. "There is nothing I treasure more than having you inside me, Cadegan. Take your time and let me love you until you're blind from it."

He thrust deep, burying himself to his hilt, and held her there, without moving.

Kissing his cheek, she cradled his head in her arms. His breathing ragged, he stared at her with his half-hooded eyes that seared her. He whispered something in medieval Welsh before he captured her lips and began to slowly, methodically make love to her. All the while, he stared at her as if she was the sole light in his darkness.

No one had ever looked at her like that before.

Jo struggled to breathe as he delivered fierce stroke after stroke to her. He held her effortlessly while he savored her body. She ran her hand over the muscles in his back and shoulders that bulged. Nothing had ever felt better than his hard body against and inside hers.

In that moment, she never wanted to go home. Never wanted to be without him.

Cadegan pressed his cheek to hers and inhaled the scent of her hair. If he could, he'd die right here and now in this one perfect instant of bliss. This instant where he was warm and happy. Where he felt loved and desired.

*It's a lie.*

It had to be. Yet it felt real. If she was lying to him, he hoped that he never found it out. He'd much rather live in this lie than deal with the reality that had been his life.

Crying out, she dug her nails into his back as she came for him. He quickened his strokes until he made her sing from the pleasure of her release.

And he waited until she was completely done before he joined her there.

Completely satiated, and feeling calmer than he could ever remember, he carried her to the bed and placed her in it. He slid in beside her and gathered her into his arms as a storm began striking against the castle windows.

She lifted her head. "That's normal rain, right? It's not like a swarm of angry piranha locusts or something, is it?"

He laughed at her panic. "It does storm here. And we do have the occasional swarm of angry locusts that devour the harvests. But that just sounds like a small autumn shower."

She let out a relieved breath. "Good. I'm not sure I could handle any more excitement today." She leaned over him and began to nibble the whiskers on his chin.

He arched a brow at her actions. "What are you doing?"

Wrinkling her nose, she gave him an evil smile. "You didn't think I was done with you, did you?"

"I did, indeed."

She shook her head. "Oh, sweetie, I've only begun. Before this night is over, you're going to be begging me for mercy."

He took her hand into his and led it to his cock that was already starting to swell again. "Methinks I'm up to that challenge, me lady. Let us see how well met you are to your word."

By the time dawn broke, Cadegan had to cede victory to

his lady vixen. She did indeed wear him out and leave him begging for the mercy of a few hours of sleep.

But it was far from peaceful. His dreams tortured him with nightmares of his father's legions coming for her and ripping her out of his arms. Of having to watch her die before him.

When he awoke, he felt as though he hadn't slept at all.

"Cadegan?"

He scowled at the deep masculine voice in his ear. Opening his eyes, he found himself spread out over a man's body.

What the hell?

Furious and stunned, he pulled back, ready to battle. Then he froze in all-out shock.

That was *his* body he'd been lying upon.

And he was in Josette's.

# 9

Jo was terrified to be staring at her own body, from the outside of it. "Cade? Is that you? Please tell me that's you I'm looking at."

"Aye, lass . . . that be *you* in me body?"

She nodded. "What's happened to us?"

Cadegan held his hands up to inspect them. Then, the moment he realized he had female breasts and that they were exposed, he snatched the sheet to cover himself.

She laughed at his actions. "Awkward doesn't quite cover this, does it?"

He shook his head.

"Oh, hello!" She jumped as a part of *her* anatomy hardened unexpectedly. Cringing, she bit her lip. "So that's what *that* feels like. It's not exactly comfortable, is it?"

"Nay, love, and especially not when 'tis obvious to others."

Likewise, he was grimacing, and crossing and uncrossing his arms.

"What?"

Making a very unattractive grimace, he squeezed his biceps over "his" breasts. "How can they be in the way and yet be so small and squishy?"

"Hey now! I could make that . . . well, okay, you're seriously not small, but still! That's rude! And for the record, I am a solid B cup."

"B cup?"

"Means those," she pointed at his breasts, "are normal size. Average. They're not *that* small."

He grinned, only it wasn't nearly as charming on *her* face as it was on his. In fact, it was extremely creepy to look at yourself from another body.

How could Tabitha and Amanda cope with this as twins? She'd always thought it would be cool to have an identical twin.

It wasn't. She hated looking at herself. It was like a vicious, cruel mirror that pointed out every single flaw, from every single angle. "I am so going on a diet when I get back in my body. And you better watch what you eat, bucko, while you're in there. If I gain so much as one pound, I'll . . . figure out some way to punish you for it."

She moved to scratch an itch on her thigh and cringed as she brushed her hand through the hair there, and especially the hair under his arms. "Oh my God, I need a bush hog, in the worst way! Some serious manscaping needs to be done to this body. How do you stand being so hairy? It's everywhere, except on your head where it's supposed to be." She started scratching all over, and in particular, her face and chest. "It's like having fleas."

"Don't you even take that tone to me. I promise you 'tis no comparison to the itchies I have in me nether regions. What is *that* and why?"

She paused in her scratching. "Oh yeah, I haven't had the money to get *that* waxed lately. You're right. It's itchy there too. We're even. Kind of." She dropped her hand to her lap and sucked her breath in sharply as she accidentally racked herself. Oh holy God and his saints!

In utter misery, she fell sideways in the bed and groaned in agony.

"Breathe, lass. It'll stop in a moment."

She couldn't speak as she writhed on the bed, cupping herself. When she finally recovered enough to draw breath again, she looked at him with tears in her eyes. "I'll *never* laugh again when a guy gets racked in a movie. Holy cow! I barely touched it! What happens when you actually get kicked there?"

"There's one lesson you don't want to learn. Ever."

"No kidding. Protect the jewels! I think my first call to action is a super-industrial cup. I see now why men liked codpieces."

Suddenly, the color washed from Cadegan's face. "I have no powers. Are they with me body?"

That couldn't be good. Her heart pounding, she met his panicked gaze. "I don't know. How do you use them?"

He shrugged. " 'Tis the same as moving a limb. I think it and they do it."

She closed her eyes. "Now what?"

"Picture us clothed."

She did, and when she opened her eyes, she burst out laughing.

Cadegan not so much, as he stared at her in his body, wearing a lacy pink V-neck tee and jeans. "That is an abomination on me body. Could you please have a little respect for it and me dignity? I've so little enough that I can't spare to lose any more."

"Sorry." She changed her clothes to a white man's shirt,

then grinned. "I have to say, though, that *I* look rather hot in chain mail. I like that look."

He snorted. "You say that, but your muscles are so weak, I can't lift me arms. How do you cope with no more strength than this, lass? Uh, this is hell!"

She daintily plucked at the mail sleeve on "his" arm. "Well, for one thing I don't walk around in a hundred pounds of armor every day. There's a good reason my boyfriend's so buff."

He paused at her words. "Boyfriend?"

Jo cringed at what she'd inadvertently said. "Sorry, I didn't mean to assume anything."

He smiled at her. "I like the sound of that. Except, I think I'm more of your girlfriend, right now. *Duw!* This is so disturbing, and in so many ways." Hissing, he placed his hand to his stomach. He grimaced and groaned.

"Oh yeah. PMS. Sucks, don't it?"

" 'Tis like a wicked stitch from running."

"Yeah, one with steroids. Just breathe through it. It'll pass in a second." While he followed her advice, she put him into a shirt and jeans that were more suited to his tastes.

She reached out and touched his face that was her face. "You're right. This is so disturbing and yet . . ." She leaned in to kiss him. "Want to try something kinky?"

"I don't understand."

"I've always wanted to know what it was like to make

love as a man. Haven't you ever wondered what sex feels like for a woman?"

"Nay, not really. I haven't had all that much of it as a man. And from what I have, they didn't seem to enjoy it near as much as I did."

There was a strange note in his tone. "What? Were you paying them for it, or something?"

He blushed.

"Oh my God, you were!" She shook her head. "Cade, there's a big difference between sleeping with a prostitute and a woman who's attracted to you."

"That I wouldn't know, lass. You're the only woman I've ever touched who wanted me to for any reason other than coin or shelter."

His words choked her. How could any woman *not* want this man? Heck, for that matter, if she was a prostitute, she'd pay *him*. She couldn't imagine a male this hot and gorgeous not fighting off every female who laid eyes on him.

"I will always want you, Cadegan, and never for any reason other than love. I don't care what you look like or where we are." She kissed him again and laid him back on the bed.

She tried to remove their clothes with her powers, but she still didn't have the hang of it. Rather, she resorted to peeling him out of his jeans and tee the old-fashioned way.

Cadegan shivered at the sensation of her scraping his

body with her whiskers. "Remind me, I need to shave more carefully for you."

She looked up with an arched brow. "What?"

He fingered her lips. "I never realized how harsh me beard was on your skin, lass. It's like sandpaper."

"Yes, but I like the sensation." She dragged her chin over his breast and around the nipple.

Cadegan sucked his breath in sharply as chills exploded over his body. "Aye, I can see the appeal now."

She laughed. Until he reached down to cup her.

Jo couldn't breathe at the sensation of the exquisite pleasure that went through her as he gently squeezed her body and danced his fingers down the length of her. "Now I know what to do for you down there. Wow! I had no idea how good this feels for a guy."

He nodded. "Sadly, I've had a lot of practice working it on me own."

She gaped as she realized what he was telling her. "So you should have gone blind by now, huh?"

Laughing, he kissed her. "Well, there's not much else to do, truth be told. Only so many times you can throw the dice without losing all sanity, eh?"

She tsked at him. "You didn't tell me this little nugget when I asked what you did for fun."

"Not exactly something one admits the first time they

meet a stranger. Hey man, what's your favorite pastime, alone? Tossing me oats in me sheets, of course. . . . Aye, nay, that confession doesn't appeal to me."

"Tossing me oats in me sheets," she repeated, then laughed. "I love the way you explain things."

"Like a wombat in a cornfield."

They were both laughing now.

Until she kissed him again.

Cadegan breathed her in and shuddered at the emotions she awoke. Happiness. Joy. Warmth. Protectiveness. For centuries, he'd lived in a numb cocoon. Feeling nothing. No laughter. Just survival.

But she was like sunshine to his darkness. Breath to his lungs.

And when she slid inside him, he cried out.

"Nice, huh?" she breathed in his ear.

Yes and no. Honestly, he wasn't quite sure what to make of it. "This is so peculiar, lass."

"Yeah, it's really weird, but not. Same, but different."

Yet it wasn't just the pleasure in his body that made this moment unique. It was the warmth in his heart that came from being held by someone who cared about him. Someone who didn't look at him with disdain or fear.

Or worse, bored indifference.

That was why he'd mostly avoided sex with women. With the exception of Æthla, he'd known they were watching the half-hourglass while he was there, just biding their time until it ran out or he finished with them.

And while Æthla had shared her body with him, he'd felt her reserve every time they were together. Her fear. Since he'd never slept with anyone other than prostitutes, he'd attributed it to her noble, innocent status.

Never to cold, blind hatred. Or to her ruthless ambition that drove her to use his desperate, bleeding heart to keep herself and her family safe, while wishing him dead and buried.

But this was so different. Josette gave herself to him openly. Without reservation.

With humor and love.

And best of all, Josette didn't just love him.

She actually *liked* him—it was unfathomable.

Most of all, it was exceedingly dangerous for all his kind. Throughout history, his species had been laid low by the gentle hand of a maid. He'd already come close to losing his life over one.

Now . . .

He couldn't stop himself from wanting her. From needing to feel her touch his flesh. *She will be the end of me.*

But could there ever be a better way to go?

Jo closed her eyes as she buried her face against Cadegan's neck. This was the strangest moment in her entire life. No wonder men craved it. She was nestled in utter warmth. In tender softness. A blanket of limbs. But there was more to it than that. She felt so safe with him. Accepted. In all the world, even when her life was quickly diving into hell, she felt him pulling her out of it.

Yeah, it made no sense. She was still losing her house. Still without a real job.

Yet she knew as long as he was with her he'd do anything to give her shelter. He'd protect her with the last breath of his life.

"I love you, Cadegan."

"And I love you, lass. More than you'll ever fathom." He barely spoke the words before he cried out in orgasm.

Jo laughed at the sound as she surrendered herself to her own. But she wasn't sure how she felt about it. Yes, it was awesome.

Still, it was *so* weird.

Panting and content, she rolled from him and started laughing. "So does this make me a lesbian, or just *really* narcissistic?"

"A lesbian?"

"Woman who craves women."

"Ah . . . I have no idea. But were I a woman, I'd definitely be one."

She arched a brow at him. "Really?"

He ran his hand over the arch of her brow. "Aye. You're the only man I'd ever do this with."

She laughed at his gentle teasing. "You're so wrong."

"'Tis true though."

She rubbed her nose playfully against his. "I've got to get my body back. While I like wearing you, I'd rather wear you as a blanket on top of me and not the skin I'm walking around in. It has this whole Hannibal Lecter aspect that's really creeping me out."

"Hannibal Lecter?"

"It's a TV show and book character. Not really important. Like a wombat in a blender."

He snorted. "I'm not sure what this blender is, but I think I should be feeling bad for that poor wombat."

She burst out laughing. "I adore the twisted way you see things."

"And I adore *you*." He picked her hand up and as he started to kiss it, he scowled fiercely. "I never realized how revolting I was."

"What are you talking about?"

He rolled her over to touch the scars on her back.

Something that made her realize just how deeply scarred he really was. There had been so much damage done to his body that she could barely feel his hands on her skin. It was an odd, numbish sensation.

How badly would he have to be beaten and tortured to destroy the nerve endings in his flesh like this?

"I'm disgusting," he whispered. " 'Tis no wonder everyone ran. That no woman ever wanted me."

She turned back to him. "You're not disgusting, Cade. You're one of the most handsome men I've ever seen."

He fingered the scar at his neck, and as he did so, something weird happened.

She saw in her mind the injury that had caused it.

Suddenly, she wasn't in the room with him. She was lying quietly in an Anglo-Saxon bed in a stone bedchamber with a rib-vaulted ceiling over her. There were two deerhounds sleeping on the floor in front of a large hearth.

Naked and exhausted, she, or rather, Cadegan, lay in bed, listening to the fire crackle. He'd been battling for almost a solid year with his brother's army. Not against Saxons or Mercians.

*Demons.*

Someone had unleashed a large nest of them and they'd been warring against humans. Because of the oath he'd taken when he joined Leucious, he wasn't allowed to breathe a word of his duties to anyone.

He was sick of the blood and battle. Sick of arriving too late to help the innocent. Of burying their remains while guilt choked him that his own father had caused much of it.

But Leucious had finally given him a reprieve for a full sennight of rest. He'd come immediately to Æthla's. His intent was to marry her so that he could keep her safe and away from the horrors and dangers of their world.

He'd already asked her father and been given permission to seek her hand. First thing on the morrow, he intended to lavish her with the gifts he'd bought for her. Samite, jewels, and the ivory hair combs she'd seen earlier that day and had remarked upon.

On the verge of sleep, he'd barely heard the door open. With nerves ravaged by war, he rolled, ready to battle. Only to relax as he saw the image of an angel.

Dressed only in a pale green kirtle, Æthla had left her long blond hair loose to flow around her curvaceous body. With a serene expression, she'd approached him slowly.

Instantly hot and aching, he'd returned his dagger to the stand by the bed and turned the furs back in invitation for her. "Is your headache better, love?"

"Nay, 'tis much worse now."

"Then you should be resting." He plumped her pillow for her. "Come, and I'll guard you while you sleep."

She hesitated. The firelight played across her face, making her look even more angelic and sweet. Precious. In all the world, she was the only comfort he'd ever known. "I just spoke with my father."

His stomach drew tight in fear that her father had spoiled his planned surprise. "Did you?"

"Aye. He told me that I'm to be your bride."

Cadegan cursed at the bastard's timing. But more than that, he'd expected her joy, not this sad reservation. "I've no intention of forcing you, love. I thought you wanted me for a husband."

"Why would you think that?"

The anguish in her tone cut him worse than a demon's claws. Confused, he tried to understand what her body was telling him. "You allowed me your maidenhead. You've always greeted me with pleasantries and warmth whenever I've visited you. I assumed you did so because you loved me."

"Loved you?" she sneered. "How could anyone love a monster like you?"

Those words had slapped him harshly. "Monster? I risked all to save you and yours. When have I ever been anything save tender toward you?"

Once he'd joined his brother's army, Leucious had forbidden him to take part in any human battle. They fought for a much higher calling and weren't to risk themselves for petty human politics.

Any such violation of oath was met with stringent punishment. Leucious brooked no insubordination from anyone. As his brother, Cadegan was held to an even higher standard, and punished much more strenuously whenever he violated Leucious's laws.

Yet when he'd stumbled across her and her family hiding in a ditch while his own people had burned down their Mercian hall, he'd violated every oath he'd ever made.

For her.

Æthla's fear had touched a heart he hadn't even known he possessed. There in that field, he'd quieted her and promised her that he would make sure no one found them. That he would keep her safe from any harm.

He'd battled his own people for the daughter of his human enemies. For the daughter of a race that had done its best to destroy his. A race that had ruthlessly burned down his monastery and slaughtered cloistered monks who had no way to defend themselves.

Once he'd made it safe for her, he'd escorted her family to shelter. Had paid for their lodgings and food with his meager coin, and made certain they returned safe to their noble relatives in the north.

"My father made me give myself to *you*, so that you would continue to help us. But I've never been able to stomach your touch. You make my skin skitter."

Those words had pierced him like battle lances.

"Now I'm told that I'm to be sold to you like chattel or my father will cast me out to whore for a living. I told him I'd rather whore for a leper's colony than suffer one more night of *you* inside me. He told me that if I didn't do this, he would kill me for it." Pure unadulterated hatred had burned in her eyes as she glared at him. "I hate you!" She'd launched herself at him.

It was only when he felt the dagger slicing into his neck that he realized she'd concealed the weapon in the folds of her kirtle.

Screaming, she'd stabbed him over and over again as her dogs stirred in anger.

Even then, Cadegan had only sought to free himself from her slashes and the bites of her hounds. He'd knocked her back at the same time his door crashed open to show her three brothers.

"He's raped me!" she sobbed at them, showing her brothers the blood on her that was his. "Help me! He said he'll kill me this night!"

He should have used his powers to flash himself out. But Leucious had made him swear that he'd never reveal his abilities to the midlings who feared their magick. More than that, he wasn't a coward and he couldn't stand being accused of something he hadn't done. Especially something so foul.

"I did no such!"

"Liar!" Her eldest brother had charged first.

As they beat and slashed at his naked body, he'd made the mistake of looking to Æthla, who watched on with a sick gleam of satisfaction.

"I want his heart for what he's done!" she shouted. "I will not wed a demonic bastard!"

At her harsh condemnation and rebuke of his heart, something inside him had snapped in twain. Fury the likes of which he hadn't tasted since the day he saw the monastery's remains tore through him, and awakened the demon he did his best to keep leashed.

In keeping with his oath to his brother, he didn't use his powers. He didn't have to. With skills honed on hundreds of battlefields, he'd fought her brothers off until he stood over their dead bodies.

Æthla had screamed like a banshee as she saw it. "Monster! Son of Perdition! You're inhuman! Revolting! You disgust me!"

Her insults had melded together as he came to his senses and saw what he'd done. As the horror of his actions washed over him and left him heartbroken.

*I am a monster.*

Born for no other reason than to end lives.

Shattered and numb, Cadegan had dressed as her father finally came and called for his soldiers to arrest him. But he knew even if they hanged him, he wouldn't die, and he'd expose to the midlings a truth they weren't ready to handle.

He'd fled the hall and returned to his brother's camp.

The moment Cadegan entered his tent to tell him of the events and Leucious saw him, his brother turned pale. His vibrant eyes had gone from blue to green to a deep, demonic red. "What have you done?"

"He killed humans," Misery, one of Leucious's breeders, had whispered as she materialized by his side. "Midlings who were trying to protect their sister he coveted for his own."

His eyes filled with condemnation, Leucious glared at him. "Is this true?"

"Aye, but—"

Leucious had backhanded him. "There are no buts! You swore to never draw midling blood again. Is this how you uphold your sacred oaths?"

Cadegan bit back his fury. "They attacked me first."

"You are the son of Paimon! No midling can truly harm you. You know this! A bloody nose or black eye you will survive."

He wanted to argue, but Leucious was right. He should

have used his powers and left. Never should he have fought back. "Forgive me, brother. 'Twas a mistake."

Leucious shook his head. "Nay, the mistake was mine for thinking for one minute that you were something more than the mindless beast you were born to be. You disgust me! I can't believe I put my trust and faith in *you*."

Those words shattered his heart. "Please, Leucious—" His brother stopped his words by grabbing his throat and cutting off his breathing.

Cadegan choked as pain racked him. Leucious's hand was buried in the same wound Æthla had given him.

"For crimes against Our Lord, for breach of my trust, I condemn you to the shadowed lands of your mother. No more are you to walk this earth as a living being. You will spend eternity remembering what you've done and regretting your actions. You are no longer one of us. For that, you are sentenced and banished from the world of man. Forevermore."

Cadegan tried to pry off his grip. To beg him not to send him to the shadow lands. To tell Leucious why he couldn't damn him there. It would be the worst mistake. Worse than even falling into his father's hands. If Morgen were to ever learn his secret, the world of man would be destroyed.

But it was useless.

Leucious threw him against the small looking glass he kept near his bed.

Instead of falling into it, he fell through it . . . into the hell realm of Terre Derrière le Voile.

Cadegan had pounded against the glass, begging for release.

Leucious had coldly turned away and covered the portal so that he'd never again have to look upon Cadegan's face.

Betrayed and bleeding, Cadegan had picked his helm up from the ground and bravely gone to face this new hole he'd been cast into.

He hadn't gone far before Morgen's fey army had overpowered him and dragged him in chains to her court in Camelot.

The lush blond witch had tried to seduce him with her wiles and body. But he knew better than to believe a single word from the witch's tongue. "Son of Brigid. Tell us where your mother has hidden your grandfather's shield."

When he'd refused to give her what she wanted, she'd moved straight to torture.

Cadegan had begged for death. Had wished it a millionfold. But there was no relief. No quarter. Not for the likes of him.

Not until an attack had distracted his guards while they'd been transporting him back to his cell. He'd fled Camelot for the only refuge he could think of.

Through treacherous land and avoiding Morgen's hounds, spies, and soldiers, he'd made his way to the Isle of Avalon.

For one heartbeat, he'd breathed in relief as he saw the shining castle where Merlin and Arthur's surviving knights lived, while continuing to fight against Morgen's evil.

Until the knight Ademar and three others had appeared and blocked his way. Swords drawn, they had forced Cadegan back.

"What do you want here, demonkyn?"

"I need to see the Penmerlin."

Ademar had shoved the tip of his sword so deep into Cadegan's throat that it'd drawn blood. "We don't allow Morgen's dogs here."

Exhausted and still bleeding from his torture, Cadegan had thrown himself on their mercy. "I'm a waremerlin. Charged with the Shield of Dagda . . . I needs see it to the Penmerlin before I succumb to Morgen's torture." Then he'd done the one thing he'd never done in his life.

He begged.

"Please, have mercy on me! I need shelter. At least for a single night, let me lay me head in peace so that I can heal for a bit."

Ademar had kicked him back. "Liar! No keeper would entrust an object of Arthur's into the hands of a demon! What kind of fool do you take me for?"

Cadegan had tried to argue, but they'd summoned more knights and beaten him back to the gray shadow lands. And there he'd spent a thousand years, trying to avoid the demons sent to claim him for his father and Morgen's beasts. Most of the time, he was successful.

When he wasn't, he endured their torture until he found a way to escape it. And all the while, he'd silently kept an oath that had been forced upon him without his consent. An oath to a mother who had cast him away within an hour of birthing him.

And all for Brother Eurig, who had given him Dagda's Shield when the king had commanded him to war.

*"This belonged to your mother. She told me that I was to give this to you should you ever be forced to leave here. Whatever you do, boy, never let evil have it. Swear it to me!"*

Jo couldn't breathe as all of Cadegan's memories played through her head. As the full weight of his true horror crushed her.

"Josette?"

She pulled him into her arms. "I'm so sorry."

"What did you do?"

Tears filled her eyes. "Not for what I've done. For what has been done to you." She buried her hands in his hair and held him close against her. "I will get you out of this hell, Ca-degan. I don't know how, but I swear I will."

"I wish you luck with that, lass. In truth, I am a bit weary of it all."

For once, she didn't have to imagine. She knew exactly how tired he was. How beaten down and defeated in spirit. Yet he let no one know. Ever. He bore his inner scars with the same dignity and grace that he did with the ones that marred his body.

External scars that did, indeed, remind him of the inner ones, every time he saw them.

*It matters naught, my ass.*

Now, she knew the truth with a crystal clarity that was terrifying. "Ever my strong, fierce warrior," she whispered against his lips.

Before he could respond, the walls around them glimmered.

Cadegan pulled back to fight, then cursed as he remembered he wasn't in his body and had no powers.

*Alfred's hairy bullocks!*

Gwyn appeared in the room with one of the demons Cadegan knew served his father.

"What is this?"

Gwyn ignored him. "She'll have his memories and blood,

now. But she won't be able to fight or use his powers against you." He clapped the demon on the back. "Good eats."

"You bloody bastard!" Cadegan snarled. He launched himself at the fey king, but before he could reach him, the room shifted and he was sucked violently out of it.

# 10

"Oh thank God, you're all right!"

Cadegan scowled as a strange woman threw herself over him and hugged him close. She was joined by an entire herd of other females, who assaulted him with questions and comments in the strangest collection of accents he'd ever heard. Some were so thick, it rendered their words utter gibberish to him.

Completely disoriented and confused, he didn't know what to make of it.

Until he focused on the tall blond man, standing near a large mirror.

Rage darkened his sight as his blood boiled in his veins.

"You bloody lamb-fucking bastard!" Forgetting that he was still in Josette's body, he launched himself at Leucious.

Leucious grabbed him in an iron grip and held him with an ease that was as infuriating as it was frustrating. Damn his strength!

"Hey, hey, hey!" Leucious said. "I saved you and you attack me for it? What'd they do to you, woman?"

"It's not Josette you saved, Leucious! You stupid wanker whoreson!" He broke off into a string of curses.

Leucious grabbed his throat and held him immobile against the glass. "Cadegan?"

"Anyone know what they're speaking?" a black-haired woman asked.

"Yeah, it's old Welsh. But their accents are so thick, I can't really follow it. Plus, I have a feeling, given Jo's shrill tone, that she's using words not found in a standard dictionary."

Cadegan ignored them as he growled angrily at the brother he hadn't seen in a thousand years. A brother he wanted to gut. "You have to send me back. Now!"

With an expression of hell-wrath, Leucious tightened his

hold to an almost killing level before he slung Cadegan away. "What did you do to Jo? If you've harmed her, I swear I'll see you dead for it!"

Cadegan faced him with fury, wishing he had the powers to rip out his throat. "Oh, aye, *I* had to have done something to her. God knows, a demon like me could *never* have tried to protect her, that's it, isn't it? That's all I am to you, brother. Something to be hated and despised because you see yourself in me and you can't stand it!"

Leucious hit him with a godbolt so hard that it lifted him from his feet and sent him skidding across the floor.

When Leucious took a step forward, another man stepped between them and held Leucious back.

"Enough!" he roared. With short black hair and eyes that were hidden behind a mask of some sort, he turned toward Cadegan. He waved his hand, and froze all the women save three of them, who stood back and didn't interfere as they tried to understand what was happening and why. "I am Acheron," the man said to Cadegan.

Cadegan eyed him warily. As a demon, he knew Acheron had partial demonic blood. But it was a different breed than his. And there was a lot more power to this creature than a demon normally wielded. The power to freeze a human was on the level of a god. So he held himself in check, in order to learn what it was he was dealing with. "What are you?"

"Concerned about Jo. Where is she?" At least Acheron wasn't judging him. Rather, he was only trying to get to the truth of the matter.

"Me enemies swapped our bodies so that they could torture her to get me grandfather's shield. I was trying to fight them from her when you ripped me here. I have to get back to her before they hurt her. Send me back there, now!"

Leucious gestured toward the mirrors, where Cadegan saw Josette's beautiful face staring back at him. "Look at yourself, man! How do you plan to fight them like *that*? They have your powers and you're in *her* body. Do you really think you can stand alone? What are you going to do? Sneeze on them and hope they die of a sinus infection in a month?"

"I hate you!" But Leucious was right. Like this, he was useless. Tears filled his eyes. "All the times I prayed for release . . . I never wanted me freedom for this cost."

Acheron placed a comforting hand on his shoulder. "Breathe, little brother. We will get her back. I swear it to you."

Aye, but how?

And in what condition?

Terrified for her, Cadegan dug the heels of his hands into his eyes in an effort to banish the memories that shredded him. "What if they've already begun her torture? Just send me back now. Maybe I can offer them something, *anything* to protect her."

"I'll go." Acheron started for the mirror, but Leucious stopped him.

"You can't, Ash. If you enter that realm, it'll strip your powers from you. Immediately. You'll never get them back."

"What?"

Leucious nodded. "You know the laws of your kind. A . . ." He glanced to the women and seemed to catch a slip he was about to make. "A being such as yourself can't simply traipse into the nether lands of another pantheon without dire consequences. . . . Not to mention, the entire place was set up to contain and restrict the powers and magick of strong creatures." He glanced to Cadegan. "I'll go. You rally an army, and I'll do what I can to hold them off until they get there."

Cadegan was aghast at Leucious's stupidity. "Are you out of your mind?"

Leucious met Cadegan's gaze. "Always." He turned back to Acheron. "Call Fang and have him gather Cael, Amaranda, Zeke, Ravenna, and Tristan from our side. You'll need fighters skilled with swords, and Dark Age tactics. Demon, Daimon, and fey powers are fine. No one can go in who has a drop of god blood in them."

Acheron nodded. "Give us an hour to get there."

Leucious held his hand out to Cadegan. "Do you trust me, brother?"

"Only to stab me in the back." He glanced to the three

women, who watched them with concerned frowns. He didn't know who was who among them, but no doubt they were part of the family Josette spoke of with such warmth and love. "Swear to *them* that you'll see Josette home."

"Don't worry. They know I will. Karma would have my balls for dinner."

"Karma?" Cadegan asked.

"The scary bitch right here," the shortest of the women said. "Jo's like a sister to me. I'll kill anyone who harms her."

"I'll have her back to you, now, in a minute. So swear I."

As they started through the portal, Acheron stopped them. "Sim? Human form."

The dragon tattoo that peeked out from his short-sleeved shirt rose up from his skin. The shadow transformed into a skinny demon with black wings and jet hair. Yawning, she scratched at her eyes like a small child.

"Akri!" she whined through her yawn, "the Simi was just getting to the good part of the dream. I was being stalked by them Nutter Butters dipped in hot sauce. Yum! Yum! Now you done gone and wokested me." She yawned again. "The Simi hopes it's important! Otherwise your baby will be very put out with her akri!"

"I need you to go with Thorn and protect him," Acheron grimaced at Cadegan before he spoke, "and . . . the woman with him."

She blinked at Cadegan, then frowned. "But she not a woman, akri. He done got frozed in there and not real happy about it, neither."

"We know, Sim. Protect them."

"Okie, akri." She skipped over to them. "Where we going, Thorny man?"

"Where there are lots of demons for you to lunch on."

Jumping up and down, she clapped her hands together in glee. "Goodie!" She pulled a bib out from her coffin-shaped bag and smiled. "Well, less go! The Simi be starving! Don't wants to wait."

Without another word, Thorn opened the portal and went through it.

Still not sure if he could trust his brother or not, Cadegan followed, and the demon pulled up their rear.

The minute they were back in Glastonbury, the demon made a face of total disgust. "Ew! The Simi done gone and faded out. Well, poo! What an unattractive skin color. Who done thought this was a good idea? I look like a refugee from a talkie!" Pursing her lips, she glanced to Cadegan. "But on you it look real good." She burst into laughter. "No, it don't. The Simi be lying, trying to make the two demon men feel better about being suddenly ugly."

Cadegan scowled at her. "Is she a bit touched in the noggin?" he asked Leucious.

Snorting, Leucious shook his head. "No. Simi's a Charonte demon. They're an ancient, fierce race we're lucky we never had to fight, and she makes me look like an infant in comparison to how old she actually is. But that being said, and thanks to Acheron's overindulgence of her, she's the human equivalent of an extremely spoiled and pampered young adult."

"Psst," Simi whispered to Leucious. "The term now is 'new adult.' The Simi knows you old and all, Akri-Thorny, but you gots to keep up with them changing times."

Smiling, she wrapped her hands around Cadegan's biceps. "And Thorny demon-man is right. The akri done gone and made the Simi rotten to the tips of her Demonia boots. But, in a fight, the Simi cleans the house and burns it down with her fire burps." She gave him a fanged grin.

Still not quite sure what he should make of her, Cadegan looked over to Leucious. "We need to get to Gwyn ap Nudd's castle. He's the one who did this to us."

Leucious scowled. "The sharoc king?"

Cadegan narrowed his eyes at the bastard. "You seem to know a lot about this realm."

Leucious glanced away.

"What's that look mean?"

Simi leaned in to whisper loudly. "It's called guilt. The Simi's seen it a lot on many human people's faces. Some other species, too, but not so much." She stood back. "You two needs to kiss and make up now."

Cadegan growled at her suggestion. "I'm not kissing him and I'm damn sure not doing the other with him either! He can rot in hell for what I care."

"No! Not make out. That's gross! The Simi mean for you to forgives him. He's your family, after all. If akri-Styxx can forgive and love akri, you can forgive your family, too. He only locked you up for one thousand years. Akri-Styxx was in his icky place for over eleven thousand! Eleven thousand . . . that's like forever, and the Simi know 'cause I've lived even longer. So see, you gots no reason to be hating. Somebody always gots it worse. Now admit to the Simi that he's your family."

"Family I wish I'd never met."

Leucious shoved at him. "Don't take that tone with me, like I'm the one who screwed up. *You* killed humans! *You* violated our oath."

"Then we're even."

"How so?"

Cadegan grabbed Leucious's shirt and jerked him to a stop. "You held your hand out to me and promised that you would be the family I'd prayed for. That you'd never throw me aside and walk away. Not for anything. Family backs each other, that's the lie you sold me, and like a fool, I bought it."

"You left me no choice."

Cadegan laughed bitterly. "You had choices, Leucious. I'd have rather you killed me than lock me here, with nothing." Cadegan shoved him away and started for the castle.

"It wasn't easy for me, either, you know!"

Cadegan laughed bitterly. "Go fuck yourself, Leucious. And your self-righteous indignation."

Thorn winced at the hatred in Cadegan's voice. Cadegan was right. He hadn't even allowed him to explain himself. He'd acted rashly, and condemned the boy without a hearing.

Too used to being betrayed by everyone and everything, Thorn had lashed out in fear. As powerful as he was, he knew that Cadegan was one of the few creatures who could kill and replace him in their immortal hierarchy. It was why he'd never allowed Cadegan into the Nether Realm where he and his grandfather lived.

Unlike Thorn, who had a human mother, Cadegan was the son of a goddess.

*Wait a second*...Thorn froze as those words played through his head. The boy was a demigod. "Cadegan!" he called, running to catch up to them.

Cadegan didn't slow down even a bit.

"Wait!" He pulled Cadegan to a stop. "You're a demigod, right?"

Jerking his arm free of Thorn's grasp, he sneered at him. "Aye."

"Yet your powers work here? How?"

Cadegan curled his lip. "Are you telling me that you sent me here thinking I'd be powerless to fight the others?"

"Not powerless. Just without the god part of your abilities."

He cursed under his breath. "You're a dodgy pile of shit, aren't you?" He started forward again.

Thorn growled in his throat. "You didn't answer my question."

"I don't owe you answers. A stern ass-kicking and some knocked-out teeth, maybe."

Never had Thorn wanted to thrash anyone more. But then, he'd hurt Cadegan badly and he knew it. Wishing he could change things, he caught up to the boy again, and tried not to let the past burn him so much.

Cadegan sneered at him. "Not that you deserve the knowledge, but . . . me mother was born of the Tuatha Dé Danann, the gods those here pay homage to for their powers. Therefore, they can't strip me god powers without taking their own. This is the realm of me family."

A family that wanted nothing to do with him.

Aching for the boy, Thorn narrowed his eyes as a new thought came to him with this new nugget. "Simi? Can you relay that to Acheron? Tell him to bring Talon?"

"Okies, sure, akri-Thorn."

He handed her the key he'd used to bring them in. "You'll need this."

She took it and flew off toward the portal.

Thorn turned back toward Cadegan. "I don't understand. If they can't drain your powers, what happened to your mother when she came here? I always assumed she became a midling."

Cadegan rolled his eyes. "Morgen turned her to stone. She still lives . . . as a permeant resident in Morgen's garden of people who pissed her off."

"What?"

He passed an agitated stare to Thorn. "She came to reclaim me shield, and leave me here defenseless against them all. Only she couldn't take it from me, as she'd given it to Brother Eurig on me birth, and he'd given it to me when I was forced to war. Only the true owner can transfer it. It must be given, never stolen or taken."

"She came to free you. She told me as much."

"Nay. Only as a matter of negotiation. She came for the shield first, and she told me as much. She didn't trust me to keep me word that I wouldn't give it over to them." He let out a short, bitter laugh. "I learned her good on that, didn't I? She wasn't the first to make that offer to me. And she wasn't the last. And still I have me shield. 'Tis the only thing ever given to me I didn't bleed for."

"I don't understand. Why didn't you give it to her when she came for it? You could have been free."

"Free?" He raked a sneer over Thorn's body and shook his head. "It's all what ever protected me without fail. Why would I let it go, and be with nothing?"

Thorn didn't want to think about that. "Where's the shield now?"

"As if I'd *ever* tell *you*? I'll go to me grave with it. Then the rest of you can fight for it, for all I care."

Thorn sighed as Cadegan moved at almost a run to get to Jo. He would use his powers to teleport them, but since he didn't know the castle, he could do them more harm than good. It wasn't worth the risk.

And as they hurried, in the back of his mind, he saw the boy as Cadegan had been on the day they first met.

Barely a man, Cadegan had been captured by a group of demons Thorn had been chasing. He'd finally caught up to them and thought it was a mere mortal they held.

As he'd entered their camp, he found Cadegan chained and bleeding from where the demons had tried to torture him for information on his grandfather's shield. Because he'd been unaware of his true birth in those days, Cadegan had no idea of the powers within him. No idea how to fight the demons who'd been sent for him and Dagda's Shield.

With a courage that baffled Thorn to this day, Cadegan had been defiantly trying to break free. And when those hate-filled, furious blue eyes had looked into his, he'd seen Cadegan's father in the boy.

Had felt the untapped powers Cadegan would one day wield.

For either good or evil. Cadegan's choice alone.

Thorn had killed the demons with ease and freed the lad, even though his common sense had told him to cut Cadegan's throat before he learned the truth of his birthright and used it against humanity. It was what he'd promised Cadegan's mother he'd do should the boy ever escape his monastery.

It was something that needed to be done now that Cadegan had taken human life.

Yet no matter how much he tried, how much he knew it'd be for the best to kill the lad there and then, he'd decided to recruit Cadegan instead.

Rubbing his wrists, Cadegan had eyed him with suspicion. "Who are you?"

"I'm called Leucious of the Brakadians."

"I don't know your people."

"You should know them."

"Why?"

"Because I'm your older brother."

Cadegan had stood and moved away. "You lie. I have no family."

"Aye, you do. Our mothers are different, but we have the same father."

Scoffing, Cadegan had reclaimed his sword and dagger from the remains of the demons. "I have no father. I'm bastard-born."

"Everyone has a father, otherwise you wouldn't exist."

Cadegan had moved to saddle his horse. "I appreciate your aid, but I needs find me lord and report in afore they mark me off as a deserter."

"What if I gave you another army to fight for? A far nobler cause?"

Cadegan had completely disregarded his offer. "I can think of nothing nobler than driving the Mercian *cythral* from good Cymru lands."

"There's a much darker threat to your people than just the Mercians and Saxons. One that won't stop until it lays waste to this earth and holds all of humanity in thrall."

Cadegan shook his head before he swung up into his saddle. "I'm sure you can find others to fight your battles."

Thorn had grabbed the horse's bridle to keep Cadegan

from leaving. "Nay, lad. This enemy requires warriors with very special skills and breeding. We are few and they are legion. And I'm always looking for good, worthy men to join my army."

"And who do you fight?"

"Our father and those he, and others like him, send out to do their bidding."

Cadegan had scowled. "I don't understand."

Thorn had allowed his eyes to turn to their natural demon red.

Cursing, Cadegan had crossed himself and tried to spur his horse.

But Thorn had held him. "I am not your enemy, brother. Like you, I was conceived by our father to wage war upon the world of man. To conquer anyone who got in my way. It's why you're undefeated in battle. Have you never once wondered why you have an unholy skill for war?"

The narrowing of Cadegan's eyes had told him that he was right.

"For a time, I mindlessly served our father. Until I couldn't do it anymore. Humans need our protection, not our ownership. We fight for all the children like us. Those who only want to live in peace and to have family."

Cadegan had scoffed bitterly at him. "I know nothing of family."

"Join me and I will change that. I will be the family you have prayed for. And I will stand at your back, and never fail to protect it." He'd held his hand out toward Cadegan. "Family defends each other. In all things."

Indecision had darkened his brow. "Everyone has abandoned me. Why should I put faith in *you?*"

"Because I won't throw you away, little brother. Not for anything. I will always be here for you. Come with me, Cadegan. I will show you how to master your powers and use them for good. How to stamp down the darkness that begs for your soul with every breath you take. We do not have to be the monsters we were created to be. No one determines our futures, save us."

Still, Cadegan had hesitated. Finally, he spoke. "Know that I don't trust lightly or with ease. But I will put my faith in you, Leucious. Do not betray it, for I will not be forgiving if you do."

"And I am putting mine in you, as well. Know that if you betray me, I will rain down a hell's wrath upon you so severe, you will beg me for death."

Thorn winced as he realized how justified Cadegan was to hate him. He'd fulfilled the wrong promise. Instead of seeing Cadegan's true heart, he'd let fear and prejudice blind him.

In the bitter end, he'd been no better than the rest. Cadegan was right. He should have killed him, rather than imprison him here in this bleak, hopeless hole. But he'd hoped that he could one day forgive Cadegan.

And so years had passed with him longing for Cadegan at his side again. With him hoping he'd find the strength to put the past behind them and move forward.

Yet every time he'd started to let Cadegan out, he'd reminded himself that the boy had coldly murdered three human beings. Cadegan had to be punished for that. Not just for the sake of his own soul, but to make sure that none of the others Thorn commanded dared to breech their oaths to him. Cadegan had served as a needed example that no one would be immune from punishment. No matter their excuse.

Now that he was with the lad again, he remembered why he'd always sought Cadegan's company while they fought together. What he'd missed most once it was gone.

There was a quiet comfort Cadegan possessed that was contagious. An accepting serenity from within that kept him from complaining or accusing others. Rather, he focused his attention on what needed to be done and what he was doing.

He only hung on to betrayals. And only so that he'd keep from ever trusting his betrayer again.

*Fool me once, shame on you.*

*Fool me twice, shame on me.*

Cadegan broke out into a run as they reached the castle grounds, leaving Thorn to keep pace.

As he approached the gate, four sharoc confronted him.

"Out of my way!" Cadegan snarled.

They refused to move.

"Gwyn!" he shouted up at the parapets. "You'd best open this gate, or so help me . . ."

The king appeared right in front of him. He passed a smug look from Thorn to Cadegan. "You're too late, demon."

"Meaning?"

"She's gone."

Thorn watched the horror play across Cadegan's face as he digested those words. "Explain yourself."

Gwyn gave him an insidious smile. "Morgen could never break you. But once I knew you had a woman you were bonded to, it was an easy thing to switch you out with her while you were here. However, I thought it would be more challenging to get her to Morgen, but once you vanished . . . easy enough."

"She's with Morgen?"

"That she is."

# 11

Cadegan turned on Leucious with a furious growl. "You'd best be glad, you goat dick, that I'm too much of a lady to slap you."

The bastard had the nerve to laugh.

Shoving him out of his way, Cadegan started to leave, then turned back. "I want two of your Adar Llwch Gwin," he demanded of the king.

Gwyn laughed at him, too. "You're in no

position to make *any* demands on me. You've nothing to barter or threaten with now."

Before Cadegan could punch the impudent louse, Leucious stepped forward. "That's completely untrue."

"How so?"

Leucious threw his arm out and used his powers to bring Gwyn into his massive paw of a hand. "He has a perpetually pissed older brother who has no compunctions about ripping off body parts you will miss . . . and often. Now give him whatever it is he wants, or I'm going to ruin the rest of your life. Might even shorten it to three minutes. Maybe less."

Cadegan snorted. "Trust me, he's good at ruining lives and shedding no tears for it. At all."

Leucious scowled at him over his shoulder.

"Well, you are. Just agreeing with you."

Leucious slung the sharoc away. "Fetch the blah-blah-blue-bluch whatever for him."

"Adar Llwch Gwin," Cadegan repeated.

Thorn rolled his eyes. "Easy for you to say."

"I never understood your reluctance to learn Cymraeg given that shite you speak, that *no* one else knows."

"Not true. Acheron, Simi, and Savitar all speak it. As does our grandfather."

"Talk to him much, do you?"

"Avoid it like leaking crotch-pox." Leucious frowned even more as he watched Gwyn slam his hand against the stone wall of his castle. Instantly, two of the muscled gryphons broke away from their perches on the parapets and took corporeal form.

"Happy?" Gwyn asked Leucious.

"Delirious. An emotion I usually celebrate by sautéing the entrails of any paranormal annoyance around me." Leucious raked a meaningful glare over Gwyn, but spoke to Cadegan. "And behold, little brother, the gods have gifted me with dinner."

Cadegan had never seen the king beat a hastier retreat.

Trying not to be amused or impressed, Cadegan approached the Adar Llwch Gwin nearest him, and held his hand out so that the beast could catch his scent. "We'll be needing saddles to ride."

The Adar Llwch Gwin he chose raked a most salacious smile over him as the saddle instantly appeared on his back. "Hello, beautiful. Just wrap those long, sexy legs around me and I'll ride you anywhere, any time you want."

Cadegan grimaced at a double entendre that disgusted him. "I'll be using the other one." He slapped Leucious on the arm. "This one's all yours. Go ahead, brother, wrap your long, sexy legs right around his waist and ride him all night long."

Leucious screwed his face up in repugnance.

The Adar Llwch Gwin Cadegan had spurned followed after him. "Wait! Bring that sassy walk back over here. I'm the stronger of the two of us. I can protect you a lot better, baby. C'mon, don't be that way. I can carry you in my arms, on my back. Take me any way you want me, sexy. I am *all* yours."

"Oh, shut it, Talfryn," the other Adar Llwch Gwin grumbled. "Can't you see she has no use for you." He bowed low. "I'm Ioan, my lady."

Leucious burst out laughing.

Cadegan had never wanted to commit murder so badly in all his long existence. "I swear, Leucious, when I have me body back, I'm going to kick your ass until me boots are oiled with your blood."

And still the bastard laughed.

Ioan scowled. "What's this?"

Cadegan took the reins before he mounted the winged beast. "I'm not really female. This is me lady's body. We're off to save her." He glared at Talfryn. "And you should be saying a prayer of thanks that it's me you're speaking to. Had you taken that tone to her, I'd be strangling the sharoc king over your bleeding corpse for a new Adar Llwch Gwin."

Talfryn sobered instantly.

Until Leucious took the saddle, then he acted as if he were dying. "Och! What are you made of, stone? One word for you, man . . . diet. Lay off the brisket and brewskis. Have you missed the e-mail? Steroids are really bad for your equipment."

Ioan sighed heavily. "Forgive him. He spends way too many nights watching the Lifetime Network and WWE. Weird combination, I know, but it keeps him occupied and semi quiet."

Leucious passed an irritated smirk to Cadegan. "I commend your choice of travel. You should work as an airline booking agent."

Cadegan growled low in his throat. "It's worse than trying to have a conversation with Josette. I only understand every other word with her. The three of you, it's every ninth or so."

"He doesn't get out much," Leucious said to their mounts. Then he changed the subject. "All right, brother. Where are we off to?"

"Camelot."

"No." Talfryn froze. "Oh, *hell* no. Uh-uh. Ain't *ever* going to happen!"

Cadegan frowned at his protestations. "I thought all Adar Llwch Gwin had to obey their riders?"

Talfryn snorted a hefty denial. "Let me put this into words you can understand. . . . Them be morons what said that tomfoolery about us, my lord. Morons Morgen hasn't threatened to pull the testicles off of should ever they, perchance, darken her presence again with theirs."

Ioan snorted. "Obviously, Talfryn won her over on their

last meeting, and made quite the impression with his most charming personality. I'm sure you can understand her rabid distemper with him."

"Indeed."

Leucious reached down and patted Talfryn in an exaggerated manner. "Now allow me to explain in words *you* can understand. You will obey my brother, now, or I'm going to make you wish Morgen had ripped off your balls, fried them up, and hand-fed them to you. Trust me. Much kinder than what I will do to you if you continue lipping off."

"To the north, it is." Talfryn took flight immediately.

As Ioan followed him, Cadegan held his breath and prayed that Josette was still safe and unharmed. Over and over in his mind, he relived all the things that Morgen had done to try and beat or pry the information out of him over the centuries. His heart bled at the thought of Josette being put through such hazards.

And as his mind replayed it, a thought occurred to him. "Ioan? How long have you served the sharoc?"

"Longer than I care to recall. Centuries, my lord. Why?"

"I'm thinking they used the same spell to swap me and Josette as they use with changelings. What do you think?"

"Most likely. It would be the easiest and quickest thing for the king to accomplish."

And though they didn't use that magick on adults often,

they had been known to do so in the past to swap out an elder fairy whose family no longer wanted to tend to them. "Do you know how they do it? How they put the spell into place?"

"Usually a gift is given to the child they intend to swap, and then they use it to administer the spell."

Cadegan considered that. "Gift? Like a bracelet?"

"Could be."

Cadegan cursed himself for his stupidity. He should never have allowed Gwyn to give anything to Josette.

Why hadn't he realized the significance of that earlier? *You've been a bit distracted.*

Still . . .

"Take me to the ground."

Ioan headed down.

Leucious followed after them. "What's going on?"

"I think I know how to save Josette. I need a cluster of purple foxglove and three eggshells from a raven. As fast as you can gather them."

"Can they be conjured?"

"So long as they're real and not made of something else. I think so."

Leucious quickly summoned them and handed it all to Cadegan. "What do we do with these?"

"I need a pot of boiling water, set over a fire."

It appeared instantly. "Are you planning to explain this?"

Cadegan ignored his brother as he quickly broke the eggs and cast out the whites and yolks, so that all he had were the shells. After crushing them in his hands, he threw them into the water first, then added the foxglove and boiled it until it became a thick syrup. "Cool the mixture, please."

Leucious obeyed. "Cadegan—"

"I'm undoing what was done to her. Once I complete this, and if it works, you need to get her out of here immediately. If she's still in Terre Derrière le Voile on the equinox, she will be stuck here forever. Do you understand?"

"Yeah. I get it."

"Swear it to me, Leucious. You will take her from this place, without fail."

"All right, calm down. I swear."

"You will not tarry. You will not allow her to seek me. She is to be taken from here as quickly as you can do so. Understood?"

"Yes. For a hundred thousand times. Yes."

Inclining his head, Cadegan began rubbing the solution all over his body. Once he was fully coated, he lay down on the ground and closed his eyes before he drank what was left of it. He breathed in and out slowly, forcing himself into a meditative state.

And as his thoughts wandered, he conjured an image of Josette in his mind. He saw her teasing eyes as she made love to him, and imagined the sound of her sweet voice in his ear. There was nothing in his life he wanted more than to see her warm and happy.

Forever.

Just as he began to relax fully, he heard an angry, menacing snarl.

Unfortunately, it wasn't Josette. It was Talfryn and Ioan fighting over nonsense again. And it snatched him right back to where he'd started.

Opening his eyes, he glared at them.

"Are you Jo or Cadegan?" Leucious asked.

"I'm the one who hates you most."

Leucious sighed. "Welcome back, little brother."

But the problem was, he didn't want to be back with Leucious. He wanted to be where he was desired.

With Josette.

Most of all he should be where he was needed.

Protecting the only woman he'd ever loved.

Tears choked him as he imagined all manner of ill befalling her. While Morgen's tongue was sharp, it was nothing compared to her physical cruelty. Something Cadegan was used to.

And while Josette, with her courage and grace, could stand every bit as strong against Morgen and her beasts, he didn't want her to suffer. Not for any reason.

And most especially not for the likes of him.

Not to mention the small fact that she carried his memories now. Which meant she knew exactly where the shield was hidden. Something, that in the wrong hands, could end the world as they knew it.

# 12

Biting her thumbnail, Jo paced the giant cave Illarion called home.

In dragon form, he crouched a few feet away, watching her through hooded eyes. *It'll be all right, Jo.*

How she wished she could believe that. But with every second that passed without word, her worry fed her insanity. She couldn't stand this wall of knowing nothing. "We don't know where Cadegan is or what happened. . . . Who has him?"

What had him?

*I know, child. Would you like to go look for him again?*

"Please." She smiled at the dragon. "And thank you, Illarion. For everything."

Still in his massive dragon form, he gave her a slight bow of his head before he lowered himself enough so that she could climb onto his back. She felt him wince as she took the small saddle he'd conjured for her.

"Are you all right? Am I too heavy for you?"

He laughed bitterly in her head. *No, lass. While I know you're currently trapped in Cadegan's body, I'm painfully aware of the fact that you're not really a man. And I was remembering my precious Edilyn who once rode to battle in the saddle where you sit now. She was the last and only female I ever allowed to ride me.*

"What?" she asked. Given the note of wounded tenderness in his voice, she had a bad feeling he didn't just mean that Edilyn rode him for transportation alone.

Illarion gave her a sad nod. *It's where the legends of the virgin sacrifices to dragons come from. They weren't really our sacrifices. Rather, they were offered to us as hopeful spouses.*

*Centuries ago, my kind were used as weapons in war. To*

*entice us to fight for them, humans would offer up their sons and daughters to us, to make sure that we had a vested interest in battling in human armies, and for their causes. Many of my kind mated with the strongest of your people and we would fight together in battle as a single unit.*

"Was Edilyn your wife?"

*In a simple word, yes, but she was a lot more to me than that. She was my best friend and the very air I breathed.*

"What happened?"

*I failed to protect her.*

Her heart wrenched at the agony he betrayed. "I'm sorry, Illarion."

*Thank you, lass . . . it's the only reason I'm willing to help the two of you, when normally I'd have left you to rot. I know what it's like to live without my better half. It's a painful bit I'd wish on no one. Your courage and resilience reminds me much of my Edilyn. And I want to see you back with your Cadegan.*

She leaned forward and hugged him. How she wished she had words to soothe him. But his grief was so deep, it was tangible. "Were you there when she died?"

He nodded. *It was both a curse and a blessing. I'd promised her that I would never leave her in this life or the next. That we would always be together, and that no other would ever claim my heart the way she had.*

*When my kind bonds, we're supposed to die with our beloved. But her people had a sorcerer who'd found the magick to undo ours, so that they didn't lose the entire battle team. So in the end, my body lived on, but my heart and soul went with Edilyn into eternity. I hated her people after that.*

*The only part of my oath to her I was able to keep was that I was there, holding her hand, when death claimed her. I have never loved anyone save her.*

*And I never will.*

With her head on his neck, she stroked his scales. "I am so incredibly sorry."

*Thank you.*

Jo took the reins, wishing there was something, anything, she could do to make things better for him. Unfortunately, grief like his wasn't easy to come back from. It could destroy the person who felt it. She'd seen firsthand what it'd done to her family when Tiyana had died. Even now, her heart was broken at the loss. Not a day went by that she didn't think of Tiyana at least a dozen times.

Almost a decade later, they still mourned her.

They always would.

Just like Illarion mourned his precious Edilyn. Poor dragon. Life wasn't fair and she knew that as well as anyone. But it was now clear why Illarion had fought so hard for her when there was no reason for him to do so. Why he'd been determined to get her free of first the demons who'd come to claim her, and then Morgen's vicious mandrakes and gargoyles. All of whom had been determined to see her captured and taken to their masters. And all the while, Gwyn had stood back, letting the two groups go at each other and Illarion. She hoped that Lord Switzerland got his comeuppance some day.

Once she gave Illarion the signal that she was secure, he left the cave and took flight.

Jo continued to worry her lip as she scanned the nasty gray scenery for any sign of her Cadegan, and where he might have been taken. Reaching down, she stroked Illarion's scales. He reminded her a lot of Cadegan. It was a pity the two of them hadn't found each other before now. They could have been great friends who watched over each other.

Or committed murder.

Perhaps they were too much alike. The two of them might get on each other's nerves like Amanda and Tabitha did. The twin sisters swore they were absolutely nothing alike, and yet they were so similar, it was more than obvious they'd come from the same egg.

Laughing at the thought as they flew, Jo still couldn't believe Illarion had returned just minutes after Cadegan had been sucked out of the castle. His psychic powers had warned him something was wrong and he'd been desperate to check on them.

But for the dragon's return, there was no telling what would have become of her.

Illarion slowed and rose up like a falcon to hover over the ground so far below. *Something's amiss.*

Latching on to him with all her strength, Jo scanned the countryside. "I don't see anything."

*It's not my eyes that sense it. I feel it. A change in the air. Morgen is launching her army again. Gargoyles and man-drakes are taking flight. They're headed this way.*

"What do you think it is?"

*Dangerous. In a word. I have no idea why she'd do such. But it doesn't bode well for any of us.*

Jo frowned as she caught sight of something off in the distance. "Is that part of her army?"

Illarion turned to look. *Not sure. Those creatures were once servants of King Arthur, but have been enslaved by others since his death.*

"Others, like . . . ?"

*Our friend Gwyn.*

"Should we attack them and see if they can help get my body back?"

*Are you up to a battle?*

"I am Cadegan, right? I have his powers. No idea really how to use them, but I'm willing to give it a go, *if* you are."

He snorted. *Hold tight and pray.*

Illarion headed straight for them.

Jo hung tight and stayed low to his neck as they flew. She felt something rumbling in his stomach. "Hungry, sweetie?"

*Getting ready to breathe fire if I need to.*

"So it comes from your stomach?"

*No. I have anatomy you don't. Let's leave it at that.*

Okay then. She wasn't sure she wanted a dragon biology lesson.

As they neared the giant, muscular gryphon birds, Jo saw the two riders on their backs. This couldn't be good.

Preparing for attack, Illarion dove for them.

But as they drew closer, she realized one of the riders was extremely familiar.

"Wait! It's Cadegan!"

Illarion pulled up. *Are you sure?*

"Pretty much. I think I'd know my body anywhere."

Laughing in her head, he projected his thoughts to the riders.

The moment he did, the one in her body headed for them.

"Josette?" Cadegan called.

"It's us, Cade!"

Illarion led the way to the meadow below. The huge gryphon birds landed not far away, while Jo jumped down from Illarion, and then ran to meet them.

A part of her didn't really believe it was Cadegan until he

was in her arms. She buried her face in his neck and held him for everything she was worth. "I thought you were gone forever."

He was actually trembling in relief. "I thought Morgen had you. We were on our way to assault Camelot."

Jo laughed as she glanced at his massive army of two. "Assault how, honey? You wouldn't have stood a chance without your body and powers."

He winked at her. "I hadn't quite mastered the plan in me mind. Was hoping for a bit of inspiration once I arrived."

"You are so nuts." She kissed him.

Until her gaze fell to the man with him and she recognized him from Cadegan's memories.

All humor fled as bitter rage took hold of her better sense.

"Hi." He held his hand out to her. "I'm—"

Before he could say another word, she punched his jaw as hard as she could. Then cursed as pain shot through her hand with a ferocious pounding. Wow, it looked so much easier and less painful in movies.

"Oh my God, I think I broke my hand." She cradled it to her chest.

With an arched brow, Cadegan moved to inspect it. "Not broken, love, but remind me, I need to teach you how to hit someone."

Thorn glared at her as he rubbed at his bruised jaw. "What the hell was that for?"

"You bastard!" she snarled at him, wanting the power to beat him blue. "It's for what you did to Cadegan. How could you!"

"You don't know what happened."

"No, Leucious. *You're* the one who doesn't know what happened! I have Cade's memories. You worthless son of a bitch!"

He didn't speak as his gaze dropped to the scars on her arms. Scowling, he moved to her back.

Jo pulled the T-shirt off so that he could see the full range of damage done to Cadegan's body. And most of it was done or had happened because of *him*. "Proud of yourself?"

His face pale, he met Cadegan's gaze. "What did they do to you."

Cadegan put the shirt back over her. "It matters naught."

Jo reached to slap Leucious, but Cadegan stopped her.

"Let it go, lass."

Let it go, her left foot! How could he be so forgiving of such an asshole? "Why are you with him?"

"He's a friend of your cousins'. He's here to take you home."

She stepped past Cadegan to poke Leucious in the chest with her index finger. "No. You're taking *us* home. I won't leave here without Cadegan."

"Lass . . ."

"I mean it, Cade. Unlike your worthless family, I will *never* leave you. Especially not alone in this hell."

Cadegan pulled her into his arms and held her close. How he wished he could believe her. But he knew that life had a nasty tendency to make liars of them all, and lay ruin to any and all intentions. He kissed her cheek. "We'll worry about that later. First, we have to switch ourselves back."

Leucious screwed his face up. "This is disturbing, isn't it? Hearing your words coming out of her body? Yeah. I think I'm getting a migraine."

"Could be a tumor," one of the birds said. "Or aneurysm. I was watching a show on that just—"

"Would you shut it already, Talfryn!" the other bird snapped at him. "Can't you ever learn to read the room?"

"There's no room here." Talfryn glanced around. "Are you daft?"

Jo scowled at them before she looked back at Cadegan. "Should I ask?"

"Nay, lass." Cadegan quickly introduced everyone.

Once they were done, Jo tapped the bracelet on her arm. "Do you think this has anything to do with this *Invasion of the Body Snatchers* episode we're experiencing?"

"Aye, and I say we go back to the castle and beat the shite out of Gwyn until he fixes this."

Leucious snorted. "Now there's the Cadegan I remember. When all else fails, beat them with a stick."

*Works for me.*

Cadegan inclined his head to Illarion. "I have a suspicion that you and I shall be good friends."

Leucious snorted at his brother. "Why don't we just pull the bracelet off and see what happens? Shall we?"

Ioan moved forward to stop him. "That might not be wise. Who put it on her, and why?"

"Gwyn, to ensure that we returned to Galar by fey vespers." Cadegan sighed. "I agree with Ioan. It's possible it could hurt her. I trust Gwyn even less than I trust *you.*"

Leucious glared at him. "Like you wouldn't cut my throat."

"Aye, I would. If ever given the right and proper chance." Cadegan took Jo's hand.

Just as he started for Ioan, the sky above them darkened.

Jo looked up and gasped. Morgen's dragons and gargoyles filled the sky.

And they were headed straight for them.

# 13

Without thinking twice, Cadegan grabbed his sword from Josette's hip and prepared to fight them to the bitter end of his strength. Even though she was in his body, he pulled her behind him as the dragons and gargoyles descended to attack them.

The moment he did, a strange red haze rose up from the ground and formed a dome over their small group. A dome that Morgen's soldiers slammed into, and recoiled off. If not for the fact that this could be an even bigger threat to them, it'd be comical.

Scowling, Cadegan looked at his brother. "That you, with a shield?"

Leucious shook his head. "Definitely not me." He glanced to the Adar Llwch Gwin. "Frick? Frack? Can you explain?"

Slack-jawed, they shook their heads in unison.

Illarion pulled back to help shield Josette and Cadegan. *It feels fey, but not as dark as Morgen's magick.*

No sooner had he pushed that thought to their heads than the ground below their feet opened up and swallowed them.

Cursing, Cadegan wrapped himself around Josette to cushion her fall as they tumbled into a deep, dark cavern. For a minute, he feared it to be bottomless.

Until he struck a hard, black floor. Though it was dark, the walls around them glistened with glowing vines.

Josette landed on top of him.

He let out a harsh groan. "I'm the one what needs to lose weight, me lady. Oof! I weigh a mighty ton. How do you stand me weight atop of you?"

Her face turned red before she shifted to speak in his ear. "I love your weight on me. But not like this."

He kissed her gently before he let her go to see what new dangers lurked for them.

Josette slid from his body. He pushed himself to his feet while the others followed suit.

"Well, well, what have we here?" a woman asked from inside the dark.

Retrieving his sword, he took Josette's hand to hold her near him.

"Why have you trespassed upon my lands?" There was a shrill note to the woman's irritated tone.

"We meant no disrespect." Leucious spoke up first.

"Actions are far more important to me than words that profess intent, as those actions, more oft than not, betray your real heart. Case in point . . ." A red mist appeared before Cadegan and Josette. "You two protect each other, without a single word. Does this mean that you don't care for one another?"

When Josette started to speak, Cadegan squeezed her hand to warn her not to. At least not until they knew more about what they were facing.

The mist went to Leucious. "Who do you protect?"

"None of your business."

The mist solidified into the body of a beautiful woman. With long black hair, she had an oval face and large, dark eyes. "You like your words, don't you?"

"They've been known to serve me well."

She scoffed at Leucious before she came over to Cadegan and Jo. A slow smile curved her lips as she danced her gaze over Cadegan's handsome body. Until she cocked her head and studied their locked hands. "Now you, *you* must have significant value for your lady to covet and protect you so."

Before either of them could speak, Jo was ripped away from Cadegan. Cadegan, still in her body, rushed for her.

As Jo tried to reach him, a twisted golden cage came out of the ground to surround and hold her in a tiny room. Similar cages sprang up to imprison Illarion, Ioan, Talfryn, and Leucious.

The woman moved to confront Cadegan, who was in Jo's body. "Do you know who I am?"

"Queen Cordelia."

She inclined her head in approval. "So you know of me?"

"Everyone in Glastonbury knows the tale of Gwyn and his wife, Creiddylad."

She wagged her finger before his face. "Nay, not until *All Hallow's Eve*. For now, I belong to Gwythyr ap Greidawl, who won me again last May Day." Sighing heavily, she cast her gaze back toward Cadegan's caged body. "And I grow weary of my place as trophy. There was a time when I would have given up my very soul for Gwythyr. But those days have long passed, and now I long for another to hold. A man worthy of the title, who will always win my hand above the others."

The queen's speculative gaze went back to Cadegan's

body before she returned to face Josette's body. "What say we fight for your man and the best lady keeps him?"

Cadegan hesitated. Did she not know they were in each other's bodies?

Was this a trick of some kind?

Unsure, he scowled at her. "Fight how?"

"A joust. You against my champion. If your love and heart are true, you will win back your man. But be warned . . . if you've spoken falsely of your feelings, all will know you have lied, and you will surely lose."

In his own body, with his strength and skill, Cadegan would have been more than prepared to take down any opponent. But lying to the fey queen seemed a stupid prospect. And he valued Josette's life too much to gamble with it.

"Majesty, do you know who I am?"

She gave him an insidious smile. "Do *you*?"

Fair enough. Honestly, he barely knew himself most days. And today was a particularly confusing one. But the one thing he didn't doubt was his feelings for Josette. "I know me heart."

"Then a joust it shall be."

"No!" Josette shouted in denial as she fought against the gold bars that held her. "I won't have it! What if you're hurt?"

Cadegan took her hand into his and pulled it to his cheek.

"I will heal." He turned back to the queen. "But there is one thing I want for this."

Cordelia arched a brow. "And that is?"

"Win, lose, or draw, Josette returns to her true home, intact. Body and soul."

She took a moment to think the offer over. "Only if you agree that should you lose, I shall own Cadegan forever. Body and soul."

It was a steep price, but he was willing. "Done."

"No!" Josette screamed. "No! I won't agree to this. I refuse it!"

Cordelia snorted. "Not your bargain to make. The deal is done." She stepped back and clapped her hands.

A whirlwind swept through the cavern, blowing all of them around. It plastered their clothes to their bodies and forced a severe chill into the room. Suddenly, a golden stallion appeared. It had red eyes and a shimmering mane as it stamped at the ground and eyed Cadegan with malice.

In the blink of an eye, gold armor encased his body, complete with a basinet helm, red plumage, and war lance.

The horse glared at Cadegan as he pulled himself into the saddle to fight whatever opponent Cordelia demanded.

Borne by fey magick, the lance rose from the ground to hover by his side until he took it into his grasp. As soon as he gripped it, his opponent appeared at the opposite side of the glowing list. Wrapped in silver armor with blue plumage and riding a silver horse, the rider glared through his helm at Cadegan with red, demonic eyes.

Cordelia manifested a huge, thorny throne at the same time a pixie with wings appeared near the field, holding a flag.

Cadegan waited for the pixie to drop the banner. The moment she did, he kicked his horse forward. He held the lance at the ready for a fair strike and braced himself for the blow.

Just as he should have struck, his opponent vanished into thin air. His horse galloped past, and as it did so, Cadegan was no longer on the field.

Nor was he in Josette's body.

He was in the distant past. A frightened boy among the king's soldiers.

Cadegan froze as he heard them speaking those words that had no meaning to him. As they cast scornful glances in his direction as if he was a mongrel dog about to shite their shoes.

One of the knights threw a basket of rusted chain mail at him, and a sword that appeared to have been scraped from the bottom of the Thames . . .

And smelted back together as a child's learning project.

Confused, he'd looked up at the man who'd sneered words at him he couldn't understand, but the tone said that it was all the likes of Cadegan deserved.

The others had laughed at his new armor the king had instructed them to find for him since he hadn't any of his own.

Still, they laughed at him.

Alone and homesick, Cadegan had dug through the basket, only to realize the other knights had soaked all the contents with their urine. And they laughed even harder while they watched him curl his lip in repugnance.

Worse, it still bore the blood of the last knight who'd worn it, or rather, given the size of the hole in the side, had died in it.

Unwilling to let the others know how much their words and actions cut him, Cadegan had washed the armor as best he could, and patched it with leather straps he'd cut from the top of his shoes.

On their first day of battle, he'd donned the armor and ignored their ridicule and disdain, and was grateful he could only ascertain their biting tones and not their actual words. One was bad enough. He definitely didn't need the other.

Since he had no horse, they'd left him to fight on foot, with only the damaged sword and no shield.

None of them had allowed him to be part of the army group. One by one, they'd pushed and jostled him until he'd been relegated to the side of their forces, to fight alone. No one at his side.

No one at his back.

It was the worst moment of his life. Because all the soldiers had refused to train him, he'd known nothing of war. He'd barely known how to properly hold his sword. But the moment the Mercians had attacked and blood had flowed thick on the field at their feet, Cadegan had held his own with everything he had. Determined only not to die that day.

However, his opponents had mercilessly sought to lop his head off and knock him to the ground.

He'd refused to give them their desire. He had no intention of going down. Not this day or any other.

As he fought, he'd seen one of the mounted Powys knights fall from his mount. The Mercians had set upon him like a pack of starving wolves. Ferocious. Merciless. They had hacked until they knocked his helm free.

It was the same man who had cast the soiled armor at Cadegan and laughed while he did so.

For the merest heartbeat, Cadegan had gloated at seeing the man's fate.

Until his mind flashed on Brother Eurig, who'd used his hands to lovingly and patiently instruct him on decency and mercy. *"Honor is what separates man from beast. The greatest way to live with honor in this world is to actually be what we pretend to be. Let others laugh and mock those of us they perceive beneath them, but remember, good Cadegan, honor lies inside our hearts and it is that which makes us act with mercy and compassion against those who have most wronged us. Even if the jackal wounds your pride, do not reward such knavery by surrendering your honor to him. Only then have you truly lost all. Never let anyone take your soul, for they are not worth your eternity or your heart."*

Instead of walking away and leaving the knight to die as cruelly as he'd lived, Cadegan had charged forward and bravely sought to protect him from their enemies.

Though the knight had survived that encounter and Cadegan—wounded himself—had carried him to the physicians to be tended, the knight's injuries had been such that he'd died the next day. But an hour before his death, he'd summoned Cadegan to his bed.

His gaze warm, he'd offered his hand to Cadegan and had given him his own sword, armor, and helm, and told the soldiers with him that he wanted his horse to be Cadegan's as well.

It was that knight's sword that Cadegan carried to this day. A reminder to himself that even those who appeared the cruelest and most evil in the world were never above salvation. That, by the right actions, anyone's heart could be changed. And a reminder to Cadegan that *all* people deserved the utmost respect. To remind himself that he never wanted to be the one who brought such pain to another living creature's misery.

As Brother Eurig so often said . . . *"No one ever gets over great pain, of any sort. It merely carves the soul into a stronger, better person."*

He would never dishonor Brother Eurig or his teachings.

"Would you give your honor for your love?"

Cadegan froze at the queen's disembodied voice. "Pardon?"

"What do you value most?" she asked him.

"Me lady. Always."

"Then prove it. Remove your clothes."

Cadegan shook his head. "I am in her body, and I will not dishonor her. You asked if I would sacrifice me honor and so I would. But what you ask of me now is to sacrifice hers, and that I will not do."

"Not even to save your life?"

"Nay. My life holds no value to me. I will never dishonor me lady."

Cordelia grabbed him by the throat and slammed him against the wall. "I will rip out your heart!"

"You promised me that you would not harm Josette. Win, lose, or draw, me lady goes home alive and intact. Your word to me." A strange fissure went through his body.

The queen narrowed her gaze on him with rancor. "And now?"

"Now what?"

"You have your body back, Lord Cadegan. Will you give me your honor for your lady?"

Cadegan looked down to see that she was correct. He was him again. "I will give anything for her freedom."

She inclined her head to him. "You will have three passes at my champion. If you are unhorsed, you will surrender yourself to Morgen. No questions asked. No escape. If you lose, you belong to me as my slave. Forever."

Cadegan would rather they kill him. But he had no doubt that he would win. He'd never once lost in a joust. "Done. But are we going to actually complete the match this time?"

She clapped her hands.

Cadegan was again on his horse. It was the moment right before they would have crossed lances, when his opponent had vanished. This time, his opponent's lance slammed into his shoulder, sending a piercing pain throughout his entire body.

He fell back on the horse, and almost came free of the saddle. It was sheer force of will that kept him in place.

But awww . . . it hurt. The pain of that single blow was searing, and while her champion's lance had been snapped in twain, Cadegan's remained perfectly intact.

The urge to cry foul overwhelmed him. Yet he knew better than to utter those words.

Cordelia wouldn't care. This wasn't about fairness. It was about winning.

Unlike her and the dark forces she served, there was no victory he wanted badly enough that he'd cheat for it. He rolled his shoulder, trying to ignore the pain of it, as he turned his destrier back toward the list.

The pixie appeared again with her flag.

She looked at the giant he'd tilted against, then him. With a quick nod to the queen, she lowered her banner.

Cadegan spurred his mount forward. This time, he took aim for the giant's heart, and again leaned into the blow. He struck his opponent straight and true. The giant reeled back, but caught himself before he fell from the horse.

Leucious and Josette cried out in happiness at Cadegan's clear victory.

Cordelia's eyes darkened, warning that she wasn't through with them, nor would she take loss lightly.

Cadegan tossed the remains of his broken lance to the ground.

Jo bit her lip as she watched Cadegan take another magical lance from the air and prepare for their final pass. He was incredible. She could just imagine how terrifying it would be to face him in battle with those skills.

He lifted his helm's visor to smile and wink at her.

Wrapping her hands around the gold bars, she prayed that he won this last round so that they could get out of here. But as he headed into the next match, a bad feeling went through her.

This was too easy.

Something that proved to be all too true as the giant rose

up during the last pass to kill Cadegan. When it did so, she saw something even more frightening.

Cadegan's armor went flying in all directions. He emerged out of it like a demonic butterfly from a cocoon. His eyes glowing yellow, he now had long blond hair, and claws. Huge fangs. His skin turned an unholy mixture of yellow and orange. Large, black wings sprang out of his back.

Leucious cursed as he saw Cadegan's sudden and extreme transformation.

"What is it?" she asked breathlessly.

"We're in deep, serious shit. They've just awakened the addanc."

"The what?"

He met her gaze through the bars, and by the paleness of his features, she saw his real panic. "It's why I trapped Cadegan here." He jerked his chin toward the monster. "It was to keep *that* from being unleashed. Each demonkyn holds in his heart his true form. The soulless bloodthirsty beast that is virtually invincible. One that cannot be stopped." Wincing, he cursed again as deep sadness marred his handsome features. "The addanc has swallowed him whole and we're next on the menu."

# 14

With a string of profanity that left Jo blushing, Leucious stepped back from the bars of his cell. "Jo? Look at me. I'm about to do something really fucking stupid. When I do this, I need you to remember three words for me. *Omni rosae spina.*"

She scowled at him. "Every rose has its thorn?"

"Good, you understand Latin. Yes. Commit those words to memory in the event I lose control. Okay?"

She didn't like the sound of that. In any way. "Lose control of what?" She hoped it was just his bladder.

Until his eyes turned a vibrant green, laced with red. Then, she almost lost control of hers as she looked into the face of his true demonic form.

"This." One moment Leucious was human, the next, he, too, was a demon. Complete with wings and gold armor that reminded her of a Roman general's.

Talfryn went wild in his cage. "Help us! Someone! Rambo! We've got to get out of here!"

"Why?" Jo asked.

Before he could answer, Leucious channeled his powers and blasted them from their cages. Illarion rushed to her side to protect her as Leucious and Cadegan attempted to murder each other.

Laughing, Cordelia turned on Jo's group with a smug smile. "Thank you for allowing me to own the one weapon neither Morgen nor Merlin can stop. He's mine now!"

One moment they were in the cavern, and the next, all of them, including Leucious—who was still a demon—were back in the house, on the other side of the mirrored door.

To her shock, four of her cousins were there, too, with a small group of people she'd never met before.

Still in his demon's body, Leucious turned on them all and let out a fierce howl. He moved in to attack them.

*Say the words!* Illarion warned her.

*"Omni rosae spina!"*

The moment she said them, Leucious threw his head back and cried out as if he were in pain. He froze as if he were fighting himself even harder than he'd fought Cadegan.

His demonic body slowly melted back to his human one. Tears streamed down his face as he visibly shook and gasped for breath.

Without a word to them, he wiped the back of his hand over his face and left through a side door.

Karma followed after him.

Selena grabbed Jo up into a fierce hug. "This is you? Right?"

"Yeah. Why?"

"After that crazy guy who was here in your body, I just wanted to make sure."

"Cadegan," Jo said, irritated at the way Selena talked about him. She looked at Illarion and paused at the sight of the mighty weredragon, standing there. He was here, in this realm. In human form. Somehow the fey queen had finally freed him from Glastonbury. But that being said, he wasn't as happy about it as she would have thought. Rather, he seemed very confused and disoriented.

He stared at one of the blond strangers as if he was seeing a ghost. Likewise, the blond gaped at him.

"Illarion? Is it really you, little brother?"

Tears gathered in Illarion's eyes before he nodded and pulled the other man into a tight hug.

By the way they looked at each other, she knew they were talking with their minds and the rest of them weren't invited to the conversation.

Not until Illarion looked past his brother to meet Jo's curious gaze.

*Josette, this is my brother, Maxis.*

She inclined her head to him. "Nice to meet you."

"And you. Thank you for helping my brother." He gaped at Illarion. "I still can't believe you're here. I thought you'd died with the others."

While they stepped aside to talk, Jo returned to Selena. "I have to go back for Cadegan."

When she started toward the mirror, three Leuciouses appeared to block her way. "You cannot release him now."

Jo glared at the being, who was about to meet the bad Cajun side of her. One thing about Southern women, they were tough. No one said no and got away with it. Especially not when it came to a loved one. "I will not leave him in there. Alone. If I have to go back by myself, I will."

Leucious returned to the room with Karma, as the three images blocking her way vanished. He cast his glance around the people gathered there. "For the love of God, will someone *please* talk sense into Queen Hard Head?" He glared at Jo. "You can't go into Terre Derrière le Voile and release a banished demon into the world of man."

Anger tore through her. Before she could think better of it, Jo rushed Thorn and shoved him back. "You should never have banished him there! This is all your fault!"

"I had no choice," Leucious growled at her. "He was slipping from us every day, turning slowly more bitter and angry. I saw it in his eyes. I did everything I could to keep him grounded and anchored, and then when he came to me that night to tell me what he'd done, I saw that he was just about to blossom into the addanc you saw earlier."

Jo couldn't believe what he was telling her. How could he do something so cold? "So you abandoned him to it?"

He winced before he met her gaze again. "You really want the truth, Jo?"

Yes, she did.

Leucious held his hand out to her. "Take it and I'll show you *exactly* what it is you're dealing with."

In that moment, she hesitated as a bad feeling went through her. She didn't really trust Leucious, and there was something very peculiar about all of this. Something she wasn't sure she wanted to know. Reaching up, she fingered the medallion Cadegan had given her.

For protection.

Cadegan wasn't a demonic beast. She knew it. No one who loved as deeply as he did could be what Leucious claimed. Leucious was the bad guy here, not Cadegan.

Unwilling to be intimidated by him, she took his hand.

The moment she did, her head spun. No longer in the house, she was in an old medieval stone monastery.

A monk she recognized as Brother Eurig and an abbot stood to the side of a modest bed where a woman she knew from Cadegan's memories as his mother was just giving birth. With dark hair and tonsures, the clergy were both dressed in plain black robes.

Cadegan's mother was ethereal and beautiful. Her long dark hair was soaked with sweat from her labor, but it didn't detract from her looks in any way. With one final push and scream, her son entered the world and slid into the waiting midwife's hands.

"Holy Mother of God!" Brother Eurig crossed himself.

The midwife cringed and recoiled from the newborn. She all but dropped it onto the bed between its mother's legs. "What is *that* thing?"

"Kill it!" the abbot snarled.

"Nay!" Scrambling to reach the child, Brigid grabbed up her infant and cradled him to her breast. She wrapped her wool shawl around the baby, as if to protect it.

This was not the same callous mother who'd gone to Cadegan to take his shield from him. The one who'd tried to barter his freedom for what she wanted.

The baby screamed for air.

Stepping closer, Jo gasped as she saw Cadegan's inhuman features. Though winged, he was humanoid, with orange, scaly skin and eyes of bright yellow. Strangely cute, the small lizard-like creature cried for comfort. Brigid pulled him to her breast and suckled him. He calmed instantly.

The abbot curled his lip. "'Tis the son of the devil! We must kill it, now, before it grows."

She shook her head. "He is the son of the Tuath Dé. Grandson of the Dagda. A god in his own right. To kill him would unravel the universe as we know it and unleash a bounty of demons upon this world that no one can fight. Do you want to begin Armageddon?"

The abbot shook his head. "We cannot allow it here."

She snatched at the abbot's robe until they were almost nose-to-nose. "You have no choice. Do you understand? If he is kept from evil, he will know no evil. He will be a force for good. So long as his heart is pure and uncorrupted, his father will never be able to turn him and use him against us."

"And if he turns evil?"

Her brow drawn together by worry, she looked down and stroked the baby's cheek while he suckled her. And as he drank from his mother, he slowly turned human in appearance.

"He will destroy this earth and all who dwell here. The only one capable of killing him would be the demon Malachai."

Brother Eurig sucked his breath in sharply as he crossed himself in terror. After a moment, he cast a speculative look to the babe. "Can he destroy the Malachai, my lady?"

She considered it for a few minutes. "As an adult, he would have those powers, aye."

The monk locked gazes with his abbot. "Wouldn't it make sense to care for such a weapon so that we might use him should the Malachai threaten us?"

" 'Tis too dangerous."

Still Eurig was insistent. "All weapons are deadly when in the wrong hand, Father. But when used by a good one . . ."

The abbot scoffed. "You're mad! Both of you."

"Nay. These are bad times." Brother Eurig toyed with the same rosary that Cadegan kept by his bed. "The Sephiroth is lost to us. But if we could have another to aid our side in this battle, we might turn the tide. We could win this war. Once and for all."

Still, the abbot refused his request. "A dog always returns to its vomit."

"And the Lord works in mysterious ways." Eurig jerked his chin to Brigid. "His mother is saintly. There is no reason to assume his father's blood would be stronger than hers or her father's, never mind the two combined."

"You're willing to bet our lives on it?"

Eurig nodded. "I will take the child in hand and guide it. I will never allow it to falter."

"*He* and *him*," Brigid corrected. "He is my son, not an it."

Eurig met the abbot's stern scowl. "We can keep him from evil. I believe that."

"I consent, even though I have a bad feeling future generations will curse us for our parts in this day." The abbot narrowed his gaze on Eurig. "He will be your responsibility and there will be harsh penalties for you whenever he leans toward the dark powers."

"I will give him the strength to stay true. Teach him how to avoid temptation. I truly believe we are meant to do this."

Leucious appeared by Jo's side in the monastery, and pulled her attention away from the scene. "Cadegan was the sole reason they took a vow of silence and became cloistered. They wanted to keep all evil away from him as best they could. Before he was sent to Terre Derrière le Voile, the monastery was his shelter from his father's temptations."

While she could appreciate what they'd tried to do, surely

they had to know better. "You can't do that, Leucious. Evil always finds a way in."

"I know." He took her hand and led her to that fateful night when Æthla had turned on Cadegan and sought to end his life. "This is what *I* saw when he came to me."

Leucious, who was more commonly called Thorn to remind himself of why he must avoid unleashing the demon inside him, was sitting at his portable desk, reviewing reports of the Malachai and his army. An army Thorn had been fighting for thousands of years. The darkness that threatened the entire world was growing faster than he could put it down.

In the last week alone, he'd lost fifteen of his Hellchasers to the Malachai's forces. Two had been massacred when they'd foolishly gone to beg to free the Sephiroth so that Jared could fight with them.

"What am I going to do?" he breathed.

Thorn glanced to the mirror where the night before, his own father had written a threat in Hellchaser blood against both him and Cadegan.

Every day brought them closer to defeat. And every day, they lost more ground.

Even Malphas was currently lost to their side. In the hands of their bitterest enemy. If Thorn was lucky, that would be the most merciful fate that awaited him.

The other . . .

He couldn't even bring himself to contemplate what would happen if he allowed his father back into his heart.

Thorn knocked the parchment to the floor with a swipe of his arm. "You won't win, Father! So help me. I won't cede this world to you and to those you serve."

Taking his goblet, he'd just downed the last of its contents when Cadegan entered his tent. Thorn's stomach wrenched at the sorry sight of him. His eyes were their natural demonic color. They glowed bright reddish-yellow in the candlelight. Something Thorn had never seen them do before.

Human blood stained his armor. Cadegan's hands trembled as if he was barely holding on to the part of him untainted by Paimon's cruelty.

His skin rippled with demonic flesh.

Thorn felt his own powers surging to fight as he saw the darkness within Cadegan. It was growing even before his eyes. He tried to stop it, but his own eyes began to change. "What have you done?"

Ashamed, Cadegan looked away at the same time Thorn's servant, Misery, appeared by his side. While he didn't trust the sultry demoness at all, he knew she never lied to him.

She only withheld the truth.

"He killed humans," she whispered in Thorn's ear. "Midlings who were trying to protect their sister he coveted for his own."

Nay! Thorn winced at the fear that Paimon, after all Thorn's attempts, had won Cadegan away from him, too. The betrayal and hurt cut deep. In all the world, Cadegan was all he had left.

All he loved, who still lived.

Hoping, praying it was a lie, that Cadegan wasn't turning, Thorn glared at his precious family. "Is this true?"

"Aye, but—"

Enraged as his own demonic blood ignited, he backhanded Cadegan. How could he do this? Cadegan knew their laws and why they had them. Theirs was a tenuous truce with the Arelim and Seraphim. One misstep and all of them would be banished to the hell realms they'd populated with enemies who would do anything to lay hands to them. Enemies who would tear them apart and grow even more powerful. So powerful, the others would never be able to stop them.

Thorn didn't care what they did to him, personally. He'd more than earned his damnation and he'd come to terms with that long ago, but the others who'd loyally served him . . .

They deserved the salvations they'd earned.

"There are no buts! You swore to never draw midling blood again. Is this how you uphold your sacred oaths?"

Cadegan's eyes had turned completely from human to demon. "They attacked me first."

Thorn winced as he felt his brother turning even more toward the darkness. Justification for cruelty was the slipperiest of slopes. Once begun, there was no turning back. Evil fed upon such blameless behavior and it thrived with it in the heart of its tool.

"You are the blood of Paimon! No midling can truly harm you. You know this! A bloody nose or black eye, you will survive."

Cadegan lowered his head. "Forgive me, brother. 'Twas a mistake."

Thorn wanted to believe him. He really did. But he'd been deceived too many times.

Tears choked him as he looked into a set of eyes identical to his father's, and realized that Cadegan was his downfall. He'd allowed this child to come too close to his heart. That was how evil worked. Never from enemies you saw coming. Only those closest to you could destroy you. The ones you mistakenly trusted.

The ones you allowed to mislead you because the pain of living without them was greater than the pain of tolerating the lie.

By forsaking his blood oath, Cadegan had taken that first deadly step toward the darkest forces. If he took one more, he'd be so powerful that none of them could stand against him.

*None of them.*

Thorn's gaze went to his desk, where the Malachai's name was carved in the wood as a reminder of how powerful a beast he was.

Should the addanc merge with the Malachai . . .

All would be forever lost. This world would be theirs and the only thing Thorn would be able to do is stand back and watch it burn at their united command.

No matter how much Thorn loved Cadegan, he couldn't allow that to happen. Not after all the horrors he'd witnessed.

And especially not after the promise he'd made.

Thorn shook his head. "Nay, the mistake was mine for thinking for one minute that you were something more than the mindless beast you were born to be."

Cadegan's entire face changed as the demon in him was ignited even more. Gone was any hint of compassion in his eyes.

Thorn curled his lip. "You disgust me! I can't believe I put my trust and faith in you."

Cadegan's face returned to its human appearance—as others before. A trick for compassion that almost always worked, and weakened the fool who loved them. "Please, Leucious—"

Thorn grabbed his throat to stop those words before they succeeded in changing his mind and allowing him to forget how dangerous Cadegan was.

Not the innocent child he loved.

The monster that innocent child had foolishly unleashed

this night. A monster who hadn't been able to withdraw from those too weak to fight him.

Cadegan had bathed in their blood. He'd unleashed the inner demon at full wrath. Of all creatures, Thorn knew that euphoria much better than he wanted to. He couldn't allow Cadegan to become what Thorn had been.

No one would be able to reach Cadegan then.

One man, even this beloved child, could never be more important than the welfare of the entire world.

Thorn tightened his grip and prayed this was the right decision. That Brigid would finally do what she should have done centuries ago.

Welcome her son to her realm, where she could watch him and keep him from his father's grasp.

"For crimes against Our Lord, for breech of my trust, I condemn you to the shadowed lands of your mother. No more are you to walk this earth as a living being. You will spend eternity remembering what you've done and regretting your actions. You are no longer one of us. For that, you are sentenced and banished from the world of man. Forevermore."

Cadegan tried to pry off Thorn's grip. For the merest instant, Thorn almost relented.

Until Cadegan's hand became a claw. Terrified of unleashing the addanc onto the world, Thorn threw him against the small mirror where Paimon had promised just the night before to devour the world through Cadegan's blood.

Cadegan went instantly into his mother's realm. He pounded against the glass, begging for release.

Thorn forced himself to show no emotion. To stand strong against the love that hated him for what he was doing.

*It must be done.* There was no choice in this matter.

Unable to stand himself for his actions, Thorn turned away and covered the portal so that Cadegan's face wouldn't weaken his resolve.

*I love you, child.*

Unable to bear the pain of it, Thorn threw his head back and roared with agony. . . .

For a full minute, Jo couldn't breathe as she pulled out and stared into Thorn's eyes. A demon who really did love Cadegan.

The events looked so different from his perspective. His fears, past, and duties had colored his vision and clouded his judgment.

Just as Cadegan's had done.

"He would never have turned against you, Thorn."

"Would you have taken that chance if you were me?"

Honestly? She didn't know. Everyone made mistakes. Everyone put their faith in the wrong person at some point.

Æthla had been Cadegan's blind spot. And Cadegan was definitely hers.

"I'm sorry I misjudged you."

"We are all guilty of that, Jo. But now you know why we have to leave him where he is."

She shook her head in denial of his solution. It wasn't that simple and she knew it. "We can't. We've awakened the addanc within him. He is the very weapon you once feared unleashing. What if your enemies find him now? Are you any more able to kill him today than you were then?"

Thorn looked away.

"That's what I thought. Before all this started, Cadegan was dormant in his cave. Alone and safe. You and I have awakened his demon side, and it's up to us to do what you should have done a thousand years ago."

"Kill him?"

"No, Thorn. *Save* him."

# 15

"Given what we've been going through with the current Malachai, I agree with Jo. I think the most irresponsible thing we can do is leave Cadegan in Terre Derrière le Voile without supervision or protection. We've awakened the demon inside him. It's our duty to watch over and guard him."

Every head in the room stared at Acheron

as those words left his gorgeous lips. Some were happy about it.

Some, not so much.

Jo wanted to kiss him for backing her wishes. The expression on Thorn's face said he wanted to choke him. Karma, who'd been lobbying to banish Cadegan to an even bleaker realm, was furious.

Fang, a handsome, dark-haired wolfwere who worked as a Hellchaser for Thorn, exchanged a gaping stare of disbelief with his blond werebear wife, Aimee. Their group was currently meeting in the back room of the bar and grill on Ursulines, Sanctuary, that the two shapeshifters owned in conjunction with Aimee's Were-Hunter family of shapeshifting bears.

The room they were in was a bit cramped with Karma, Selena, Tabitha and her twin sister Amanda, along with Tabitha's husband Valerius, who'd once been a Roman general, and Amanda's husband Kyrian, an ancient Greek general who'd been killed by Valerius's grandfather. Then there was Talon, an ancient Celt who'd once worked with Valerius and Kyrian, who sat between them.

Just in case.

While Kyrian and Valerius had learned for the sake of their twin wives and five children to let bygones be bygones, they still had a tenuous relationship at times. One Jo had never understood the root of, until today.

How ironic, really. She'd steadfastly denied the existence of a paranormal world that existed side-by-side with the one she walked in every day. It blew her mind now to know that she had eaten many meals in this establishment that was owned and run by an entire clan of were-animals. That she'd unknowingly spent countless hours with men who were thousands of years old. It was impressive that her cousins had kept their secrets so well, and it made her seriously wonder who the father of Karma's son really was.

Some of the covert glances she'd caught between Karma and Thorn definitely told her there was much more to them than just mere friendship.

Could Thorn be E.T.'s father? Was that even possible?

While they discussed Cadegan's future, Simi sat beside Acheron, eating a plate loaded with barbecue chicken while Acheron's twin brother, Styxx, kept adding french fries and coleslaw to her meal whenever she ran out.

Styxx and Acheron were an odd couple, indeed. They were identical in absolutely every way, except hair color and style. Acheron's black curly hair was cut just below his ears and fell around his face. Styxx was blond and brushed his short curls back, out of his eyes. Acheron's clothes were black on black and as Goth as a 45 Grave audience . . . including his black titanium wedding band that had skulls and crossbones on it. On the flip side, Styxx had a preppy style and wore a dark blue shirt and jeans. His yellow gold wedding band appeared to have Egyptian hieroglyphics on it.

Also in black, Thorn sat beside Jo while Illarion and Max leaned against a wall next to Ioan and Talfryn. Zeke had stepped out only a few minutes ago to take a call, while they discussed what to do about Cadegan.

Thorn sighed heavily. "You didn't see him, Ash. He is the addanc. Fully morphed. Are you really willing to unleash him into this world, where we might not be able to stop him?"

Ash met his brother's gaze. "I've learned to reserve judgment on people for their actions, especially when they've been wronged by family." He turned back to Jo. "What do you honestly think? You've spent the most time with him out of us. And remember, if you guess poorly, you'll probably end the world as we know it."

She snorted at Acheron's words. "No pressure there, right, buddy? Wow, Ash. I know why you don't have your own self-help show . . . *Lifestyles of the Morbid and Terrifying*. Stay tuned, folks. This week we learn how to end the world with a flourish and get rid of those pesky dog flea problems, all in ten minutes."

Talon and Styxx burst out laughing.

"Hey!" Simi said. "No picking on the akri! He not the one who gots us into this . . . for once."

Offended, Acheron snorted. "Thanks, Sim."

"Anytime, akri. That's what the Simi's here for. Make sure you don't get one of them big heads."

Ignoring their segue, Illarion stepped forward. *I haven't known him long, but he seemed decent enough. For a demon. And I've known many of them over the centuries. I think we can trust Jo. She is his anchor, from what I've seen. There's nothing he won't do for her. He even spared my life at her command. So long as she lives, I think he's safe.*

Ash put his hand on Simi's shoulder. "That's the one truth of demons. They are all enslaved to their hearts. So long as it remains flesh and not stone or ice, we can control them."

Karma shook her head in denial. "But you're talking about someone who's been locked away for a thousand years. How will he acclimate to the modern world? You can't just let him loose and say, hey, dude, welcome to the Electronic Age. Make sure you don't put your finger in an outlet."

Styxx waved his hand at her in a gesture that said to take it down a notch. "Lower the disgust in your tone a bit. As one who was locked away in solitary confinement for eleven thousand years, I can say that no, it won't be easy. You people are effing nuts in this day and age. You make as much sense as a blind rat in a shifting maze. But with a guiding hand, we're not psychotic. I think Julian, Seth, and I have proven that. We have yet to run screaming naked through the streets . . . though tempting it is at times."

Selena grinned. "Your sessions with Grace must be going well."

Styxx nodded. "She's helped a lot and we can get Cadegan the same counseling. Plus . . ." He glanced over to his brother. "We could set him up in one of our temples to live. There are still plenty that sit vacant on the hill."

Ash arched a brow at Styxx's suggestion. "You want him that close to your wife and toddler?"

A slow smile spread across Styxx's face. "I'm pretty sure Bethany can handle it. I have no fear for them. From this, any-way." He glanced over to Jo. "If we can save him, I think we should try. I stand with Acheron and Jo on this matter. We unleashed him. We police him."

Talon nodded in agreement. "If he really is the grandson of the Mórrígan and the Dagda, that makes him the first cousin to my wife. Family is family. We protect that always."

Karma sighed. "Normally, I'd agree with you all. But do we protect him at the expense of the rest of the world? Is there not any way to bind his powers?"

"Duct tape?"

They all cast a droll stare to Fang.

"Oh, don't give me that look. Like none of you have never wondered why a witch doesn't use that in a binding spell. Nothing gets away from duct tape without losing half their skin and all their hair."

Thorn snorted. "Really don't want to know about your kinky sex life, Wolf. Your wife handles my food, and now I'm grossed out."

They laughed.

Acheron turned back toward Talon. "So, Celt, does anyone in your camp know Cordelia personally?"

"My mother-in-law probably does. She's a member of the Tuath Dé. Technically so am I, and my wife. But Starla lived among them in her youth. She knows everyone who's still living in their pantheon."

"Tuath Dé . . ." Acheron repeated that under his breath as he narrowed his gaze on Jo.

"Does that ring a bell?" Kyrian asked.

Acheron pulled out his cell phone and dialed a number. "Yeah, it does, and not for the obvious reasons." He held his hand up to let them know the person he was calling had picked up. "Hey baby, how's my girl?" He paused to listen before he laughed. "Give them both a big kiss from Grandpa and tell them that I'll be by later to tuck them in." With his inhuman, swirling silver eyes, he stared at Jo in a way that was really making her uncomfortable. "Yeah, actually I could use you for a minute. Can you pop over for just a few minutes?" He nodded. "I'm at Sanctuary. Back room. You can ask Dev when you get here and he'll show you in. Thanks, precious. Love you." He hung up.

"Kat?" Styxx asked.

Acheron nodded again. "She'll be . . ." The door opened to show an insanely tall, gorgeous blond woman who appeared even older than Acheron. "Walking in the door, right now."

Wide-eyed at the number of people inside, Kat cast her gaze around the room. "Hi, Daddy." She moved to kiss Acheron on the cheek before she hugged Simi and Styxx. When she went to steal one of Simi's french fries, the demon gasped in horror.

"You won't share fries with your sissy?" Kat asked the demon.

Simi eyed her with mock ire. "Good thing I love my baby sissy. But . . . Daddy akri, akra-Kat stealing your Simi's fries! Make her stop!"

Laughing, Acheron shook his head. "Don't make me put you two in separate corners. Play nice."

"Yes, sir." Kat stepped to the side.

Simi handed Kat another fry before she laughed and returned to her barbecue.

Acheron jerked his chin toward Jo. "Does she remind you of someone?"

Screwing her face up, Kat licked the ketchup from her fingers. Suddenly, recognition lit her green eyes and she gasped. "Are you thinking Brit?"

"Yeah."

Kat nodded. "Spitting image of her. But I haven't seen her in centuries. It's why it took me a while to realize it."

Jo frowned at their discussion. "Who's Brit?"

"Britomartis," Acheron answered. "She was a cousin of the goddess Artemis. They played together when they were girls on Olympus."

Kat nodded. "She's the one who gave my mother her famous nets that no one can escape from. As a thank-you for them, my mother gave her an enchanted mirror that had once belonged to Apollo. The mirror could show events of the past, present, and future. But most of all, it showed Britomartis the true heart of those around her."

Acheron nodded. "She was gazing in that same mirror one day when she fell in love with a Welsh prince and demigod named Arthegall ap Tyr, whose face she saw while he was jousting against another knight."

A chill went down her spine. "I saw Cadegan in the mirror before we met. It was how I ended up falling through it and into Glastonbury Tor."

Thorn rose slowly to his feet. "That's one hell of a coincidence, isn't it?"

Acheron nodded. "And I don't believe in them."

Kat moved closer to Jo. "Brit had a son and daughter, and both she and Arthegall gave up their godhoods so that they could live out their lives in peace with their children."

Karma folded her arms over her chest as she jerked her chin toward her cousin. "Jo could always see things in mirrors. She used to accuse us of planting it in her mind, but she's a born scryer."

"I have no powers."

"Would you let us test your blood?" Kat asked.

Jo hesitated. "Test it how, Draculina?"

"A little prick?"

Talfryn snorted. "Little prick's what got her into trouble."

Ioan shoved at him. "Shut it."

"It's true. Just saying."

Kat ignored them. "Can we?"

Jo held her hand out toward the woman. "Sure."

Kat pulled out a small knife and lightly pricked the edge of Jo's finger. She pooled the blood on the knife's blade before she took it to her father and handed it to him.

Acheron dipped his finger into the blood, then tasted it.

Jo screwed her face up in absolute repugnance. Nasty!

After a second, he nodded. "It's the same bloodline as Artemis."

"You sure?" Thorn asked.

He gave Thorn a droll stare. "Yeah. Pretty sure. I've tasted it before. Jo is from Zeus's bloodline."

Jo scowled at all of them. "What does that mean?"

Kat winked at her. "We're very distant cousins."

"For another," Acheron continued, "there's something much larger at play here. Your ancestor was pulled into Terre Derrière le Voile by a mirror to meet her future husband who was a Welsh prince and demigod."

Just like her. A chill ran down Jo's spine. Was any of this possible?

Did she dare hope?

"You think the two of them are reincarnated?" Selena asked.

Talon passed a knowing look to Acheron. "It happens, and you don't want to get in the way when it does. Two lovers will not be denied."

"Then how do we get him out?" Jo asked.

Talon stood. "I'm part of the Tuath Dé, so I'll lead us in."

Styxx nodded in agreement. "Since we're trespassing into another pantheon's realm, I think we should keep the group small. Jo has to go, because we'll need her to deal with Cadegan. Thorn's Frick and Frack, since they'll follow us in anyway." He grinned at Talfryn's disapproving growl over their nickname. "Thorn and me."

Simi looked up from her food. "No Simi?"

Styxx kissed her on the forehead. "Not this time. I don't want to risk you, and I know your father agrees with me. We need you here to protect our small sons and Kat's son and daughter."

That placated her. "Okies. But you have to let me put hornays on Baby Ari."

"Sure, as long as they're detachable."

She blew him a raspberry.

*I will come, too.*

Max tensed at his brother's offer. "Then I will go."

Illarion glared at him.

"You've been too long alone. I won't let you do this without a wingman."

Styxx nodded. "That actually works. It leaves a mount for each of us."

Anxious and breathless, Jo stepped forward. "Then we're going after him?"

Thorn inclined his head to her. "May the gods have mercy on us all. The last thing we need is to face an even stronger creature."

# 16

Cadegan dove beneath the blackened waves as he sought some sort of refuge from the hell that had become his world. Hatred and bloodlust pounded through him without letup. He wanted to taste the entrails of every creature dumb enough to approach him. While he'd never been friendly, this was completely different.

He had lost all ability to feel for anyone or anything.

Opening his eyes, he breathed in the water and scent of blood that still clung to him. The giant had been his first victim.

Too bad Cordelia had run screaming before he had a chance to finish the giant off and add her to his menu. Since then, he'd flown over the countryside, looking for more food. How he loved the musical cadence of screams echoing in his ears.

Truly, there was no better sound.

Drunk on the panic he'd induced, he dove deeper into the water. This was what he'd needed. The water's caress. The sound of his heartbeat echoing in his ears.

He froze his muscles as his instincts picked up on the sound of creatures approaching.

Curious, he tucked his legs and floated to the surface. With only his eyes out of the water, he scanned the banks until he saw Morgen's men. Fey Adoni armor glistened in the grim, gray light. Armed with crossbows and spears, they sent out lures to flush him to the top.

Did they think him as mindless as he was soulless?

Hah! They were about to learn the truth of his kind.

"Cadegan?" Morgen called. "We are here to free you."

Her gown was the only color in the dreary landscape. Bright bloodred, it clung to the voluptuous curves of her body. Something that brought out a new hunger inside him as she stirred his lust.

"Come to us, love. We will care for you in ways you cannot imagine."

Tempted, he moved his gaze to the MOD on Morgen's left-hand side.

Bracken. His uncle who'd once tortured him at Morgen's behest. He wanted to spear the bastard through his missing heart. But he refused to give them his location.

Especially since half her army carried nets he knew were there to capture him.

"Cadegan? Come, child. Let me care for you."

He went perfectly still at the sound of a voice that was identical to his mother's. For the merest instant, he was a boy again, sitting on the edge of the tower window as he counted down to the bell toll. As he looked out upon the endless land and wondered if his mother was out there, somewhere.

If she ever gave a passing thought to the child she'd left behind.

Furious, he started forward, wanting more blood.

But as he moved, the water caressed his demonkyn skin like the hand of a lover.

It caressed him like . . .

He struggled to remember. It was important that he recall the sensation.

*'Tis nothing. Devour them!*

He pulled back. Placing his hand upon his cheek, he heard the faint memory of laughter.

Gentle teasing.

*Like a wombat in a cornfield.*

"Josette," he breathed as he remembered feeling something other than burning hatred and the stinging hunger for death and blood.

*I will never leave you.*

But she had left him. Just like everyone else.

His rage built even higher. It was true. She'd betrayed him. Abandoned him the first chance she'd had to go home.

And here he stayed. With no one and nothing.

*Morgen wants you.*

Nay, she did not. He was not so stupid as to be that easily fooled. She wanted to *use* him. Like everyone else.

No one ever wanted to keep him. Not in reality.

"Cade?"

At first, he thought himself dreaming. Imagining the sound of a voice that was forever lost to him.

"Sweetie? Where are you?"

It was Josette. His heart pounded as a hope he despised filled his entire being.

*'Tis a dodge from the Queen Bitchtress, herself. Another lying ruse. . . .*

A slight movement on his right, caught his attention. Crouched low in the shrubs and staring at him was the last person he'd ever expected to see.

Josette.

She stretched her hand out toward him. "I'm here to take you home with me. Come, my lord. I won't let anyone harm you."

Cadegan started forward instinctively. Until he saw that she wasn't alone. Three men were with her. His bastard brother and one he knew was related to him, and another who favored Acheron, but this one wasn't demonkyn.

He scowled at their small group. He wasn't sure how he knew that the one was related to him, but he'd always been able to sense any member of the *Tuath Dé* what came near him.

Morgen's forces saw them and moved to attack

Suddenly, two dragons and two Adar Llwch Gwin swooped down from the sky to engage Morgen and her army.

Exploding into action, Morgen's forces flew at the new-comers. Shouts and curses rang out as the two groups clashed. The scent of blood filled his nostrils and the call to war was more than he could bear.

Without thought, he went for them all.

Jo swallowed as she watched Cadegan rip through Morgen's mandrakes and gargoyles without hesitation or mercy. No wonder they feared him so. In his demonic form, he *was* a killing machine.

In that moment, she seriously doubted the sanity of bringing him into her world. Everything Thorn had said about his abilities, rang in her ears. Who or what could stop *that*?

Yet as she watched, she remembered the quiet man who'd protected her from harm. The tender man who'd teased and made love to her. She had seen his heart from the outside, in.

*Violence resides inside us all.* She knew that. She also knew the restraint Cadegan was capable of.

But there was only one way to know for sure.

*Are you out of your ever-lovin' mind? Don't you dare!*

*He's worth it,* she told herself. He wouldn't hurt her. Even in this form. She knew that.

It was time to prove it to everyone.

Even herself.

Breathing steadily and summoning every piece of courage she could, she ran toward Cadegan as Morgen and her army fled his wrath, and he turned his ferocity onto the Adar Llwch Gwin.

"Cadegan!" she shouted before he could hurt Ioan or Talfryn. "Stop it! They're not your enemy."

With a fierce, demonic hiss, he turned toward her and

made her really glad in that heartbeat that he didn't have the power to breathe fire. Or she'd be Jo Toast.

The look in his eyes said that he was about to put her on his menu, and not in the way she wanted him to.

Styxx, Thorn, Max, Illarion and Talon moved to protect her.

She pushed her way through them.

"Do you mind? He doesn't trust any of you."

Still in his terrifying addanc form, Cadegan landed before her and circled her on the ground like a lion bent on Jo Tartar. "Why should I trust *you*, little morsel?" he growled low in his demonic voice.

Jo met his gaze without flinching. "Because I love you and you know that beyond a doubt. I promised I wouldn't let them have you and I meant it. Come home with me, Cade. Let me give you the love you deserve."

Cadegan pulled up short at those words and the strange chord they struck inside him. He blinked twice as he remembered her warmth.

The kindness of her touch.

*Nay! She's lying to you. 'Tis the worst sort of dodge ever handed you, lad. Don't be an imbecile.*

But he saw no deceit in her eyes. Heard no tremble in her voice.

Did he dare believe it?

Before he could stop himself, he moved closer to her. He expected her to scream when she saw what he looked like. Horned, winged and foul. Even he'd glimpsed himself and thought, *that can't be right.*

Yet it was. His outside now betrayed the truth of his blood. It telegraphed to the world exactly what a monster he'd been born.

Like the warrior she was, Josette didn't flinch at his approach. He saw no condemnation in her dark eyes. Only a kind acceptance he'd never known anywhere, other than her arms.

She again reached for him. "I'm here for you, baby. I'm not afraid to love you."

He pulled back. "Don't look at me. I'm hideous."

"There is nothing about you I find repellent."

The moment he felt her hand on his skin, he calmed down to that quiet serenity that eased him deep inside his soul. Gone was the violence that wanted blood. With her courage and her love, she tamed him completely.

He no longer wanted to kill. He only wanted Josette.

She wrapped her tiny hand around his miscolored, clawed one. "Ever my hero. Thank you for protecting me from Morgen's army."

Cadegan stared at their laced fingers. As always, her skin was the perfect porcelain blend. Soft beyond imagining. "Aren't you afraid of me?"

She shook her head. "I will never fear you. I see you, Cadegan, for what you really are, and not for this exterior skin that you can't help. Your outside isn't important to me. It's your heart and your soul I love. The real you, only I know."

Before he realized what she intended, she kissed his scarred lips.

Jo tried not to think about the fact that he could tear her apart as he lifted his hand to cup her face while he kissed her. Her body went from cold to hot faster than she was prepared for. More than that, he kissed her with an unbelievable passion.

When he pulled back, she expected to look into reptilian eyes again.

They were again his vibrant blue. She smiled at him as she danced her gaze over his perfect, male body. He looked just as he had before. Human in every way.

Slowly, his gaze locked on hers. Like an exhausted cat, he laid his head on her shoulder, and pressed her hand to his cheek.

"Me precious Josette."

She brushed her hand through his hair. "My beautiful Cadegan."

Cadegan struggled to breathe as she held him and he realized that what he wanted could never be. That they were born of two incompatible worlds. She was light and color, and he was banished to a dark gray hell. "I still cannot leave this place, me lady. I am forever damned here."

"No, sweetie. I've come to get you. I can take you through the portal, the same way we took Illarion earlier."

Lifting his head, he met her gaze. "Do you swear to me?"

"Every effing day." Smiling, she held her hand out to him. "Come home with me, Cadegan. Back into the light where you belong."

He glanced to his brother, who watched them with a worried expression. "Are you here to stop us?"

Leucious shook his head. "I'm here to help."

Cadegan wished he could fully believe that. But his experience with Leucious was such that he knew better than to put faith in anything his brother said.

"And you are?" Cadegan asked the blond man beside his brother who favored Acheron.

"I'm Styxx. They brought me along because I have Asshole Brother issues, too. And can relate fully to yours. Case in point, mine, as well as his goddess girlfriend, locked me in a hole for eleven *thousand* years. I know *exactly* how hard it is to trust again. And I know the hunger you have to be free of this place. Forever. Come with us, and we'll take you somewhere you'll never be alone again."

"Will you be there?" Cadegan asked Josette.

She nodded. "I promise I will never leave you and I never break my oath."

Still, it seemed too easy. And nothing in his life had ever come that way.

Cadegan looked to the other blond with them. The one who was related to him somehow. This male creature bore the markings of the Mórrígan over his body.

"I'm Talon of the Morrigantes. My wife is the granddaughter of the Mórrígan and the Dagda. We're cousins, and I swear on every bit of me good Celt blood that this is no dodge, brother. You can trust in us."

His hand trembling, Cadegan held Josette's palm against his cheek, as he debated on whether or not to believe her and the others. He wanted to, desperately. But a broken oath from her would destroy him.

In the end, he came back to one truth.

Without Josette, he wasn't whole. She removed the pain inside him and filled his heart with unimaginable warmth and happiness. Against all sanity and reason, he needed her.

"Take me home with you, Josette. 'Tis the only place I wish to be."

Thorn stepped back as he watched Cadegan, now in human form, kiss Jo's palm. It was the damnedest thing he'd ever seen.

One minute, Cadegan had been a full fledged, blood-crazed demon.

The next, he was perfectly calm again. Serene even. Acheron was right. So long as they had Jo, they had a leash for Cadegan. She was his anchor to humanity. Perhaps it would work out, after all.

But as Thorn opened the portal and allowed them to walk through it, he knew it wasn't this easy.

Something bad was going to happen. It always did.

# 17

Cadegan hesitated at the portal as the others went through first. Styxx stayed behind with him and Josette.

On the other side, Leucious turned to face them. His expression seemed sincere enough. But Cadegan wasn't accustomed to trusting him.

Not for anything.

"I am here for you, little brother."

That only made Cadegan more apprehensive. Leucious killed or banished creatures like him. He didn't suffer them to live among the world of man, and he damn sure didn't help them to reach it.

Unsure, Cadegan met Josette's dark gaze, and tightened his grip on her delicate hand.

"I trust him, Cade. He won't betray you. And if he does, I promise to serve up a part of his anatomy that he'll definitely miss."

He smiled at that.

"I am here for you, sweetie. Always."

Those words touched a part of him he'd never met before and they choked him. In that moment, he craved her with a madness that made the demon inside him tremble in fear. Cupping her cheek, he kissed her and wished they were alone so that he could ease the other ache inside him that begged for her touch.

With a breath for courage and her hand in his, he stepped through and waited for the wall to slam shut in his face. For him to walk into a solid mass that kept him banished where he belonged.

In hell.

But it didn't.

Holding his breath, he opened his eyes and found himself in a horrifically bright room. Unused to actual daylight, he flinched and held his hand up to shield his squinting eyes. Even so, he reveled in the pain of it.

Sunlight. Real and true. He could even feel the warmth of it on his skin.

Amazed, he held his hand out and let the rays dance over his flesh.

"Dang it, Karma! Close your curtains. Fast!"

A woman who looked similar to Josette ran to obey.

Jo bit her lip as she watched the awe and marvel play across Cadegan's handsome face. He was like an infant discovering his feet for the first time.

And he looked so out of place here with his black monk's robe and chain mail and spurs.

Karma raked a sneer over him, but he didn't pay a bit of attention to her. Not while unbelievable joy spread across his face, as he turned a small circle and glanced around the brightly painted room and decorated bookshelves.

He met Jo's gaze. "Where am I?"

"Karma's house."

Cadegan digested that news slowly as he continued to look about. Scowling, he paused and cocked his head at the sight of a familiar stranger.

In the far corner stood Acheron, who was indeed identical to Styxx, except his hair was black and his eyes a swirling silver, instead of Styxx's deep blue. This time, Acheron didn't wear the strange mask that had covered his eyes earlier.

"Severe Asshole Brother issues," Styxx repeated in Cadegan's ear. His voice was filled with humor as he cracked a wide grin. "Every time you think you have it bad, just remember, you don't see Thorn's face every single time you stumble in front of a mirror."

Cadegan snorted at something that wasn't really funny. "I concede this issue to you, me lord. By far, yours is the greatest indignity."

He clapped Cadegan on the shoulder. "If only you knew, my brother. If only you knew." Rubbing his arm affectionately, Styxx went to Acheron's side. For all of Styxx's protestations, he and Acheron seemed to get along well.

In fact, Acheron embraced him. "Glad you're back. I was starting to worry."

Patting him on the shoulder, Styxx indicated them with his chin. "Acheron, I present to you, Cadegan. In his real and true form."

Acheron inclined his head respectfully. "Welcome back, my lord."

He seemed sincere and decent enough. But Cadegan was suspicious of the demon blood he sensed inside Acheron. Blood Styxx didn't share.

What was he? Why would one twin be demonic while the other wasn't?

"We have clothes for you," Acheron said graciously. "Whenever you're ready, Styxx or I can show you to your new home."

Cadegan arched a brow. "My new home?"

"In a realm called Katateros."

His stomach wrenched as his anger grew. So he wasn't free after all. He'd only gone from one prison to the next. That was what he got for trusting them. He should have known better. "Then I'm not to stay in this realm?"

The men stepped back in trepidation.

Jo placed her hand on his and calmed him as she saw the demon rising to the forefront. She placed her hand on his face and forced him to meet her loving gaze.

His eyes went from yellow back to blue as quickly as they'd switched before. "Shh, Cade. That's not what they meant. You'll have the freedom to come and go as you wish. And I'll be with you the whole time. If that's what you want."

"You will?"

She nodded. "I will be with you so long as you want me. Just promise that if you want to get rid of me, you'll tell me and not cut my head off or something equally mean."

"I would never do such, lass." He pressed his cheek to

hers before he stepped back to eye Thorn. But at least this time, he remained fully human.

Jo wrinkled her nose playfully at him as he held her hand. "Your eyes are like an old-fashioned mood ring. The moment you get angry, bang . . . the demon rears its ugly head and stares at me. Kind of scary."

"I would never cause you harm, Josette."

"You mean you hope you'd never harm her."

They all turned to Thorn, who'd spoken. Unrepentant, he explained his point. "The demon in our blood isn't always under our control. For that reason, Jo, you need to learn when to run from it. Lest you be harmed, and he be devastated by his own inability to control himself."

"Really?" she asked, suddenly apprehensive of Cadegan.

Acheron nodded. "I almost killed my wife once in the throes of it. And I'd sooner cut out my own heart than make my Tory frown."

Cadegan hesitated at those words. Since he was so seldom around others, and never someone he loved, he hadn't even considered that. "Is this true?" he asked Leucious.

"Sadly, yes, brother. But you know that. It's what led me to banish you. You unleashed the demon within and killed without reason."

Aye, he had. But, unlike Josette, those humans had meant

nothing to him. Suddenly, fear rose up inside him. He tightened his grip on her hand. "Then I should be apart from you."

"Not on your life, bucko. Call me Velcro. You go, I go. I promised you that, and I never break my word, either." Her eyes darkened as she passed a knowing smile to Styxx. "Would you mind showing us to our new home now? I should like to introduce Cadegan to my three children."

He choked and coughed at that. Was she serious? "Pardon, lass?"

Jo blinked innocently as she heard the panic in his voice. "Didn't you know, sweetie? You're a father."

The expression on his face was priceless.

"Only you could make stark cold terror look sexy, Cade." She kissed his cheek. "Relax, sweetie. It's just my three dogs. You'll love them."

Finally relaxing, he shook his head at her.

Laughing, Styxx returned to their sides. "If you're ready?"

Cadegan nodded.

One second they were at Karma's with all the group that had rescued Cadegan. The next, they were inside an ancient temple that had been built on a steep hill, nestled among others of a very similar style. Bright sunlight cut across the white marble foyer where they stood.

Confused, Cadegan glanced to Styxx for an explanation.

"That is where I live with my family." Styxx jerked his

chin toward the window that showed the temple closest to this one, farther up the hill. "My wife, Bethany, is the Atlantean goddess of woe. She and I and our youngest son live in her temple, all year long. Our oldest son, Urian, lives in the small temple, just through those trees, whenever he's here and not with his wife's family in Minnesota. The building on top of the mountain is Acheron's home, and it's where Simi, her sister, and his friends stay. Since Acheron's wife was human, they tend to spend most of their time, with their sons, in New Orleans . . . in a house not far from Karma's. Whenever you're settled and ready, I'll introduce you to everyone."

Styxx offered him a kind, patient smile. "I know exactly how overwhelming all of this is . . . For now, my Beth has set this temple up for the two of you to live in. You should have everything you need . . . if not, we're only a call or visit away." He folded his arms over his chest. "We all thought this would be an easier adjustment for you than moving straight into the human realm. Though you are welcome to live there if you desire, I should warn you, modern humans are fucking nuts."

Jo laughed at something that baffled Cadegan. But then if those people were anything like what he'd met thus far, he could deduce Styxx's meaning.

"They're short a few bales?"

Styxx clapped him on the back. "Oh, the stories I will tell

you when you're feeling up for mead and beer, my friend." He started for the door.

Cadegan frowned. "Styxx?"

He paused to look at Cadegan. "Aye?"

"Thank you. For everything."

Styxx inclined his head to them. "If either of you need anything, just let me know." He vanished instantly.

Finally alone, Josette turned to face Cadegan. "How are you doing with all this? Really?"

It wasn't in him to confide in anyone. Yet when he looked into her dark eyes, he was lost and the truth poured out of him. "Much *moithered,* lass."

She nodded in understanding. "Too much hand-holding?"

It took a second to realize what she meant. "*Moithered,* not mothered."

She mouthed the two words as if struggling to comprehend them. "Yeah, you say that like there's no difference in the two words. . . . No, silly, it's dip, not *dip.*" She elongated the second word to comical effect. "See, you sexy wombat you, it makes no logical sense."

Snorting, he shook his head. "Confused, lass." He sobered instantly and swung his arm out to indicate the temple around them. "By all this."

"You're really not bound, Cade. I made them swear to that. You can always leave here. But we all thought you'd prefer to take baby steps back into the real world so that you'd not feel out of place there."

Her compassion stung his heart. It was why she meant so very much to him. No one else had ever considered his feelings before. In any matter. They merely ordered him about, regardless of his opinion. But never his Josette.

To her alone, he mattered.

"That I would, love. Thank you."

"Yah! We guessed right." Laughing happily, she tugged at his hand and led him through a door into a small solarium. The moment they were in it, three huge white dogs with vibrant blue eyes came running up to them with happy barks and licks.

Kneeling down, she gathered them into her arms. Her bright smile was even more blinding than the sun. "My furry little babies!" she said in the same high-pitched tone most people reserved for speaking to infants. "How have you been, huh? Did you miss your mommy? Your mommy missed her babies! Yes, she did! My little baby punkins! I love you so! Yes, I do! Come here, my babies! Gimme me kisses. Lots and lots of kisses!"

She cuddled and loved on each of them before she introduced them to Cadegan. "Henri's easy. He's our only son." She rubbed noses with the largest. "Then we have Belle." She clucked her tongue at the smallest, who also had a patch of gray around her eyes. Then she draped her arm over the back of the third one. "And last but never least in my heart is my precious Maisel, or Maisy Waisy, as I often call her." She went back to her baby talk. "You're just a beauty, aren't you? Yes, you are, my sweet Maisy Waisy." She hugged them again, then gestured to Cadegan. "Go meet Daddy! Go on. Say hi! Tell Daddy you love him, too."

They assaulted him instantly.

Cadegan stumbled back, unused to such furry attention. "They're a little . . ."

"Spoiled is the word you want. And yes. They are very. I've worked hard to make them that way."

Laughing at the way her dogs openly accepted him without question, he looked up, and the minute their gazes met, he saw in her eyes the same hunger that had gnawed at him since she'd held her hand out to him. His humor died instantly as it was swallowed by an overwhelming need to be alone with her.

She raked a hot stare over his body. "Why don't we get you out of those clothes, huh?"

He arched a brow at her bold words. "Meaning?"

"You know my meaning, hot stuff." Chewing her nail in the cutest of ways, she scowled at the multiple doors. "I wonder which one goes to the bedroom." She headed for the nearest one, which turned out to be a closet. "Oops. Too small."

Laughing, he watched her explore and become more and more frustrated as she ran afoul of her plans to molest him.

When she finally found the door to a hallway, she took his hand, and together, they went in search of a bed. Strange how she made the search fun. Every time she guessed wrongly, she stripped a piece of his clothing from him.

He watched as she pulled his gauntlet from his left hand. "I've never played this game before."

"Strip Christopher Columbus?" She paused to rake another look over him. "Yeah, I guess you haven't. You predate him, too, don't you?"

"You make me feel old, lass."

"You are old."

"But do you have to remind me? And so often?"

She grinned evilly as she finally found the right room and pushed him into it, near the giant bed. "Yes, I do." She pulled the robe over his head. When she struggled with his mail, he used his powers to strip them both.

Nodding in approval, she nipped at his chin. "That is still my favorite power of yours. That and the one you have that makes me horny every time I look at you."

He laughed. Until she dropped to her knees in front of him. Just as he started to ask what she was doing, she cupped him in her warm hand.

All thoughts scattered as pleasure sent him reeling. For a moment, he feared his legs would buckle and send him to the floor. Thankfully, the wall was behind him so that he could catch himself, otherwise he might have fallen.

His breathing ragged while she thoroughly pleasured him, Cadegan buried his hand in her hair as she slowly, methodically explored every inch of his hard cock with her mouth. "Lass, you've no idea what you do to me."

She laughed deep in her throat as she cast an impish glance his way that told him she knew exactly what she was doing. And that she meant every bit of it.

In that heartbeat, he knew how much he loved this woman. How quick he'd die at her bidding. There was nothing else in this world that mattered to him.

And he would never be able to take another day without her.

Even though it was the last thing he wanted, he withdrew from her and swung her up in his arms to carry her to the bed.

Jo held her breath at the fierce expression on his face. While there was no sign of the demon, he held an almost possessed quality to him. "Are you okay?"

He answered her with a kiss so hot, it left her breathless and weak. He literally ravaged her mouth as he pressed his body against hers and parted her thighs with his knees.

His hands and lips took turns exploring and teasing her with pleasure until she came from it.

She was in the middle of her orgasm when he entered her and heightened it even more. Screaming out his name, she clung to him as he thrust himself against her hips.

He laughed as he cupped her cheek in his hand and stared down into her eyes. She saw the hunger inside him. But more than that, she saw the love and adoration. No man had ever looked at her that way.

"I love you," she breathed.

"And I, you." He took her hand into his and kissed it. Holding it against his cheek, he buried himself deep inside her and came.

She watched ecstasy play out across his face before he collapsed against her and held her tight.

"Thank you, lass."

"For what?"

He lifted his head to stare down at her with a searing sincerity. "For keeping your word to me. No one has ever done that before."

Her heart broke for him as she fingered his whiskers and lips. "They were great fools, me lord," she said, trying to duplicate his accent.

He rewarded her with a bright, impish smile. "Your fake accent is terrible."

"And yours isn't. I could listen to you speak all day."

His eyes gentle, he kissed his way from her lips to her stomach, where he placed his cheek and sighed. Jo played in his hair while his breath tickled her skin. In a matter of seconds, she felt him relax and realized he'd fallen asleep with his body between her legs.

Smiling, she laughed. Her poor Cadegan. Like this, he seemed so harmless and sweet. But she knew the violence he was capable of. The rage.

This wasn't a man she'd let into her heart. He was one of the fiercest demons ever born.

More than that, he was a demigod.

*What have I done?*

Jo held her breath as reality crashed into her and she glanced around a room that was the temple of a god in a mystic land that existed outside of human time and space.

*You don't believe in this crap.*

Yet she could no longer deny it. This was as real as the demon god sleeping in her lap.

Holy cow. She hadn't merely dipped her toe into the paranormal pool, she'd cannon-balled it. And Cadegan would have enemies after him for the rest of his life.

Thorn had warned her of that. It was part of the reason they'd decided to put him here, where no one and nothing could reach him. Only Acheron and those he invited directly could access the Atlantean heaven realm. Here, they would always be safe.

At least that was her thought until a bright light appeared beside them.

One moment, Jo was lying peacefully with Cadegan. In the next, she was ripped from his arms and pulled from the bed.

# 18

"Brit? Is it really you?"

Jo blinked at the incredibly beautiful red-haired woman in front of her. "Excuse me?"

The woman gripped her chin and angled her head so that she could peer deep into Jo's eyes. "It is *you!*" she breathed with a bright smile. Tears spilled down her face as she seized Jo into a happy hug and held her there.

Bug-eyed, Jo stared over her shoulder to

where Cadegan was now rising from the bed to confront the woman holding her.

"Release her!"

The woman turned around and snorted dismissively. "And you!" She pulled him in for a tight hug. "I've missed the two of you terribly!" Growling at them, she shook her head. "Why did you ever want to be mortal? I've never understood your reasoning. And you must have reconsidered, otherwise you wouldn't be you now, would you?"

Cadegan exchanged a baffled grimace with Jo. "And here I thought *you* were the one who confused me most, lass."

Sadness darkened the woman's vibrant green eyes. And now that Jo thought about it, she looked a lot like Acheron's daughter Kat. "You don't remember me at all, do you?"

"Artemis?"

The joy returned to her beautiful face at Jo's guess. "You do know me! I knew you couldn't forget. Not after all we did for each other!" She pulled Jo into another tight hug. "I should never have allowed you to go to Britain. Icky place, that. Why didn't you come home?" She pouted at Jo, then smoothed her hair. "But you're back now, aren't you? Both of you!"

Jo bit her lip, unsure of how to answer.

Artemis patted her shoulder. "It's all right. You will remember me. In time. I know you will." She dropped her gaze and turned bright red as she realized Jo was standing there naked and she'd interrupted them in bed. "Oh . . . oh! I'm so sorry. I didn't even think. When Katra told me that you were back . . . I wanted to see you immediately. Forgive my intrusion!"

She took Cadegan's hand and Jo's and pressed them together. "You two were always my favorites. And this time, there will be no more of this talk of mortality. No more talk of leaving me or each other, ever again. You are two halves of a whole and I love you both too much to ever stand to see you pulled apart again. Damn the witch's curse. This will be undone. My word to you both." She vanished instantly.

Completely stymied, Jo stared at Cadegan. "Is it just me, or do I attract every weirdo in the universe?"

He laughed at that. "You attracted me, so I be thinking I shouldn't comment on it."

She kissed him then pulled back with a scowl. "Do you feel reincarnated?"

"Not really. You?"

She shook her head. "Weird, huh?"

"Any idea what she meant about the *gwiddonod*?"

"English, dude! Speak English."

Laughing, he kissed her. "Witches, love. She spoke of a witch's curse."

"No idea." She trailed her gaze over his long, muscled

body and felt the heat inside her build again. Stepping closer, she lifted her chin so that she could nip at the sexiest jawline she'd ever seen.

Cadegan closed his eyes as he savored the sensation of her lips and tongue on his flesh. Pleasure ripped him asunder. "You keep doing that, lass. And we'll never leave this place."

She reached down to cup and fondle the part of him that was already growing hard for her again. "I'm good with that."

He covered her hand with his and rocked himself against her palm, enjoying the warm pressure of her touch.

Jo frowned as he spoke in his thick Welsh to her. "What?"

"You are the light in my darkness, lass. Without you, I have no hope. No faith. I barely exist. And all I ask is that if you ever leave, you will do me the mercy of tearing out me heart, rather than leaving me lost inside the forever night without you."

Tears choked her, not just at his words, but at the honest, raw emotion that backed them. "I wish I could be that poetic, Cadegan. I suck at romance and relationships. I always have. Never have been able to find the right words at the right time. But I do love you. Now and always. And I never want to live without you."

He kissed her then, and drove himself deep inside her body. This time, when he made love to her, it wasn't soft and gentle, but demanding and fierce. As if he was afraid he might never see her again.

Jo lost herself to the sensation of him hard and thick inside her. She met him stroke for stroke as she sought to ease the pain that never left his eyes. At least not entirely.

But whenever he looked at her, it lessened. And that made her feel special and cherished.

That was all she'd ever wanted. To matter to someone. To have someone she could depend on when she needed them. Someone who wouldn't break faith with her. Life wasn't easy. It wasn't supposed to be. Yet with the right person, even the worst journey was tolerable. More than that, it could be fun. It wasn't about learning to suffer through the storm to make it to the daylight. Life was about running through the rain and laughing even while it soaked you to the bone. Dodging the lightning strikes and daring it to come for you.

That was what Cadegan made her feel. In his arms, she was invincible. Not because she couldn't be hurt, but because she knew he wouldn't leave her cold and alone. He would pick her up and fight by her side until the storm passed.

She wrapped herself around him and came in a blinding wave of ecstasy.

Growling deep in his throat, Cadegan joined her. And even then, he didn't release her. Still on his feet, he kept the whole of her weight without complaint.

And when he met her gaze, she saw the yellowish eyes of the demon inside him.

Unafraid, she pressed her hand to his cheek and kissed his lips.

Cadegan savored her taste that shook him to the core of his being. "Marry me, lass," he breathed. "Stand with me, forever."

She dipped her head to pass him a playful frown. "What is that look?"

"What is what look?"

She narrowed her gaze. "You don't really doubt my answer, do you?"

"I doubt any time me life is going good."

Nipping his chin, she squeezed him tight. "You should never doubt me, Cade. Of course I'll marry you. Name the altar and I'm there, with Selena's bells on."

"Selena's bells?"

"My crazy cousin who sews them into the hem of her skirts. She thinks it keeps evil away."

"You wear that and it would keep me away."

She tsked at him. "You're not evil. Wicked, definitely. But not evil."

Cadegan closed his eyes as he savored her acceptance. It was the first time in his existence that he didn't feel as if he were a scourge that should never have been born. He felt whole.

Most of all, he felt happy.

And that terrified him.

Happiness had always been something other men had. Never him. Happiness had run from him as if he were a leper carrying the pox and selling plague-laden bread.

He dropped his gaze to the medallion that he'd put around her neck. Picking it up, he placed it in her hand and covered it with his own. "Should you ever be without me and need me to protect you, take this in your hand and say these words . . . *Ysym arglwydd gwrdd gorddifwng ei far, gorddwy neb nyw ystwng.*"

It took her several times before she spoke them correctly.

"Can you remember all that, lass?"

"I can. But what does it mean?"

"There is to me a powerful lord of overwhelming wrath— the oppression of any, he will not tolerate."

Jo smiled up at him. "It's beautiful, and very fitting for you."

"You bring out the best in me." He kissed the medallion and rested it between her breasts. "You can only use it when you are under attack, never against someone else. For any reason. Understood?"

"Got it."

With a quick nod, he turned about and frowned as he looked for something.

"What is it?"

"Your most important room is missing. I was looking for a place to wash."

Jo laughed. "I know it's an ancient place, but . . . there must be a bathroom here, right? I would assume such a room, should it exist, would—"

"It's the door on the left."

Her eyes bulging at the unknown voice, Jo squeaked and placed herself behind Cadegan to cover her naked body. "Who said that?"

"I did." It was the stone lamp statue thing, in the corner of the room.

"Who are you?" What was it?

"I am Electra. But fret not. I'm not really sentient, but rather am a smart device, or conduit if you rather, set here for your convenience. I only activate for certain questions. Such as where are rooms, should you need lights, or if you wish to contact another person who calls Katateros home."

Cadegan approached it slowly. He reached out and touched the cold marble. "You truly can't feel?"

"Or see. I only hear and speak."

Jo pulled Cadegan's robe over her head before she joined them to inspect it. "It's kind of cool, huh?"

"Aye, but marble usually is."

"Not, cool, Cade . . . cool!"

"Ah . . . the wombat's on a horse, lass."

She laughed at him. "Poor wombat's getting his workout today." After kissing him lightly, she stepped back. "Where was that bathroom again?"

It actually pointed at the direction.

Still not quite sure about it, Jo went and found a huge, gilded bathroom with a pool reminiscent of an ancient Roman one instead of a tub. "Hey, Cade?" she called. "I think you're going to really like this."

He stuck his head in the door, then grinned like an adorable little boy. "Aye, me like."

Before she realized what was going on, he removed her clothes with his thoughts, tossed her over his shoulder, and dove into the bathing pool. She came up laughing and sputtering while he continued to swim beneath the surface.

Jo froze as she realized something. Cadegan was amphibious. Or he had the strongest lungs ever created.

When he finally surfaced, it still wasn't his whole head. Only his eyes. He kept his nose and mouth below the waterline.

"Are you breathing?"

He nodded.

"Underwater?"

Again, he nodded. He dove under, swam to her, and brushed her legs before he finally broke the surface and pulled her against his chest. "I'm an addanc demon. It's one of our powers. Most of my kind are lake dwellers."

"What else can you do?"

"In the water, I can shapeshift."

"But not on land?"

He screwed his face up. "Only into me winged demon form and a bird on land. I have many more options in the water."

"So would we have a baby or a tadpole?"

Cadegan froze at her playful question that slapped him hard.

Children. It wasn't something he'd thought about in over thirteen hundred years. Before Leucious, he'd possessed no knowledge of his demonic origins. No idea of the powers that had lain dormant within him. Back then, he'd thought himself a man, like any other, and had hoped to marry a woman and have a brood of children with her.

After that, he'd been more cautious. Until Æthla. With her, he'd planned to have one to see what sort of child it might be. Fey or human.

And after Leucious had banished him, there had been no hope whatsoever.

Now . . .

He saw a reality that truly terrified him. No wonder he'd given her the summoning words when, in theory, she shouldn't really be able to use them.

Aye, it made complete sense, and that upper connection with her scared him even more.

"Are you okay, sweetie? I was only kidding."

His hand trembling, he reached out and touched her flat stomach. Biting his lip, he smiled. "I can think of no greater honor than to have a child with you, me lady. Or a tadpole," he teased. "Mayhap even a wombat."

She laughed and handed him the bar of soap she'd found. "You're so silly. I love you."

"And I, you."

Jo watched as he returned to frolicking in the water. She wondered if Styxx and the others had known he'd want a pool. Probably. They seemed to know a great deal about him. Much more than she did.

But she was learning. And while he wasn't perfect—at times, he was downright scary—he was perfectly hers.

She wouldn't change anything about him. . . .

They spent the rest of the day just hanging out and exploring each other's bodies. Their likes and dislikes.

It was the best day of her life. She never wanted it to end. As the sun set, they walked outside to sit on the beach and watch it. Katateros was a strange place. In some ways, it reminded her of Hawaii.

In others, like some of the peculiar creatures who inhabited it, she felt as though she'd fallen down the rabbit hole.

Cadegan ran his fingers through Josette's hair as she lay

on the beach with her head in his lap. For the first time in centuries, he felt truly human. Truly alive.

For the first time ever, he felt loved and cherished.

"So what do we do now, Josette?"

"Are you hungry?"

"Famished, but not what I meant. After this day, what's to become of us?"

She took his hand into hers. "I don't know."

"You can do what Styxx does and work for Acheron."

Jo sat up with a gasp as Cadegan tensed. A few feet away from them stood a beautiful Egyptian lady dressed in shorts and a tee. Her long black hair was pulled back into a ponytail and she held a sleeping blond toddler in her arms.

With a friendly smile, she approached them slowly. "I'm Bethany. Styxx's wife." She pulled the boy off her shoulder to cradle him in her arms. "And this precious one is Ari."

Jo pressed her hand to her chest as she stared into the face of a curly-haired cherub. "He's absolutely adorable! How old?"

"He turned a year old yesterday."

"Really?"

She nodded. "Would you like to hold him?"

"Oh, I'd love to."

Bethany handed her son over.

Jo melted at the warmth of the boy in her arms. "He sleeps so soundly!"

"Always. His father is forever trying to wake him from his naps. The most you can get is for him to swat at your hand. But he never wakens when he does it. He just rolls over and returns to sleep."

His little lips worked as if he were speaking to angels. "I've always been a sucker for children."

Cadegan watched quietly as Josette cuddled the boy. Whether it was animals or children, she held a very maternal instinct. She deserved her own son. But her earlier words plagued him now.

What kind of child would they have?

Demon, demigod, or human?

"Are you all right?"

He blinked at Bethany's question. "Aye."

She covered his hand with hers. "I know. I've only been back in the human world and this one for a short time myself. Not quite two years. It's a lot to get used to." She plucked at her shirt. "The clothes definitely take some time. But you have your Josette and you have us. Friend or family . . . or irritating acquaintances, whatever you choose to call us. We are here to help you in any way we can."

"I'm not used to such consideration."

"Like my Styxx. Never trusting. Even now. But every day,

his smile brightens more as he comes to terms with the fact that this is his life now, and that no one will rip it from him."

Bethany touched the scar on Cadegan's arm. "All wounds take time to heal. But one day, you'll awaken and the pain will plague you no more. You'll go days, maybe even months before you think of it. And one day, if you're lucky, you'll never think of it at all."

Jo looked up at her. "You're very wise, Bethany."

She grinned sheepishly. "Sometimes. But I am the goddess of wrath, and as such tend to let my temper get the best of my sense at times. Never want to be near me when that happens. It's truly frightening."

Ari blinked open his eyes, then widened them as he realized Jo wasn't his mom.

"I'm right here, sweetling."

"Mama!" He quickly scampered back to Bethany's arms, where he rubbed his eyes and pouted. "Papa?"

"He'll be home soon." She kissed his plump cheek. Then, she grimaced. "Someone needs his diaper changed. If you'll excuse me . . ."

Bethany rose to her feet. "It was nice meeting you both." Rubbing Ari's back, she met Cadegan's gaze. "Don't worry about the morrow. It will come. And you will always have a place here as a member of our motley family."

"Thank you, me lady."

Inclining her head to him, she left them.

Jo scooted back toward Cadegan. "You still look . . . ill."

He let out a heavy sigh. "Not about you, lass. I will never doubt you, but . . . I have a feeling deep in me gullet. Something's coming for me. And it's not going to rest until I'm destroyed."

Shaking her head, she attempted to soothe him. "Don't think that."

Cadegan tried to smile for her, but the problem was, he didn't think it.

He knew it for a fact.

# 19

Cadegan wasn't sure about this new hell. Therapy. Just the word itself sounded awful. Like some kind of small animal pissing on him.

He froze outside the office door and screwed his face up at Josette. "I don't know about this, lass. Not sure anything can help me. Surely, I'm beyond all help, of any kind." He dropped his gaze down to the deep V of her shirt. "I'd rather go home . . . with you, and put a smile on your beautiful face."

Tsking, she dodged his kiss and, to his chagrin, kept him at arm's length. "You're sneaky one, Lord Demon Wombat, but no. You need to talk to Grace. It won't hurt you. I promise. She'll be very gentle and even has toys to play with, if you're good. The time will pass quickly and I'll be back as soon as the session ends."

A tic started in his jaw as his anger mounted. "I don't want to do this."

She tugged at the thing called a jacket that she'd put on him. "Just this once. If you really can't stand it, I'll never make you do it again. Promise. But Grace's husband is a demigod, son of Aphrodite, who spent two thousand years cursed in the pages of a scroll before she released him. They have six kids, and live in total marital bliss. That's what I want for us, and you do, too." Her gaze sharpened. "Now sac up, man, and do this. Two hours. You can handle it." She glanced around before she dropped her hand to cup him.

His eyes widened at her actions.

She leaned in to whisper in his ear. "And if you behave and cooperate for the good doctor, I promise I'll make it worth your while later, and put a really big smile on *your* face. I'll even don the lace wedgie you like best."

His breathing turned ragged as she fingered him through his jeans. It was all he could do not to find a corner and take her, right here and now. "As soon as this ends, I expect you naked in me bed."

"Willingly." Jo had just withdrawn her hand before the door opened to show Dr. Grace Alexander.

One of Selena's longtime friends, Grace had all but grown up with Jo and the Devereaux sisters. And gotten into more trouble with them than Jo wanted to think about.

It was a wonder they weren't all cellmates.

Smiling at the adorable brunette, Jo gently pushed Cadegan toward her. "Grace meet Cadegan. Cade, play nice."

Grace laughed. "It's all right. After treating the Wolves, Panthers, and Bears all these years, nothing can surprise me anymore. I promise, Cadegan, I won't make you do anything you don't want to. We don't even have to talk. Come in and make yourself comfortable."

With one last miserable glance at Jo, he went inside the office.

Grace patted Jo's arm. "I'll take good care of him. Is there anything that's concerning *you*?"

Jo glanced around Grace's shoulder before she lowered her voice. "He's been having trouble sleeping. When he does, he wakes up in a sweat and grabs for me, and he won't go near any mirror. I have to keep the one I use covered at all times. And he's really, really overprotective. He can't stand for me to be out of his sight. If I'm gone too long, he panics."

"All very normal for what he's been through." She patted Jo's hand. "Have you felt threatened by his behavior, at all?"

"My fear? He's going to coat me in bubble wrap and force me to wear his armor everywhere I go."

Grace laughed. "I have that same problem with Julian. And you don't want to know how bad Val is with Tabby." She offered Jo a kind smile. "All right, let me go do my job. We'll get him calm, I promise."

"Thank you, Gracie."

"Anytime, sweetie."

Jo paused and stuck her head in the door. "You have my number, Cade. I'm just down the street with my cousins. I promise not to fall into any mirrors without you."

"You're not amusing, love." But he smiled in spite of his words.

Trying not to worry about him, Jo headed toward the mansion where everything had started. They'd never had a chance to finish "cleansing" the place, and Selena and her friends still needed a camerawoman to record it.

Jo had given them two hours. After that, she was all Cadegan's. They had a wedding to plan. And unlike her ex, Cadegan agreed to the June wedding Jo had always wanted.

Of course, a lot of that had to do with the fact the poor man had no idea what a June Cajun wedding entailed. Or the fact that their average June temp was ninety degrees, as opposed to the sixty degrees he'd been used to in Wales and the frigid temps of Terre Derrière le Voile. Never mind the fact that it could easily reach well into the upper nineties by mid-June, but . . .

He'd said he would do whatever she wanted for the wedding. And she mentally promised herself that she wouldn't abuse his sweetness. Much, she thought impishly.

As she approached her car, she saw Thorn on the street, standing beside it with a horrified look on his face that said she'd just offered him a ride in it.

He gave her a look of supreme admiration. "You really are the bravest woman I've ever known."

She frowned at him. "Why do I think there's a veiled insult in that statement?"

His gaze slid to the car. "How long have you driven this refugee from hell?"

"Speaking from experience?"

"Speaking my mind."

She scoffed at his dry tone. "Hey, don't knock it. It still runs. Most of the time, even after I turn it off."

Thorn laughed and shook his head at her. "You know, I've had my issues with Cadegan in the past. But I do love the little shit, and his dignity has been sorely challenged enough in his lifetime. I really don't want to keep grinding his nose in it." He tossed something at her.

Jo caught it to realize it was a set of keys. "What's this?"

He jerked his chin to the shiny new black Mercedes SUV behind the Falcon. "Something I think you'll both enjoy a lot more whenever you venture into this realm. I also bought your condo out of foreclosure, and made the landlord an offer he couldn't refuse."

"Death and destruction?"

An evil glint darkened his eyes. "Let's just say, he saw the advantages of kicking everyone out of the place. The entire building is now yours, and is being renovated to serve as a single house and not multi-units."

"Leucious!"

"Relax. They were all well compensated for their troubles. Besides, I did them a favor. That place was a fire hazard, and only one toaster misfire away from tragedy. The contractor works for the Dark-Hunters so we're putting in . . . protection, shall we say, for you and Cadegan. Consider it a wedding gift."

Her heart softened at his kindness. "Thank you."

He inclined his head to her. "Just take care of him for me. Make sure he stays in the light."

"That I will definitely do."

He opened the car door for her. "I already put all your equipment in back for you."

Jo paused by his side. "Can I ask you something?"

"Maybe."

She ignored his sarcasm. "What's between you and Karma?"

"Right about now . . . three miles."

She snorted and passed him an irritated grimace. "You know what I mean."

"I know what you mean, and it's between me and Karma."

"You do know that by not answering the question, you're answering it."

He closed the door. "Maybe she just does my laundry for me. You ever think of that?"

"And hell's just a hot tub. . . . Fine. Keep your secrets. I've been in your head and I know for a fact that you're not quite the badass you pretend to be."

"But I am still the killer I was."

A chill went down her spine. That was true. "I guess a barbarian warlord never really changes."

"Just the battlefields and the causes." He patted her hand. "If you need me, I'm just one unanswered phone call away."

She laughed, knowing he wasn't serious. "Hey, Thorn?"

He arched a brow.

"I love you. You're an awesome big brother."

Squeezing her hand, he didn't say anything else as he wandered off toward an elegant Bentley on the corner.

Jo ran her hand over the elegant leather interior. Wow! "I will never say another evil word about you again, Thorn. Good demon overlord."

Thorn *froze the* moment he closed the car door. Something was wrong. *Deadly* wrong. "Josiah?"

His driver didn't turn around. He was completely in place, with blood trailing from his left ear.

Shit.

As Thorn reached for the door handle, it melted and the doors locked. He was blocked from teleportation. Furious, he knew of only one demon who would dare such with him. "What do you want?" he demanded through clenched teeth.

A dark shadow appeared in the seat beside him. "You don't call. You don't e-mail. I'm beginning to feel like you don't like me. And that really hurts me in my inner tender place."

Thorn glared at the demon. "Didn't you get the Father's Day gift I sent you?"

Red eyes manifested to glare at him. "Yes, the hands of my best demon in a pink, bloody box, middle fingers extended. How very thoughtful of you."

"Knew you would like it. Soon as I saw him on my ass, I knew it would make the perfect gift for you."

His father blasted him against the door. "Where is he?"

"Where you can't reach him."

"I know you have that little bastard shielded from me. It's just a matter of time before I find him again and take what I want."

Thorn scoffed at his nebulous progenitor. "He would die before he allowed you to have it."

"And I will kill him for it. See, we can all get what we want and be happy. Why prolong the inevitable?"

"And miss out on all these fun father-son chats we have? Why would I ever do that, old man?"

Paimon sighed wearily. "Do I have to kill you?"

Thorn burst out laughing. "Try it."

The shadow created a giant mouth with serrated teeth. Opening, it moved to swallow Thorn whole.

"That was only scary when I was a child. I've grown up, Dad. Deal with it."

He screamed in Thorn's face. "I weep at the seed I spilled to beget you!"

Thorn patted his heart. "Such fatherly love and compassion. It brings tears to my eyes." Sighing, he spread his hand out and examined his manicured nails as if bored with their exchange. "Why do you want him so badly anyway? Not like you can use his powers where you are." He looked up. "Unless you have a body?"

"Why would I tell you if I did?"

"Good. You don't. That'll save me the trouble of having to track you down and banishing you."

Paimon pinned him back against the seat. "You think you're so clever and smart. But there's something a lot worse than me after your son, Leucious. We will find him."

"No. You won't. Now begone. You're stinking up the place. And it's a six-month waiting list to get another one of these."

Paimon rushed him, then went through his body to return to the realm where Thorn had banished him centuries ago.

Sighing in relief, he leaned forward to close Josiah's eyes and whisper a prayer for the poor man.

And as he did so, Cadegan's rosary fell from his pocket. He'd brought it today to return it to him, but had refrained. He had so few things from his son that he hadn't been able to part with it.

He picked it up and pressed it to his lips. Neither Cadegan nor Jo could ever learn the truth of who'd really seduced Brigid.

Or why.

Cadegan was so much more than Thorn had ever hoped for in a son. And thanks to Josette, they were now reunited.

As brothers.

That was all anyone needed to know.

*For now.*

Jo *groaned as* she struggled with her bag and tripod. Just as she was about to curse her day like a slow-walking dog, Selena appeared to pitch in.

"Nice ride."

"I know, right? Apparently, my future brother-in-law has a lot of guilt and even more money."

Selena snorted. "Glad you're here. Everyone's on edge."

"Of course they are. It is Tuesday, after all."

She scowled. "How do you mean?"

"You know . . . Tuesday—the new Monday. 'Cause my life has so much shite in it, that one mere single day could not possibly contain the full range of horrors and degradations seeking to rob me of my sanity. . . ."

"And this particular discussion is seriously challenging my desperate need to not go to jail for murder. . . . What were you saying again?" Selena completed the quote that had been a favorite rant of Tiyana's every Tuesday when new merch came in for her store. "God, how I miss her."

"Yeah. Me, too. Sorry I brought it up. It's just every Tuesday, I hear her in my head and smile."

Selena nodded. "I'm just glad we didn't lose you, too. Don't ever scare me like that again."

"Yeah, death would have seriously mucked up my future plans."

They dragged the equipment inside.

Jo dropped it by the door and let out a groan. "So where do I need to set up?"

"Let me go check. I'll be right back." Selena ran up the stairs.

While she waited, Jo wandered into the room that had made them gasp the last time she was here.

Now she understood why. It was like something out of a museum. There were all kinds of ancient artifacts strewn about. It looked like Karma's house on steroids.

"Josette?"

She turned at the same whisper she'd heard the last time she was here. Dang, it sounded so much like Tiyana, it was scary.

Something flashed on her right.

Gasping, she turned toward it. There was nothing there. At least not until she saw the image of a woman in an old mirror.

"Tia?"

No, she was losing her mind. Yet it looked so much like Tiyana that it was frightening.

"Run, Josie, run!"

In that moment, she knew it was Tia. No one else called her Josie. She ran for the door without hesitation.

It slammed shut as soon as she reached it.

Terrified, Jo turned. The shutters on all the windows swung closed and locked with a resounding clatter and snap. "Who's here?"

"She is not the waremerlin."

The owner, Cal moved from the shadows to approach her. As he drew near, he changed into a beautiful man with pale skin and formless eyes. "She drew the waremerlin out of his prison. He protects her. You wanted your shield, Kessar. I have given you the means to procure it."

Jo heard even more whispering in her head. It was like hearing the entire world on an open channel. Never had she imagined anything like this.

Kessar was a Sumerian gallu demon. She had no idea how she knew that, but the voices in her head told her. Too bad none of them had ever coughed up winning lottery numbers.

Bastards!

She turned toward Cal, and knew he was possessed by an extremely deadly and powerful demon. One who was desperate to lay hands on Cadegan and gift him to Paimon. "Valac."

He drew up short. "How do you know my name?"

"Wild guess? You know . . . Bob, Michael . . . Valac." Jo continued to listen as something inside her snapped.

Kessar moved to subdue her.

She flung her hand out and with some power she had no comprehension of, she stopped him dead in his tracks. It felt as if something or someone had control of her. As if she was in a trance and some ancient force resided deep inside her. "Why do you seek the Shield? To what purpose would you use it?"

Baring his serrated demon fangs, Kessar tried to break free. He gurgled in his throat before his red eyes turned glassy and he spoke as if in the same trance that held her immobile. "The Shield would allow me to descend into Kalosis and protect me from my enemies so that I could kill them all, and reclaim the honor of my race from the ones who now hunt us like rabid animals for our blood."

"*You* hold the Shield!" Valac gasped. "The Dagda has returned . . ." He summoned a hole in the floor and out poured twisted, winged creatures who flew for her like rejects from the *Wizard of Oz, Zombie Edition.*

Instinctively, Jo grabbed the necklace Cadegan had given her and whispered the words he'd taught her. "*Ysym arglwydd gwrdd gorddifwng ei far, gorddwy neb nyw ystwng.*"

The moment those words were spoken, golden armor wrapped itself around her, and the necklace expanded into a giant shield.

Jo gasped as she realized that the Shield of Dagda wasn't the one in Cadegan's room, after all . . . that was the shield the knight had given him when he'd died.

*This* was the relic of King Arthur that everyone sought. This was what Cadegan had been tortured for and had never once revealed. Meanwhile, it'd been under his attacker's noses the entire time. Innocuous in appearance, it was one of the strongest of the sacred objects Emrys Penmerlin had given to King Arthur to help him rule his kingdom.

And Cadegan had entrusted it to her. To keep her safe in his absence. The one object he'd sworn would never leave him.

Now she understood why Cadegan had never used it in battle.

The toll it took on her was exhausting. She felt as if she was going to fall from the sheer weight of it. But then, it hadn't been fashioned for her. She lacked the blood needed to wield . . .

Suddenly, the Shield lightened as the demons attacked her en masse. A sword manifested in her hand.

In that moment, she felt the strength of the ancient Celts inside her. It roiled through her body, until she was stronger than she'd ever been before. With the skill of Cadegan, she began to drive the demons back and fight them off.

Kessar grabbed something from Cal's collection before he ran out of her sight and vanished.

Jo knew she should go after him, but she had to deal with Valac's soldiers first since it was obvious, they had no intention of letting her out of here.

Valac called out commands for his demons. "I want that Shield! Freedom to the one who can claim it!"

Karma pounded on the door, screaming for entry.

Grinding her teeth against the onslaught, Jo ducked one demon and sidestepped another as she fought against them. "Love for you to join the party, coz. But I'm a little too busy to unlock the door." She dodged the demon that lunged for her. Then turned and swung the sword.

Its head went flying.

Ew! Nasty!

Valac tried to reach her, only to recoil from her when he ran too close to the Shield. It arced out an electrical charge, that drove him back. Hissing in fury, he transformed into his demon's body "I want that Shield! I will have it!"

"And I want world peace and toasted M&Ms. Guess we're all disappointed, eh?"

The entire house shook as if it was in the throes of an earthquake. Suddenly, demons rolled out of the hole with a speed and intensity that she couldn't even count them all.

*I'm in a bad nightmare . . .*

Holding the Shield up, Jo could no longer fight their growing number. While she might have his armor and Shield, she lacked Cadegan's skill and experience with battling the damned. All she could do was kneel on the floor and keep the Shield between her and them.

Over and over, they slammed into her and ran at her back. Her limbs were numb from the pain.

*I'm going to die here. As wretched demon kibble.*

Just when she was sure she'd drop the Shield, the doors behind her crashed open.

Dressed in his mail and robe, Cadegan was there, shouting in a language that was neither Welsh nor Latin nor anything she'd ever heard before.

He and Thorn, with the help of Illarion and Max, and the Adar Llwch Gwin, made their way through the demons until Cadegan was by her side. His skill awed her even more, now that she fully understood the toll this kind of fighting took on a body.

With his sword in one hand, he drove the demons back while he helped her regain her feet. "Stand to me back, me love. Together, we will banish them."

Something easier said than done as the demons picked up speed. They spun around the room, howling and attacking, faster than she could even follow. Thorn and Valac were tearing into each other as if they had a grudge match of some kind.

Bleeding, but undaunted, Cadegan turned toward Thorn. "We have to banish them."

Thorn kicked Valac back. "Agreed."

Cadegan held his sword up, with a fierce battlecry. Thorn did the same. They looked at her. Following suit, she held hers and touched the blade of it to theirs.

The men began to chant. "*Crux sacra sit mihi lux! Non draco sit mihi dux! Sunt mala quae libas. Ipse venena bibas! Pax nobiscum!*"

She wasn't able to join them until the third round. And as she spoke the words, she began to understand them. *Holy cross be my light. The dragon shall not rule me. What you offer me is evil. Drink your poison. Peace be with us.*

As they spoke, a dark, whirling vortex opened, similar to the one the demons had emerged from. Fighting against it, the demons began to shriek and run. With skeletal fingers of lightning, the vortex reached out and scooped them in, one by one.

Except for Valac. When the hands reached for him, he blasted them back and laughed.

He, alone, withstood the words of banishment as he hovered over the floor, wings flapping. His eyes a vibrant, scary orange, he glared at Thorn. "We are not done, Forneus! I know you and you will bow before me!"

Thorn laughed at him as he broke from their ranks and charged at the demon. "When hell freezes!" He sent a blast of color at him.

Dodging the blast, Valac attempted to vanish. But Cadegan knew that if he did, he'd be back for the Shield he'd been sent for.

Most of all, he'd be back for Josette.

And that he'd *never* allow.

As Valac dove for the portal, Cadegan did what he'd never done before. What Thorn had banned him from doing.

He summoned the addanc inside and rushed for Valac. Thorn cried out, but he ignored him as he wrapped his body around the older demon and held him.

Valac fought for his freedom. His claws shredded Cadegan's flesh.

It mattered naught.

His fangs elongated, he looked at Josette and felt his powers surge even more. "You will not leave this place," he growled in their native demonspeak. "You will not threaten what I love. Never again."

Valac hissed and screamed as Cadegan felt his powers mingle for the first time in his life. Demon crossed the *Tuath Dé*. And as it did so, he used them to rip Valac asunder.

With one last screaming cry, the demon disintegrated.

Cadegan threw his head back and roared as his powers absorbed Valac's and he grew even more powerful.

Jo stumbled back as Cadegan's form changed into something truly terrifying. His form merged with the mangled mess that had been Valac.

Thorn pulled her behind him. His features pale, he angled his sword at Cadegan.

"No!" She put her hand on his arm and angled the blade to the ground.

Swallowing her terror, she forced herself to step around Thorn and approach the demon god. "Cadegan . . . I know you hear me. And you don't want to hurt me, do you?" She used the same tone in him that she did her puppies. "No, you're a good demon boy, aren't you? You don't want to barbecue us . . . I can't keep my promise to you if you do."

He cocked his head and frowned. For a full minute, she thought she was toasted Jo On The floor.

She reached out and touched his leg as he hovered in the air.

At first, he recoiled, then he paused to meet her gaze. "Josette?"

"That's right. You want to come down from the Halloween party now? I give you first prize for the costume, baby."

He slowly began to transform.

Thorn stepped toward him and he immediately went back.

"Quit!" she snapped at him. "Everybody, step to the rear or out of the room."

Cadegan lowered himself to the floor. Then he flew to her and wrapped his arms and wings around her body. He laid his head to her shoulder and immediately returned to his human form. Her entire body shaking, Jo handed the Shield, and as she did so, it returned to being a necklace, back to Cadegan.

He brushed his thumb over the three-headed dragon before he placed it around her neck. "You need this, lass."

She smiled up at him. "Is it over?"

He met his brother's bitterly amused gaze. "Nay, love. The war never ends for those of us who fight it. But we won this day. They won't be back until they regain strength and number."

Jo scowled at him and then glanced down to the Shield she wore. "I don't understand. How can I use this? I thought you had to be of Dagda's blood for it to work."

"You do."

She screwed her face up in distaste. "Please don't tell me we're related. Honey, I ain't *that* Southern."

Cadegan laughed at her. "Nay, me love. We are not related. But a part of us that is, currently resides inside you."

"Wombat spotting. What?"

He took her hand in his and kissed her knuckles. "The son you carry unifies your blood with mine. So long as you carry him, you can wield me shield. 'Tis why I gave it to you. So that no one could cause either of you harm."

Gasping, she placed her hand on her stomach. "I'm pregnant?"

He nodded. "The first time I touched you."

Joy consumed her. She threw herself against his chest and held him tight. "Dang it. I'll never get my June wedding."

"I will wed you any time you want. Anywhere you want."

She shook her head. "No. If I'm pregnant now, he'll be born sometime in June. I don't want him to have to compete with our anniversary. June will always be his special month. Alone."

Karma cleared her throat to get their attention from where she squatted on the floor beside Cal's body. He must have passed out when Valac jumped out to assume his demonic form in order to fight them. "Hey, Jo? Question? Did any of this shit that just happened make it to film?"

Jo sucked her breath in sharply. "No. Sorry. I didn't have time to set up."

Karma sighed wearily as she rose to her feet. "Fine. That's it, Jo. You're fired. Love you, but you suck at this."

Thorn scoffed at her. "Actually, she's better at it than you are. I'd take it easy on her. She held quite the swarm back without help. Damn impressive for a woman who has untapped powers and no ability to wield or control them." He clapped his hand on Karma's shoulder. "Now I'm off to warn Acheron and Stryker that Kessar is back and gunning for them. We might have stopped him today, but he'll return."

Karma nodded. "I'll let Xedrix know to guard his wife,

too. Kessar might try for them. Last thing any of us needs is for the gallu demons to reunite with the Dimme and Charonte. That has demon holocaust written all over it."

Thorn met Cadegan's gaze. "The war continues and worsens. Oh goodie. We still have jobs."

Jo laughed at his dry sarcasm.

"Speaking of," Ioan said as he sat back on his haunches. "You're not going to banish us back to Glastonbury, are you?"

Thorn hesitated. "You've both been a great help. But we do have a problem. You don't exactly blend here."

"Wait!" Talfryn immediately changed from his gryphon form to that of an extremely handsome man. "If we look like this, can we stay?"

Thorn arched a brow.

Ioan also transformed.

This time, Thorn gaped. He looked at Cadegan. "Did you know they could do that?"

"Of course. Didn't you?"

Thorn appeared a bit embarrassed. "I need to renew my *Mythology Today* subscription."

Talfryn ignored that. "So we can stay?"

Thorn nodded. "So long as you blend."

"Awesome sauce!" Talfryn high-fived Ioan. "Now I just need to get laid, and it'll be a perfect day."

Ioan rolled his eyes. "How did I end up as *your* babysitter?"

"Stop, bitching. I want to learn how to drive. Do you think . . ." Their voices trailed off as they wandered out of the house and onto the street, with Max and Illarion following at a discreet distance that said they didn't want to be mistaken for friends.

Mama Lisa and Karma surveyed the mess they'd made in the room. Artifacts and furniture were busted and scattered all over. Even one window had been broken out. She glanced to Cal's unconscious body. "Think we'll get paid?"

Karma scoffed. "Honestly? We'll probably be sued . . . again."

Selena slapped Karma on the back. "Good thing I married a lawyer, eh?"

As they continued to worry over the pending suit, Jo pulled Cadegan out of the room to speak to him privately in the foyer. "So how did it go with Grace?"

"We were interrupted when you summoned the Shield's power and alerted me that you were in danger, but . . . she said that I have potential. She sees no reason why I can't learn to fit in here, in this strange world you call home."

"Good. Is that all she said?"

"She also asked me what it would take to make this place home and to make me happy."

"So what did you say?"

"You know what I said."

"But I want to hear you say it."

"I don't want to say it." He placed his hand to his shield around her neck. "I'd much rather show it . . . and speaking of . . ." He took her hand in his and led her toward the door.

"What are you doing?"

"You have a promise to fulfill, me lady. One I intend to hold you to, as I was a most good boy for Dr. Alexander."

Thorn watched as they vanished into thin air, no doubt returning to Katateros.

But as they left, the news slammed into him like a fist.

Cadegan had fathered a child with a woman whose blood-line ran straight back to Zeus, himself.

Neither of them understood the importance or strength of that child. Forget Acheron's progeny.

Theirs would be much more devastating in the right or wrong hands.

Shit. The war he feared most, was fast approaching and there would be no way to stop it.

# 20

Thorn froze the moment he returned home to his bleak, dark castle in the Nether Realm of absolute evil. At one time, this had been his father's home.

Until he'd banished the bastard and taken his place.

As he entered his study to drink what he needed for nourishment, he felt a powerful presence in the room.

Thorn glared at the last bastard he wanted to deal with. "What are you doing here?"

With long dark hair and mismatched eyes, Jaden stepped out of the shadows. "I felt that which should not have been done. Valac is dead?"

Thorn sighed wearily. "He is."

Absolute horror darkened Jaden's eyes. "Only the Sephiroth has that power."

"Apparently, Jared has a friend." Thorn moved to his crystal decanter and poured himself his libation. "As the Chthonians rose from the Source as a counterbalance to the gods who were abusing their powers to prey on humankind, it seems we have a new species born to balance the demon races."

Jaden cursed under his breath. "Forneus—"

"What would you have me do? Tell me what power can destroy this one?"

"The Malachai."

"You want to pit the Malachai against him and make the Malachai all the more powerful? Is that really your plan?" He laughed. "Good one. Let's set off nukes, while we're at it. At least then, the planet would be habitable again . . . eventually."

Jaden rubbed his hands over his eyes. "You're insane. You should have killed him at birth."

"As you should have killed your progeny?"

Jaden's eyes flared with his hatred. "We don't speak of *that*. Ever."

Narrowing his eyes on the beast he hated most—the bastard who was solely responsible for Thorn's regrettable birth—he swallowed his drink. "Ditto. What do you think would happen if your boss, my grandfather, ever learned of his great-grandchild's existence?"

Well aware of *that* nightmare, Jaden glanced away. "What game are you playing?"

"The same game you are."

"No," Jaden growled, "I know who and what I am. What side of this conflict I *clearly* fall on. You dance with a darkness that will one day swallow you whole."

"For your sake . . . for the sake of the human world you love so much, you better pray that never happens."

Jaden winced as he was summoned home by his masters. His gaze dark and filled with foreboding, he paused before he left with one parting shot. "I had this very conversation with your father, once. Let us pray, that when history repeats itself, your conqueror is kinder to you."

Thorn set his drink down as those words echoed in his ears. Centuries ago, the Chthonian, Savitar, had warned him of the same thing. Savitar condemned the union that had brought him into being.

They both walked a tenuous line between opposing forces

that constantly sought their very souls. Like him, Savitar had chosen to abandon the mortal realm for solitude. It was much easier to avoid temptation when it wasn't near.

*We are all the architects of our own downfall.* Acheron's words haunted him now.

Yet, on the other side, everyone was also the architect of their own salvation and redemption.

Sadly, there was only one creature who could tell the final outcome of it all. And thankfully the one still remained dormant.

Sleeping.

For the sake of them all, no one needed to disturb that beast.

Sighing, Thorn moved to sit before his fire and stare into flames that spoke to him in the quiet solitude of his lonely home. He used his powers to pull his drink to him so that he could toast the noise. "Here's to the future. May it never bring to me what I deserve."

K*essar clutched the* ancient disk in his hand as he entered the cave where he and the last of his brethren remained hidden from the Greek Daimons who sought their blood so that they could walk in daylight and thwart the ancient god, Apollo's curse against their kind.

The Daimons had almost hunted them to extinction. But with this . . .

It was even better than the Shield of Dadga.

"What is that, my lord?" Namtar asked as Kessar walked past.

He smiled at his second-in-command. "Our salvation."

"You have the Shield?"

Kessar shook his head. "Something better."

"What would be better than . . ." His voice broke off as he read the inscription on the disk. "Is this real?"

"It is, indeed. Can you not feel it?"

Namtar grinned. "The Smaragdine Tablet," he breathed reverently.

Cupping the demon's cheek in his hand, Kessar nodded. "With this, we don't just rise. We dominate. 'Tis a new age coming. And we will be the overlords of all. Even the gods, themselves, will bow down to us."

Happiness fled Namtar's face as he fingered a part of the disk. "This has been worn down. Will we not need it to find the item?"

"A few months to repair it. That's all. Then we will leave this hole and take back our dominion from Stryker and his Spathi crew. They will weep for the day they crossed us. And we will have *no* mercy for them."

# EPILOGUE

*June 23, 2015*
*New Orleans*

Cadegan stared down into the most precious face he'd ever beheld.

His son.

And he wasn't a tadpole. Or a demon. He was a perfect infant. Fully human in appearance.

Josette held him cradled to her bosom while

he slept in total peace and security. Her cousin, Essie, who'd been their midwife for the birth, had withdrawn from the room a short time ago with the entire Flora-Landry-Devereaux clan that had been summoned the moment Josette went into labor.

They'd descended on their New Orleans condo like demon locusts to witness the event, and had forced Cadegan to put Simi on guard duty to keep them out of the bedroom until they knew for certain the baby wasn't a tadpole. Or something else that would terrify her family.

He'd even banned the Mórrígan, Leucious, Talon and Sunshine from the room until after the babe was with them. He'd wanted this to be a private affair between him and his wife. After all, the nipper had been conceived without an audience. It was only fitting he get used to his parents before he was forced to endure more strangers.

Josette was right. Cadegan was still an extreme recluse, but he'd gladly learned to share his solitude with her and their furry babies. And he looked forward to their newest addition.

Kissing her cheek, he sat down beside her on the bed.

She leaned against his chest. "So what shall we name him? I know we've argued for months now, but we have to decide for sure, 'cause *hey you* will get him seriously mocked in school."

He laughed at her words. "I'm still partial to Guorthigirn, meself."

"Let us strive for something the poor boy can spell and pronounce before he reaches college, shall we?"

"Here, here," Acheron said as he and Styxx joined them. "Take it from someone who's experienced that. I think I found the only woman in existence who doesn't mind spelling and repeating Parthenopaeus a thousand times for every person she talks to."

Styxx laughed.

Cadegan rolled his eyes. "Happy birthday, by the way."

"And to you and baby . . . name to be determined. Styxx and I consider it an honor to share our birthday with him."

"That we do."

Acheron and Styxx approached them slowly so that they could see the baby.

"He's beautiful," Styxx said.

"Like an angel," Acheron added.

Josette smiled at them. "Thank you."

Simi trounced in behind them. "Can the Simi make a suggestion on the baby akri-boy name?"

Jo smiled at the demon who'd been pacing the floors, waiting to be a big sissy again. "Sure, Simi. What do you like for a name?"

"Drystan Eurig Maboddimun!"

Jo grinned. "I like that." She looked at Cadegan. "What about you?"

"I could go with Drystan Eurig, for sure. But never Maboddimun. He is Drystan Eurig ap Cadegan a Josette. No one will ever doubt his parentage. He is *our* son. Proudly so."

Jo rubbed her nose against her son's. "You will never fit all of that on a driver's license, little one."

Acheron folded his arms over his chest. "Then how about Drystan Eurig Cadox? A Welsh shortening of Cadegan's son?"

She nodded. "I like it! I say we go for it." She smiled at Cadegan. "What say you?"

"Aye, lass. But it doesn't seem quite fair to you as you did the hardest part of the birthing. And the saints know, you disavowed me and my skeptical parentage quite a bit as you struggled to birth him."

Laughing, she kissed his cheek. "All forgiven now that we have little Drystan with us."

"Yippee!" Simi jumped up and down and clapped her hands. "The Simi finally gots to name a baby demon! Now can I give him hornays?"

"Please don't," Jo said with a laugh as she cupped the baby's head to protect it. "If you do that, the hats my mom crocheted for him won't fit."

"Well, poo. That no fun."

A knock sounded on the door.

Styxx opened it to show Thorn and Karma on the other side. "Mind more visitors?"

"Not at all," Jo said. "Grand Central Station and them some. Come in, guys. Join the party!"

By the hesitant way they walked in, she knew it couldn't be good.

Cadegan slid from the bed. "What is it?"

Thorn ignored him as he moved to touch the baby's cheek. "Have you named him yet?"

"Drystan Eurig."

The moment Thorn's hand touched his skin, the baby opened his dark blue eyes to stare up at him as if he recognized him as family.

Thorn smiled. "He's intelligent and beautiful. Hi, little Drystan. 'Tis a pleasure to finally meet you." He stepped back from the bed while Karma scooted in beside Jo so that she could hold him for a minute.

Turning to the men, Thorn moved away. "Am I the only one who finds it very odd that he was born on the Atlantean Day of Fire and shares the date with you two?"

Acheron met Styxx's gaze. "It'd . . . crossed our minds."

"And you know what this year is?"

"Blood Moon," Styxx whispered. "September 28. We're very much aware of the signs and the prophecy."

Thorn lowered his voice. "Have any of you spoken to Savitar in the last two days?"

They each shook their heads.

Acheron frowned. "Why?"

"Because your friend, Kessar, has released the Scythian Guard from their slumber."

Styxx and Acheron sucked their breath in sharply.

Cadegan scowled at Thorn. "What's the Scythian Guard?"

It was Acheron who answered. "A race of Drakaina—female dragons who were a sister tribe of the Amazons. They were so fierce, they almost brought down both the Sumerian and Greek pantheons. When they were finally defeated, Zeus had their survivors turned to stone."

Thorn swallowed hard. "On the rise of the Blood Moon, they will be able to free their queen, Echidna."

Cadegan could tell from their faces that she wasn't an easy adversary, but he'd never heard of her before. "Echidna?"

"The mother of all monsters," Styxx breathed. "One of the fiercest of the Titans." He laughed bitterly. "We are so screwed if we don't stop them."

Acheron let out a tired breath. "It's the Rise of the Dragons, we've known this day would come. The Scythians were put down before. We'll do so again. Simple."

Styxx snorted. "This is not simple, brother. Simple slaughter for us, maybe. But not a simple fix for them."

"The Simi gots her barbecue sauce and a whole passel of Brother Xeddy's Charonte. Will that help?"

Styxx arched his brow as he turned back toward Acheron. "Have the Charonte ever fought dragons?"

Acheron nodded. "And had their wings handed to them." He pulled Simi against him. "This is one enemy, Sim, you can't win against. They have all the powers you do and many you don't."

Her mouth formed a small O. "Then what do we do, akri?"

"What we always do. We stand and we fight for our families."

Cadegan looked past them to where Jo and Karma sat with his son.

Family. The one thing he'd never thought to have. But now having found it, he wasn't about to let it go. Not without a brutal fight. And brutal fighting was what he knew best.

Let the evil unleash their dragons all they wanted. They were in for one hell of a battle.

"Hey, guys?" Jo called from the bed. "Don't look so stern and serious. C'mon, you remember when we all died in 2012? And the world came to an end in 1999?"

Cadegan scowled at her. "I missed the end of the world?"

"And all the chaos that went with it." She wrinkled her nose playfully. "We'll get through this. One shiny, scary

Apocalypse at a time. After all, that's what life is. Seldom do we get to ride the merry-go-round. More often than not, we're thrown on the back of the bull right as they open the gate. All you can do, is take a deep breath, close your eyes and hold on with both hands. Either you'll tame the beast or it'll break you. But it'll only break you if you let it."

Cadegan returned to her side as Karma left the bed to make room for him. "She's right. Besides, she's already done the impossible. If she gave me back my soul, what's a few Drakaina?"

"Few dozen," Thorn said under his breath as Karma moved to stand by his side. "But who's counting?" Yet for the first time since he entered the room, he smiled at Karma. "We will get through this. After all, we have the only thing that's worth fighting for."

"Barbecue?" Simi asked.

Cadegan shook his head. "Family, Simi. It's what we put ourselves to the hazard for. And to me precious Josette and Drystan, I gladly pledge myself against any challenge." He glanced to the others. "I'm not forgetting the extended family. We will survive."

"No," Styxx said earnestly. "We will thrive, and in spite of our enemies, we will treasure what we love and be happy for the ones we have. For as long as we have them."

Jo took Cadegan's hand in hers and smiled up at him. "Here, here. As Tabby so often says, get thee behind me, bitches. Or I'm going Cajun on you. And if you think medieval is bad . . . just wait. You ain't seen nothing yet."

# Son of No One

## BONUS SCENE

"*You* bastard!"

Entering his war tent, Thorn froze as he heard Brigid's furious tone. It was nothing compared to the slap she delivered to him as soon as she closed the distance between them.

The demon in him rose up, demanding her blood for the assault. But he stamped it down, for one reason only.

He deserved it.

Her dark eyes flashed as she glared at him with the fury of her entire pantheon. Her breathing ragged, she struggled to control herself.

He licked at the blood on his lips from her blow. "I take it that you're upset with me, love?"

"Don't *you* even," she snarled in warning as she walked a circle around him, dragging her heavy brocade skirts in her tightly clenched fists.

Thorn arched a brow, still stunned that she was in his tent in the middle of the war that was raging outside. More than that . . . "I thought you swore that you'd never breathe the same air as I again." That was the polite version of her words, at any rate.

Two months ago, after she'd found out who and what he really was, she'd broken his heart, kicked him from her bed, and banished him from the only happiness he'd ever really known.

"I'm pregnant!"

Thorn felt the color drain from his face as those words hit him even hard than her hand. "What?"

"You heard me well enough!"

For one incredibly stupid heartbeat, he almost asked who the father was, but her fury answered that well enough. It was his issue, she carried. Joy tore through him at the prospect. Never once had he considered the possibility of fatherhood.

But that happiness was cut short the moment she spoke again. "You did this on purpose! What? Do you plan to offer him to your father as a gift?"

He gaped at her insinuation. "You don't honestly believe that, do you?"

"You're a demon! What else am I to believe? The whole reason you slept with me was to get to my father's shield."

Wholly untrue, but they'd already had this argument. She refused to see him as anything more than his grandfather's tool. And that was not why he'd seduced her.

There for a time, in her precious arms, he'd almost been normal.

He wiped at his swelling lips. "It wasn't the whole reason. You are quite stunning when you're not slapping me."

She glared at him.

Thorn braced himself as he considered the implication of what they'd done. "So what are you planning to do with the baby?"

"I wanted it ripped from my womb the moment I learned of it, but I've been told that it would kill me in the process. With it being of demonkyn blood, I have to deliver it."

Those words bit him to the core of his soul. Just once, he'd give anything to be something more than the despised progeny of his father. "He'll only be a quarter demon."

"One drop is as good as total."

He winced. Of course it was. He should know that by now. "Then give him to me. I'll raise him."

Her eyes flared with angry passion. "I'd sooner cut his throat the moment he's born."

"Then you are planning to keep him?"

She shook her head. "I'm planning to put him where *you'll* never find him. Hopefully, he'll be mortal and will die quickly after his birth. If not . . . I'll take care of it."

He glared at her. "That is your son you're speaking of!"

"What would you have me do? Suckle it on the milk of a goddess? To what purpose? To strengthen it?"

"Brigid . . ." He moved to touch her.

She quickly stepped away and raked him with a bitter hatred that scalded his tongue. "Never touch me again. Go to your grandfather and tell him you have failed. Neither of you will ever take possession of this child."

And with that, she was gone.

Brigid *returned to* her chambers as her fear and loathing warred with the love she felt for both the demon who'd seduced her and the child he'd given her.

How could she have been so foolish? But then that was Thorn's greatest power. The ability to deceive and to make enemies trust when they shouldn't.

Aye, he was a dodgy bastard. And she'd been so lonely these years since her husband had been slain, and Tuireann had grieved himself to death over losing his sons. Her own grief had made her weak. And she'd longed for comfort and companionship.

There for a time, she'd thought Thorn the most perfect man ever born, and he'd eased the constant agony in her heart. Had filled her days and nights with such great happiness.

Until Gwyn ap Nudd had told her what Thorn really was. Who he served.

Grandson of Noir. The oldest, darkest primal power of evil. The essence of the worst of all kind. Closing her eyes, she placed her hand over her stomach where her son was barely the size of a bean.

"In your heart, you will have the ability to do the greatest of good."

Or the worst of all evil.

"What troubles you, daughter?"

She turned at the melodic sound of her mother's voice. In the form of a maiden, the Mórrígan was as beautiful as always. Her raven dark hair was braided around her head in an intricate pattern.

Before she could stop herself, she ran to her mother and held her close. "What have I done?"

"What we've all done at times. You followed your heart

and it led you somewhere you didn't want to go." Her mother placed her hand to Brigid's stomach. "Breathe, daughter. All will be right."

"Do you know that or do you believe that?"

"Is there a difference? We make our own truth with what we believe."

Brigid scowled at her. "As spoken by the goddess of fate?"

"Who better to know the truth?"

She was right, and Brigid loathed her for that. "No one can ever know who his father is."

"Then don't tell them."

Brigid nodded. Aye, she'd keep this secret. And she'd make sure that her son was forever safe from harm. Forever beyond the reach of evil. He would be a son of the Tuath Dé, and even though she probably should, she wouldn't withhold his birthright from him. He would be the last of her sons. She felt that with every part of her goddess being.

She'd buried one son already, she would not lose another.

"I shall name him Cadegan. The son of battle and glory." And in addition to life, she would give him the one thing that she dare not entrust to any other. The one thing that would protect him from harm and keep him safe from all.

Her father's shield.

So long as Cadegan didn't shed human blood, he would be safe from his father's reach.

350

Her mother brushed her hand over Brigid's furrowed brow, smoothing it with her fingers. "Good and bad lives in the heart of us all. It is the choices we make, large and small, every day that determine our future. Have faith in your child, Brigid. For while he holds his father's blood, he also holds yours. Once he leaves you, his life will be his own. And as with all living creatures, he'll have to find the courage to face and battle what his enemies throw at him. Whether he stumbles, falls or ultimately triumphs is a decision only he can make. For there is no true failure in life, child. There is only giving up one day before we would have achieved success."

"But if he unites with his father?"

"His father was born of Paimon's blood. Yet he spurned it and is now on our side."

"For today. What of tomorrow?"

"It will come and we cannot stop that. But we don't have to fear the morrow. We only have face it." Kissing her cheek, her mother left her.

She was right and Brigid knew it. Whatever happened, she would do her best by her child and hope. After all, hope was the greatest gift, and the single greatest curse of every living thing.

*Turn the page for a sneak peek at Sherrilyn
Kenyon's upcoming League novel*

# Born of Betrayal

# 1

It was all-out war.

Prime Commander Galene Batur stared at the report of The League attack on an Andarion outpost where almost two hundred civilians had been mercilessly slaughtered.

And for what?

Human vanity? How she hated their inferior species. Humans had never brought her anything but utter misery. Now they had brought her a whole new bloody war that would cost the lives of countless Andarions. Cost her the lives of her soldiers, who would be forced to protect their repugnant species.

How she wished she could bomb them all into oblivion.

"Commander?"

She looked over her shoulder at her lieutenant commander's call. Dressed in the standard red-and-black Andarion command uniform, Talyn wasn't just her second-in-command and adjutant, he was the only male she'd ever trust at her back.

At twenty-nine, he stood head and shoulders above her, and most everyone else. Muscular and unbelievably handsome, he wore his long black hair in typical Andarion warrior fashion—tiny braids that were held away from his face by a red band. Her only complaint with him was the well-trimmed moustache and goatee he'd started wearing lately. It was a current fashion trend she didn't care for. At all. But he thought it made him look more masculine and sexy.

As if he needed help in either of those departments.

Still, his presence caused her heart to soften. It took everything she had not to reach out and cup his beloved cheek. But he wouldn't approve of such open affection before the rest of their troops.

Her Talyn was always prim and proper. Always circumspect.

"Yes?"

Talyn saluted her. "I have an urgent message for you from the royal house."

Galene forced herself not to wince. It must be the queen wanting information about the attack she had yet to gather.

Sighing that she didn't have more reports to offer, she headed for the secured line. She placed the link in her ear before she opened the channel.

Instead of Queen Cairistiona, it was Prince Nykyrian who popped onto her monitor. Unlike his fraternal twin brother, Nykyrian appeared human with his white-blond hair and green eyes. The only part of him that betrayed his Andarion roots was his set of fangs . . . along with his height and military prowess. While she might not appreciate his human half, she definitely respected his exemplary war record and battle skills.

She gave him a curt bow. "Your Highness, to what do I owe this honor?"

"I know you're busy, Commander, and I hate to take your attention away from our troops for even a second, but I have serious business to discuss with you. The Alliance has decided that we need a single military leader we can trust to oversee our joint forces and armies as we fight against The League. Your name was the first one to come to our minds, and we are all in agreement. We'd like to offer the position to you."

Stunned, she stared at him, amazed by the offer. "I'm honored, Highness."

"If you need time to think it over . . ."

Was he serious? Who in their right mind would turn this down? This was a dream appointment anyone would kill to possess. A once-in-a-lifetime opportunity.

Galene would command the single largest military movement in the history of their United System of Planets.

"No, Highness. I would love to lead Alliance forces. I only have one concern. I know that part of our forces are Phrixian and Caronese." Misogynistic troops and armies that would balk heavily at taking orders from a female commander.

"You'll be assigned a male adjutant for handling them . . . a Tavali commander. Likewise, you'll be responsible for dealing with the Qillaq directly since they won't take orders from a male."

That was certainly true.

It was rare for any army to be as integrated with both sexes as the Andarions were. Male or female didn't matter. Only competence and lethal skill did.

"When would you like for me to start?" she asked.

"Immediately. The Tavali are on their way to you right now. With a transport and your new adjutant. The two of you will be flown to their northernmost base, where The League has been making their heaviest strikes. All we'll need is for you to name your successor for the Andarion armada, until the war is over."

Galene gestured to Talyn. "We will see it done."

Nykyrian inclined his head to her. "Welcome aboard, Commander. May the gods smile upon you. Always."

"Thank you, Your Highness. I promise, I will do you, your mother, and Andaria proud."

"I know you will." He cut the transmission.

Galene stared at the blank screen as she considered this latest twist of fate.

Wow. She, the daughter her parents had callously thrown out from their house when she was just a girl, was going to lead their combined forces in the war against The League. If they won, she'd be eternally famous.

If they lost, she'd be executed for treason.

One hell of a gamble. But then, as the Andarion armada prime commander, she'd die if they lost, anyway. At least as their allied military leader, it would all be in her hands, and if they failed, she alone would be to be blame.

Thrilled and a little scared, she turned toward Talyn.

His beautiful white eyes glowed with loving pride. "Congratulations, Commander."

She smiled at him. "I shall name you the new prime commander of the armada."

He shook his head. "I will go with you to The Tavali."

"No . . . you belong here."

"I belong at your back, Commander. Protecting you. Always."

"Talyn—"

"Mom," he stressed the word, making her realize that she'd dropped their strict military behavior first, by using his given name. "I will not stay here while you interact with others who could betray you. You will need a support staff you know is loyal to you and above reproach. Now more than ever. If you think for one moment that I will stay behind while you risk your life for all of us, you don't know me at all." His gaze burned into hers. "You go. I go."

She wanted to beat him. But how could she? "You are ever my pride."

"And you are ever my cherished mother."

Smiling, she pulled his head down so that she could press her cheek to his. "I love you, *mi tana*."

"I love you, too."

She fisted her hand in his hair. "I should order you to stay."

"Only if you wish to see me court-martialed."

She tugged at his hair. "Don't tempt me, scamp." Releasing him, she stepped away with a frown. "Call Commander Ilkin. We can promote him."

"Yes, ma'am. And I'll personally assemble an Andarion security team for you."

Galene rolled her eyes at his paranoia—as if she couldn't protect herself. She would argue that with him, too, but he was far more stubborn than she was when it came to such things. Years of fighting his steel will had taught her that.

"See it done quickly."

He saluted her. "Yes, ma'am."

Her heart swelling with love and pride, Galene watched him leave to carry out his orders. In all the universe, he was the only family she had. The only family she needed.

*You should have been a surgeon, Talyn.* It was what she'd drilled into him from the cradle. But her ever-defiant boy had refused, and followed her into the military as soon as he graduated primary school.

*Evil little booger. Stubborn and headstrong . . .*

*Just like his father.*

No one could ever tell him what to do. The gods knew she had tried. Many times.

Now he would follow her into war. It was the last thing she'd ever wanted for him. But there was no way to keep him out of it. The time had come for all of them to choose a side.

*At least this way I can keep an eye on him.*

And she would tear apart anyone who threatened her baby.

Sighing, Galene took a moment to look around the Andarion command center that had been her home for years now. Talyn had been here, at her side, almost the entire time. It would be weird to adjust to a new army. A new way of doing things.

But she was nothing if not adaptable.

Okay, not really. She hated change passionately. But she liked to lie to herself about her inflexible flexibility.

Still, a whole new chapter was about to begin for both her and Talyn. She didn't know what it would hold, but she couldn't wait to see where it led her.

*An ill wind blows to all ill things.*

A chill went down her spine as she remembered her father's old saying. She only prayed that this time, he was wrong.

# 2

Fain felt his stomach shrink with dread as they dropped anchor and called for the Andarion contingency they were here to pick up.

*I fucking hate you, Jayne.* This was why he didn't have friends. Why he didn't want them. Because they invariably did shit like this to him.

His brother Dancer, and Dancer's friend Jayne, thought it was funny to volunteer him to be the adjutant for a female who hated his guts with the fire of a million suns.

It wasn't.

The last time he'd seen Galene, she'd shoved his ass into a public arena with all his business hanging out, and had locked the door behind him. Something he'd been beaten for, and not just by his parents, who'd been horrified by the indecent display.

He couldn't wait to see what Galene would do to him this time.

*Probably shoot me.*

If he was lucky.

If he was really lucky, it wouldn't be in his balls.

Sighing irritably, he stood up to get it over with. There was no need in delaying the inevitable. He might be a lot of things, but a coward had never been one of them.

And it wasn't like he hadn't been shot before. At least this time, he had on battle armor. As long as she didn't shoot him in the head or groin, he would survive the encounter.

Physically, anyway.

Dignity . . . might be a problem. They were oh-for-seven on that one.

He hesitated by the door and pulled down a helmet so that he could add an extra layer of protection between his groin and whatever might go flying at a part of his anatomy he'd like to preserve. Though, to be honest, he wasn't sure why, at this point. Not like he had many chances to use it anymore.

*Don't go there.*

Chayden clapped him on the back. "You all right, Hauk? You look like you're about to hurl."

Fain cut a glare toward his friend. Hurl? No . . .

Kill. Definitely.

"I'm fine."

Fain's little brother came out of the holding area to stand next to him. "I'm with Chay. You look a little green, *drey*."

Fain dodged Dancer's hand as his brother reached to touch his forehead, and barely resisted the urge to slap him. "I know you were just a kid when I ran off with Omira. But do you remember the fact that I was pledged to an Andarion female before I married her?"

Dancer's jaw dropped. "No. I have no memory of that at all. Who were you pledged to?"

Fain faced the ramp that was lowering in front of them. "Prime Commander Galene Batur."

Dancer's curses rang in his ears as Fain headed down the ramp toward the one female he was sure would gut him on the spot. As he scanned the gathered Andarion soldiers, he kept the helmet carefully positioned.

Just in case.

His gaze went straight to her, as if it was drawn there by

magic. *Damn,* was the first thought that went through his head. As with all Andarion females, Galene had been a gorgeous teen. But the adult warrior waiting on them had to be one of the sexiest, most beautiful of her kind.

Tall, lithe, and exquisite, she was dressed in a standard red-and-black Andarion battlesuit. One that hugged a body made to be privately worshiped by naked activities.

And often.

He sucked his breath in sharply as an involuntary image of her wrapping those long legs around him went through his mind. He hadn't been this attracted to a female in a long time. Not since the last time he'd seen her.

Every part of him was alert and panting.

And he was twice as glad now for the helmet at his crotch. *I should have worn looser pants.* Gods help him if he had to sit down with a hard-on this fierce. That pain alone might kill him.

*Focus.* Something much easier said than done.

*What the hell had I been thinking when I walked away from that?*

Young and stupid didn't quite cover it. But then, there'd been extenuating circumstances that had forced his hand. Things that had made staying with her completely out of the question. *Maybe I should have fought harder.*

Yeah, right. It hadn't been that simple.

A fight, he could have won. What they held over his head had been totally out of his control.

She looked up and met his gaze. His throat went dry as his body hardened even more and he remembered the way she used to look at him.

Like he was her cherished hero.

*And I screwed her over.* Badly.

Yeah, he'd earned the hell that had been his life. How he wished things could have been different. Especially between the two of them. While he'd been enamored of Omira, it was nothing compared to what he'd felt for Galene when they were kids.

*The worst decisions in life are always the ones we make out of fear.* He hated to admit how right his father had been whenever the old bastard had quoted that. But life had shown him just how wise his father was.

At first, her gaze swept past Fain, to the other Tavali trailing in his wake. She had no idea who he was.

Not until he pulled his Tavali mask down and exposed his face.

Galene *was impressed* by the military formation and discipline of The Tavali crew—something she'd never expected from outlaw pirates who were as famed for their blatant disregard of rules and social conventions as they were for their savagery. While they each wore different uniforms and styles of battlesuits, they conducted themselves like any disciplined army.

She'd been told that they had their own set of laws they adhered to, but she hadn't believed it.

Until now.

This was impressive. And the one leading them was a huge warrior. Tall and broad-shouldered, he was as muscular as an Andarion male.

And that swagger . . .

It was masculine and mouth-watering. Confident. She had no idea of his species, but whatever it was, he no doubt gave credit to it.

That was her thought until he stopped and stood with all of his weight on his left leg. She almost smiled at a stance that was identical to one Talyn preferred, especially whenever he was uncomfortable with his surroundings.

The Tavali's gaze held hers hostage as he slowly reached up with one hand to lower the black-and-red mask that concealed his face.

Andarion. That explained his white eyes.

Just as she was sucking in her breath in appreciation of his rugged handsomeness, recognition slammed into her. Yes, he was older and now sported three days' growth of his beard, but she knew that proud jawline. Knew those perfect, gorgeous features that had once set her on fire.

Actually, they still did. Only instead of lust, they filled her with raw, unmitigated rage.

Reacting on pure instinct, she pulled her blaster out and fired. It landed straight in his chest where his missing heart should have been.

Total chaos erupted as he fell to the ground and the other Tavali pulled their blasters out and took aim. As did the Andarion soldiers with her.

Throwing himself in front of her, Talyn pulled the weapon from her hand. He and the six Andarions he'd chosen as her guard formed a wall between her and the others.

"Medic!" a human Tavali called out in Andarion.

"Arrest them!" a Sentella soldier demanded.

Galene looked past Talyn's shoulder to see Dancer Hauk, Fain's younger brother, calling for the soldiers to secure her and her team.

Talyn moved in closer, to protect her.

"No!" She grabbed her son's arm to keep him from doing something even more rash than *her* stupidity. "Stand down!"

Talyn did, until a soldier went to cuff her wrists. "Get your hands off her!"

Before she could catch him again, Talyn had eight Tavali and two of their own bleeding on the ground at his feet. With a blaster in each hand, Talyn held the others at bay as he kept himself in front of her. "Anyone else want a free trip to the hospital and paid leave?"

"Talyn!" she snapped, placing her hand on his shoulder. "Enough! Everyone calm down."

Dancer held his blaster angled at Talyn's head. "I believe *you* started this, Commander, when you shot my brother."

"And now I'm ending it. Everyone, arms down!"

They all hesitated.

"Dancer!" Fain growled as he rose to his feet. "Drop your weapon." Biting his lip, he grimaced and glared a hole through her. "I deserved it."

Only then did Dancer lower his blaster.

"Talyn," she said gently as she ran her hand down his arm and pushed his aim toward the floor. "It's all right."

She felt his muscles flexing in debate before he glanced to her and let his weapons fall to the ground. The Tavali surged forward to handcuff him. Something he didn't protest until they went to cuff her again.

Faster than anyone could blink, Talyn knocked the two guards closest to him away and used his foot to kick his blaster back into his hand. He put himself between her and the others. "One hand to the commander, and so help me, I'll fucking kill every one of you bitches!"

Fain's gaze darkened as Talyn's weapon went back to

Dancer, who was inching toward them. With unbelievable speed, Fain attacked Talyn.

Galene's head spun as cold terror consumed her. Both Fain and Talyn were former titled Andarion Ring fighters. And right now, they fought with death in their eyes. If she didn't do something fast, they'd tear each other apart.

Dodging their blows, she forced herself between them, and pushed them to opposite sides.

"Enough!" she roared.

Dancer moved forward to take Fain by his arm.

Holding his chest where she'd shot him, Fain spat the blood on his lips to the ground. He glared his hatred at Talyn. "Aim at my brother again, and I'll rip your fucking spine out, punk!"

Talyn didn't flinch at the threat. "One hand to the commander again, and I'll rip apart every ass here, including yours *and* his, *old man*."

She sucked her breath in sharply at the double-edged insult. Not just that Fain was older, but to insinuate he wasn't Andarion . . . it was the worst sort of slap in the face for their kind.

Fain licked at his busted lip as he watched Galene place her hand over the heart of the soldier in front of him.

"It's all right, *courani*," she said in a gentle tone, using an endearment that called the male soldier her precious heart. "Stand down."

The soldier's eyes softened as he glanced at her and covered her hand with his. Lowering his head, he brought her hand to his lips, and kissed it before he stepped back.

But not so far that he couldn't shield her with his body again if he needed to.

Disgusted, Fain met Dancer's gaze and shook his head. Galene had chosen quite the boytoy for herself. The kid was large, even for an Andarion. And as much as Fain hated to admit it, the bastard could fight. It was actually impressive what he'd done.

And the ease with which he'd accomplished it.

"Isn't he a little young for you?" Fain asked her snidely.

Galene pinned him with a sneer. "I don't think it's any of your business who I live with."

Fain's jaw went slack that she'd openly admit such a scandalous relationship in front of everyone. While it wasn't unheard of for commanders to sleep with their staff, they were usually highly discreet about it. Rarely did they flaunt it.

He scowled at her. "Well, aren't you full of surprises?"

She raked him with a scathing grimace. "I learned early . . . from the best."

He took a step forward.

So did Talyn.

Galene pushed them apart again. "Boys! Enough!"

Fain curled his lip before he dropped a potent verbal

bomb on them. "You do realize that you both just attacked a member of the Andarion royal family?"

Galene gaped. "Excuse me?"

Dancer quirked a smug grin. "The queen adopted my brother a week ago."

Fain expected that to take some of the fire out of her boy-toy's eyes. It didn't. Defiant and reckless, he snorted disdainfully at the news.

"Talyn!" Galene snapped before the child could speak. "Not a word."

He inclined his head respectfully. "Yes, Commander." But his gaze said that he was struggling to hold back his opinion.

And it wasn't a happy one.

Fain returned his sneer with one of his own. "I should have you both arrested."

"Try it," the male said with an arrogant, taunting grin. "You'll be dead before they cuff me . . . If I'm going to jail again, old man, I'm going to make it count."

"Talyn!"

A tic started in his jaw as Galene reached up, buried her hand in his hair, and forced the boy to meet her gaze. Only then did the fire go out in his eyes.

She pressed her cheek to his and whispered in his ear before she kissed his forehead. Her hand lingered on his chin as her gaze held his a moment longer.

Finally quelled, the soldier took a step back.

Fain swept his gaze around the other Andarions here. The fact that none of their soldiers found this display odd said it all about Galene's open affair with her second-in-command.

Normally, Andarions never touched each other in public. Not even married couples. Unless they were fighting, it was their custom to keep a respectful distance from each other at all times.

A fierce, unwarranted hatred for the boy consumed him. He had no idea why he'd care or feel the jealousy inside his heart, but he did. And it wanted that kid's head on a pike.

While Fain's entire life had gone straight to hell after their last encounter, it was obvious Galene had been living quite the dream with her child-lover.

Galene stepped back as the medics arrived to tend Fain's injuries.

She met Dancer's glare. "We shall withdraw to my office, where I will contact the queen immediately and inform her what has happened. If she still wants my arrest, I'll surrender myself to her authority. Until then . . ." She turned her curled lip toward Fain. "I hope you die painfully of your wounds."

And with that, she walked away.

Talyn passed one more hate-filled glare at him before he followed after her. Like a dutiful puppy.

Little fucking bastard.

Yeah, okay, huge fucking bastard, but still . . .

The medic let out a low, evil laugh as she saw Fain's wounds. And especially the one at his eye that was already swelling, and burning like a mother. "I see you met the commander's bodyguard. What'd you do? Speak to her in the wrong tone of voice?"

Fain gave the Andarion female an arched brow. "Does he do this kind of thing a lot?"

She snorted as she examined his eye. "Actually, he must like you."

"How so?"

"You're still breathing. He normally kills anyone who so much as grimaces in the commander's general direction."

Dancer sighed as Fain sat down on the stretcher and allowed them to remove his chest plate to inspect the blast wound. "I'm sorry, Fain. When you said she was a nasty piece of work, I should have listened to you. I had no idea she'd hate you *this* much."

Fain looked down at the bleeding wound in the center of his chest. Had he been wearing anything other than his Tavali armor, that shot would have killed him instantly. As it was, it hurt like hell and he'd be bruised for a few days, but he'd live. "I figured she wouldn't be happy to see me again. However, I did underestimate her exact degree of hatred for me."

"What did you do to her?" Chayden picked up the helmet Fain had been holding against his groin.

Fain swallowed hard as he met Dancer's gaze before he answered Chay's question. "I broke off our engagement to marry a human."

The medic sucked her breath in sharply at his words.

As a human, Chayden had no idea what a slap that was, and what it would have cost Galene in their society. "Yeah? So?"

The medic snorted. "She must have really loved you at one time."

"Why?"

"She didn't shoot you between the eyes."

Galene swallowed hard as the door to her office closed, and she moved to call the queen. She'd no more than reached for the controls before Talyn finally spoke to her.

"So that's my father."

"Excuse me?"

He sighed heavily. "There's no other male you'd attack like that. Only Fain Hauk."

Tears choked her at his emotionless tone. "If you knew, why did you attack him?"

"He came at my mother. No one does that. I don't care who or what you are."

She could kill Talyn for his own recklessness . . . that he'd inherited from Fain. "You shouldn't have endangered your-self for me. You know better."

He shrugged nonchalantly. "You didn't hesitate to pro-tect me."

"I'm your mother."

"And I'm your son . . . as you raised me."

She was torn between the desire to hug him for that, and spank his bottom like she'd done when he was a boy. "I told you to be a doctor, didn't I?"

He gave her an impertinent grin. "You raised me to be fierce. Like you. Not to don a medic's robe and serve others."

"Careful," she warned him, "you're not so big or old that I can't still take you over my knee."

He laughed playfully at her threat. "I'd like to see you try."

She popped his butt. "Impudent boy."

His smile faded as her link buzzed. "Is that the queen?"

"Most likely."

Talyn gave her a sincere look that said he would be more than willing to die for her. "I won't let them harm you, Matarra. Not for that worthless piece of shit."

"He's your father, Talyn. I won't have you insult him."

The tic returned to his jaw as he looked away.

She moved to answer her link. As predicted, it was Queen Cairistiona.

"What happened?"

Galene bowed her head respectfully. "Forgive me, my queen. I was caught off guard and allowed my emotions to get the better of me. I had no idea that you had adopted a new son. You should have told me we had a new member of the royal family to protect."

The look on the queen's face was stern and lethal. "It's just the two of us, Galene. I want your side of this matter, before I render verdict. And I want the whole story."

Galene's gaze went to Talyn. "Before His Highness was disowned by his birth mother, I was pledged to him."

Cairistiona sucked her breath in sharply. "He left you for the human he married?"

She nodded. "Because of his actions, I was abandoned by my own family and turned out in disgrace."

"Say no more, Commander. I understand. I would have shot him, myself, in your place."

Thank the gods the queen was so understanding. But then they had decades of history together. And an unbreakable loyalty to one another.

"I am sorry, Majesty. Had I some warning about Fain's identity, I would have handled it better. But this is the first time I've seen him since the day he told me I failed to please him."

Cairistiona's speculative gaze went past Galene, to Talyn. "Is he the father of your son?"

Galene clenched her teeth. Only two people besides her knew the identity of Talyn's father. Talyn and his great-grandmother, who'd taken her in years ago when she'd been living on the street, pregnant with him.

But it was a death sentence to lie to her queen. "Yes, Majesty."

"Does he know?"

"I've never kept such secrets from my son. Talyn knows. His father does not."

Cairistiona let out a bitter laugh. "Talyn?"

He cast a concerned glance to his mother before he stepped forward and bowed to her. "Majesty?"

"It appears you are now of royal blood, child. My grandson. A prince of Andaria."

His jaw went slack. Until now, he'd lacked full lineage. As such, he'd been ineligible for many Andarion benefits, including marriage. It was something they'd both accepted a long time ago as a very bitter fact.

Now . . .

"What have you to say, Prince Talyn?"

He swallowed hard before he spoke. "I know not, Majesty."

"Yaya," Cairistiona corrected playfully, using the Andarion term for grandmother. She laughed at the stunned expression on his handsome face. "Breathe, child. Remember, you once sat in my lap to color and draw on paper, and do your homework for school. . . . I know it'll take some getting used to. Your father is having the same trouble acclimating to the title. But you will, in time."

She turned her attention back to Galene. "It appears I cannot punish my grandson for protecting his birth mother. Even from his birth father. And while I would normally have your head for this assault, the circumstances were extenuating. As such, and given the fact that Fain will live and is remarkably understanding of your motivation, I'll let this event pass unpunished. But let's not repeat it, shall we?"

"Never, Majesty."

"Cairistiona or Matarra, Galene. You are the mother of my grandson, after all. As such, I will send a contingency of royal guards for you both. And while Talyn, as prince, can be excused from military service, I'm going to assume that he has no intention of leaving your side while we're at war." She passed a questioning look to him.

"My place is with my mother."

Cairistiona smiled proudly. "Spoken like a true Andarion." Her gaze returned to Galene. "If you can refrain from slaughtering the father of your child, we shall proceed as if none of this has happened. Is that acceptable?"

"Yes, Majesty."

"Cairistiona."

Galene hesitated before she spoke again. "Cairistiona . . . I'm assuming you'll want me to step down as—"

"No. I'd like to see you continue on as the commander of our combined forces. You are still the most qualified to lead us. And I'd feel much more confident with you at the helm than a commander from one of the other nations."

"It will be my honor, Ma . . . Matarra?"

Cairistiona smiled in approval. "Very good. And have no fear that I will tell Fain about his child. That is your place." She sighed heavily. "For now, I will say that the additional guard is to make sure the two of you don't attack him. But there are certain advantages Talyn will have as prince. I'm sure both of you will want them for him. When you're both ready, let me know and I will make a public announcement."

Galene inclined her head to her. "Thank you. For everything."

"Don't thank me yet, Commander. This has all the earmarks for disaster. We are at war with The League. If we lose, all of us will pay with our lives. We have committed treason against the organization that has reigned over all our worlds

for the last fifteen hundred years. May the gods be with us."
She cut her transmission.

Indeed. Galene turned toward her son. "Funny, this was
not how I saw the day going in my mind when I woke up this
morning."

Talyn laughed. "Nor I."

Her gaze softened as she digested his new place in their
world. It was more than deserved and she couldn't have
wished better for him. "Prince Talyn. It has a beautiful ring
to it."

He scoffed at her words. "I'm not a prince, Matarra. This
changes nothing."

"It changes everything. It silences all those bastards
who have mocked you. All those bitches who have turned
their noses up whenever you've glanced their way. I can't
wait to see them choke on their own bile when they hear
this news."

And still he shook his head with blatant disregard. "I've
never cared what they thought of me."

That was sadly true and she knew it. But he had cared
what they thought of her. She'd mopped too many tears from
his beautiful face when he'd been a small child. Had tended
too many bloody noses from the fights he'd been in with those
who had called her whore and worse.

And she'd seen the silent hurt in his eyes when females had viciously spurned him because he had no paternal lineage. Only his mother's broken one.

He had suffered so much because of his father's actions. That, more than anything, was what she hated Fain for. She could handle her own humiliation.

It was what had been unjustly given to Talyn that burned bitterest.

What her son had been forced to endure that made her crave vengeance from his father. Her proud, precious baby had deserved none of it.

Tears choked her. "You have ever been my brave champion." When everyone else had abandoned her, Talyn had stayed by her side. Ever the dutiful son.

Maybe not verbally. He did have his father's limited fuse, and a smart mouth that had tested her temper and restraint on many occasions.

But his heart had always been loyal. Always loving.

Always ferocious. Her fierce little lorina.

"You deserve to be a prince."

"Titles mean nothing to me. You know that."

Only his rank as her adjutant had ever mattered to him. He'd worked insanely hard to achieve his rank as fast as possible so that he could be with her and watch over her.

Something that had been twice as hard for him since he'd lacked his father's prestigious military lineage. It was why he'd become a prizefighter for the Ring as a mere boy. With every title he'd earned, his military rank had advanced to match his proven martial skills. Most of the time, anyway.

But even without his father's lineage, even with her being harder on him than she was on her other soldiers, he'd risen to become one of the youngest officers in the Andarion military. Had attained his current rank at an age when most were only beginning their obligatory service.

He had done her proud.

"You may think nothing of them, Talyn. However, that's not true of others, and I know how much you want to marry and start your own family."

He looked away, but not before she saw the bitter yearning that lived inside him for something he'd been denied.

"Exactly. I do know *you*, my son. As prince, you will have your choice now of any female who meets your fancy."

He scoffed at her words. "If I wasn't good enough for them without a royal title, I damn sure don't want them because of it. Besides, I love my Felicia. She is everything to me. I am grateful and lucky to have her in my life."

Galene bit back a scoff at his words. While she adored Felicia for taking care of Talyn whenever he was allowed liberty, she knew the truth.

Felicia was a paid companion. A contracted mistress who lacked lineage, too. One Talyn had been forced to pay top dollar to keep in a style that was unheard of for others of Felicia's birth-standing. And the unfair terms of Felicia's original contract still sickened Galene. No other Andarion male would have been forced to sign such a travesty, or spend the credits he did for her services.

Or to buy out her contract from her agency because they hadn't wanted Felicia tainted by Talyn's bastard status. Galene flinched as she remembered *that* particular nightmare.

But because of her and Fain, Talyn's social standing ranked below even that of a slave's. It didn't matter how many fighting titles he'd earned. How many citations and awards he gained as a military hero, he was still unable to legally marry.

Even a paid companion.

Worse? Only one companion brokerage in all of Andaria had been willing to contract with him at all. The rest had rudely slammed their doors in his face, leaving him with no other options for a female in his life.

Title and lineage were all that mattered to their people. The purer the lineage, the better, and the more choices an Andarion had.

Had Fain married her as he was supposed to, Talyn would have had all the pride and dignity of a military prince.

Instead, Fain had abandoned them and taken his lineage with him.

But now that Fain had a new family lineage, Talyn might be able to salvage the rest of his future. "Your father's blood gives you everything I never could."

"You've given me the only things that matter."

Cupping his cheek, she shook her head. "You should have married long ago. We should be planning the Endurance for your eldest child by now."

He snorted. "I don't need a wife nagging me. I have a viciously overprotective mother for that."

Before she could respond, her office door pulsed open. She glanced past Talyn's shoulder to see the beast himself entering without being announced. Her lips curled involuntarily.

Talyn pulled her against his chest and held her so that she couldn't attack Fain again. "Don't kill him," he whispered in her ear. "The queen won't forgive you that."

Laughing, she hugged him close. "All right." She kissed his cheek before she let go.

"I'll be just outside." Talyn passed a threatening glare to Fain. "Call me if you need anything, Commander."

"I will, Talyn. Thank you." Forcing herself to remain calm, she faced Fain. "What are *you* doing here?"

Fain watched Talyn until the door was closed behind the brat. "You just can't keep your hands off him, can you?"

She arched a brow at the jealousy she heard in that deep tone of his, and couldn't resist egging it on. "You should have been in here a few minutes ago when I was physically spanking his little ass. I think you would have enjoyed it. I know I did."

He twisted his lips up in disgust. "You really live with him?"

"Yes. I have for years."

"And what? Do you have to burp him after you feed him, too?"

"I've been known to."

Fain was nauseated by her and her lifestyle choices. How could she be so flagrant with a boy almost half her age? Did she have no dignity whatsoever?

"What happened to you, Galene?"

"I was stripped of my family and forced to live on the street. You?"

That took some of the fire out of him. "I never meant to hurt you."

She gave him an arch stare. "Wow. If the damage you did me was without effort, I shudder at what you could do if you actually applied yourself. What did you think would happen when you left me for a human? That my parents would throw me a parade? Send flowers and celebrate?"

"I assumed you'd pledge another male. Chrisen. Actually."

Galene looked away as old memories flared. Had she

not been pregnant . . . had Fain not been disowned over a human . . . she might have survived the scandal. But once her pregnancy showed and after Fain's mother had publicly disavowed him as a traitor to their people, no family would accept her. Not while she carried an unlineaged baby.

And no matter how much better *her* life would have been, she couldn't bring herself to destroy her child. Nor could she have given him up. Not with what happened to abandoned Andarion children. They were relegated to a caste so low, even slaves pitied them. She'd refused to save herself by sacrificing Talyn. His conception had been *her* mistake.

Not his.

While she regretted every minute she'd ever known Fain, she'd never once regretted Talyn in her life. No matter how hard or awful it'd been, one look at his precious face had made everything worth it.

"Well?" Fain asked. "Why didn't you marry Chrisen?"

"Chrisen wanted nothing to do with me after you left. I was a pariah to everyone, Fain. So deformed, they all claimed, that I drove the male I was pledged to into the arms of a pathetic human female. Instead of shoving you into that auditorium, I should have killed you where you stood. That would have saved my social status, and *that* is my sole regret in life."

"Really? That's all you regret?"

She laughed bitterly. "You're right. I do have one more."

"And that is?"

"That I didn't aim at your head on your arrival."

# 3

Talyn drew up short as he left his mother's office to find his "uncle" waiting in the secretary's lounge. A few inches shorter than him, Dancer looked a lot like his father. Enough that it made him want to punch the bastard out where he stood.

But unlike his father, his uncle had red, glowing eyes, instead of the typical Andarion white.

It was a rare genetic defect that caused

Dancer's eyes to glow red like that. One that meant his uncle was overly possessive and loyal to his female. A trait that was inside Talyn, too. Ironic really, as that was a deformity most Andarion females would sell their souls to have in their males.

And here all but Felicia had rudely turned him away.

If they only knew . . .

Dancer raked him with a less than complimentary stare. One that turned into a stern frown as he finally focused on Talyn's features, which were very similar to both his and Fain's.

Just as Dancer opened his mouth to speak, a tall Hyshian female swept into the office with a bright smile.

One Talyn returned immediately as she grabbed him into a fierce bear-like hug. At least she made his day better since she was like a second mother to him. "Jaynie? What are you doing here?"

Her back to Dancer, she cupped his face in her hands. "I heard Lena shot Fain on his arrival and had to tel-ass immediately to see for myself." She frowned as she saw the bruise on his eye, courtesy of his father. "What happened to my sweetie?"

Talyn shrugged. "Same as ever. I bumped into a fist."

Tsking, she continued to examine it. "I thought you were retired from Ring fighting?"

"I am. But not from asshole fighting. . . . So how's Hadrian and the kids?

She rolled her eyes at him. "All good. Sway's been nagging me to let him go camping with you again. I don't know what the two of you did last time, but he really enjoyed it."

"Traded porn mostly. You know . . . typical guy stuff. Kid gets tired of swimming in the estrogen pool."

Chucking him on the arm, she laughed.

"You two know each other?"

Turning around, Jayne finally saw Dancer in the room. "Hey, sexy! I didn't see you there. Why you hiding in a corner?"

He jerked his chin at Talyn. "Keeping my eye on him."

She laughed. "I must have missed one hell of a party."

"That you did," Hauk said drily. "Fain failed to explain to us exactly what a powder keg the commander would be. We were extremely ill prepared for her hot reception."

She turned back toward Talyn. "So I have to know. Fain refused to tell me. What is this prank your mother supposedly pulled on him in school?"

"Mother?" Dancer asked incredulously.

Talyn ignored him. "On their graduation day, she shoved him naked into an auditorium full of witnesses."

She covered her mouth with her hand. "No, she didn't."

He nodded.

"Why does she hate him so much?"

"They were pledged," Dancer answered. "She's the one Fain left for Omira."

Jayne sucked her breath in. "Damn, Hauk. Why didn't you tell me that before I stuck them back together?"

"I had no idea until Fain opened the door on our arrival here. I was just a kid when he was disinherited. I didn't know anything about a previous pledge . . . but, in retrospect, that explains a lot about my mother's hostility toward him."

Dancer narrowed his suspicious gaze on Talyn. "I'm surprised your father married your mother, given that."

Talyn had to force himself not to roll his eyes at his uncle's density.

"Lena's not married," Jayne said before Talyn could stop her. "She's never been married that I know of."

Dancer went pale as he mentally did the math and realized who Talyn's father had to be.

"Yeah," Talyn said drily. "You're so bright."

Seeing the look on Dancer's face, Jayne scowled. "What?"

Dancer looked sick as he struggled to accept the truth. "Why didn't she say something?"

"To whom?" Talyn asked defensively. "Who in your family would have given a single shit?"

Dancer raked a hand through his braids. "Does my mother know?"

"Know what?" Jayne asked. "What do you two know that I don't?"

Crossing his arms over his chest, Dancer jerked his chin at Talyn. "That he's my nephew."

She snorted derisively. "Impossible. Keris would have been . . ." Her voice trailed off as she finally put it together. "Oh my God, no wonder she shot him. I'm just surprised she didn't go for his head."

Talyn scoffed. "I'm surprised she didn't go for his crotch. It explains why he was holding a helmet there when he came off the ship. She must not have changed much since her youth."

Dancer approached him slowly. "I knew you looked like Fain. But damn . . . I just thought that was why she'd picked you for a boyfriend."

He screwed his face up. "That's my mother you're talking about. Do you mind?"

Dancer laughed. "No. No wonder you attacked us like you did. You were protecting your mother." He tried to pull him into a hug, but Talyn shoved him back.

His uncle took the rejection in stride. "Fain's going to shit when he finds out. I can't believe he has a son."

Jayne's evil laughter joined his. "Who's going to tell him?"

Stepping back, Dancer shook his head. "Not me." He cupped Talyn's cheek in his hand so that he could examine his features.

Talyn slapped his hand away. "I'm not your whore, boy. Get your hands off me."

Again, Dancer shrugged his insult away. "The guilt from this is going to destroy Fain."

"Good." Talyn stepped out of his uncle's reach. "I hope he chokes on it."

"Careful. That's my brother you're talking about, and he's a good male. He's stood by me when no one else has."

"Nice to know he can be loyal to someone. The gods know, he never showed that side of his character to my mother."

Jayne came between them. "Whoa, guys. Breathe and stop before you say something you're going to regret. You both are entitled to your feelings. But Dancer, you don't know how hard their lives have been. I love every one of you. You're my family. But Fain hurt them. Badly. And Talyn . . . you've no idea what your father's been through. Trust me. Fate got him back. With interest. He hasn't lived a fairy tale, either. There's a reason he's in a Tavali uniform."

"And I don't really give a shit, Aunt Jayne."

The door to his mother's office opened. His father came storming out.

Fain curled his lip at Talyn, then turned his attention to Jayne and Dancer. "I cannot work with that . . ." His voice trailed off into a choked sound as he gestured at the door. "She's impossible!"

Talyn grabbed him. "Did you hurt her feelings? What did you say to her?"

As his father went to punch him, Dancer came between them. "Stop it! Both of you!"

"Talyn!"

He froze at his mother's sharp tone and withdrew from the fight.

"Yeah, you better keep walking, *boy*."

"Fain!" Dancer snapped through gritted teeth. "Bite it."

He held his hands up in surrender. "Call Nyk. I'm out of this." With long, furious strides, he quit the office.

Dancer let out an elongated breath as he locked gazes with Galene. "I know you hate my brother and I'm sure you're entitled to it. But you should both know that while you had each other, he had absolutely no one. He didn't even have a country to call home."

Galene curled her lip. "What about his *human*?"

Dancer's gaze turned sharp and biting. "Let's just say that out of the two years they were together, his happiest memory is probably you shoving him naked into an auditorium full of family and friends, and locking the door behind him." And with that, he followed after Fain.

Galene couldn't breathe as those words echoed in her ears.

*Two years?*

*What?*

She looked at Jayne for an explanation. "What happened to his wife?"

"Before or after he caught her screwing a human male in their bed?"

Bile rose in her throat. "You're serious?"

Jayne nodded, then pulled her into a comforting hug. "I had no idea Fain was the one who left you."

"I had no idea you were friends with his brother." Because of her less than legal activities and associates, Jayne never talked about her friends or family in anything more than the most abstract of terms. She never mentioned anyone, other than her husband and children, by name.

Without commenting on that, Jayne glanced to Talyn. "How are you holding up, sport?"

He shrugged. "I'm Andarion."

"That's really not an answer."

"For him it is." Galene rubbed his arm. "Notify the team that we'll try this again tomorrow with The Tavali. I need the day to mentally regroup."

"Yes, ma'am." He gave her a sharp salute before making an about-face and leaving them to carry out his orders.

Jayne snorted. "I'm so used to him as a civ that I forget how military our boy really is when he dons that uniform."

Galen smiled proudly. "I'm far more likely to break protocol than he is."

Jayne let out an elongated breath. "I'm really sorry about this, Lena. I'm the one who suggested you for the position. I had no idea what I was getting you into."

Sadness choked her as she thought back to the day she'd learned she was pregnant with Fain's child. It had been one of the tiny handful of perfect moments in her life. They had been pledged on his sixth birthday. Just a few days apart in age, they'd been raised together and had gone to the same school. Since he was to be her husband, she hadn't even looked at other males.

Back then, Fain had been her entire world. A renowned and regaled athlete and champion, he had been destined to become a war hero like his father, and she'd planned on med school like her parents. Their wedding had been set for the fall, following their graduation.

And Talyn had been conceived on Fain's birthday. Her virginity a gift to her fiancé.

Instead of becoming a delighted father and devoted husband as she'd expected, Fain had shattered her heart and thrown her love away as if it was meaningless. She'd never recovered from his betrayal.

"I hate him so much," she whispered. "But he did give me the greatest gift of my life. I couldn't ask for a better son."

"He's just like his father."

She quirked her brow at Jayne's comment.

"He is," Jayne said defensively, with a nervous laugh. "Now that I know, I see it clearly. I don't know how I could have missed it, all these years. Talyn's not Fain's son so much as he's his clone. Driven. Fierce. Stubborn. Loyal."

"I will argue that last bit."

Jayne shook her head in disagreement. "Something happened, Lena. Something really bad. I know Fain and have for years. If he broke pledge with you and you don't know why, it was something foul. He wouldn't have just walked away for no reason. That's not the male I've known. There is no one more honorable or loyal than Fain Hauk."

"He was in love," she spat the word. *With a human.*

Jayne screwed her face up. "Maybe, but here's a question for you, and you're from a medical family so you'd know the answer better than I. Both Keris and Dancer are stralen. What are the odds that gene missed Fain entirely?"

She shrugged. "Genes are strange things."

"Yes, they are. And it is a rare trait, but . . ." Jayne walked away.

"It's possible he never loved either of us," she whispered under her breath. However, if that was true, why would he have left his Andarion heritage behind to marry a human?

He wasn't *quite* that stupid.

As much as it pained her to admit it, Fain's life would have sucked as much as hers did without his prestigious lineage. He'd been military royalty before the scandal.

In the blink of an eye, like her, he'd lost everything. And Jayne was right. As rare as that gene was, for two brothers to have it, it would be extremely unlikely for it not to be in Fain, too.

Of course, there was one way to know for sure.

*Tell him he has a son.*

Regardless of his feelings for her, his body chemistry would kick that gene into overdrive if he thought his son was threatened.

Not that it mattered. She wouldn't risk Talyn's life to find out. Fain wasn't worth it.

Still . . . it did give her something to think about.


W*e need you* to do this."

Fain cursed at Nykyrian, who sat behind an ornate black desk in front of him. "Ryn is The Tavali ambassador—"

"Whose mother is in charge of the Wasturnum—fourth generation to rule that branch—and his beloved little brother is the Caronese emperor. The UTC won't see him as impartial, and you know it."

Still, Fain argued against his appointment to serve with

Galene. "I'm now an Andarion prince. Won't they have issues with *that*?"

"It's not the same, and you know it. You weren't raised by my mother and have no real loyalty to her. You're not blood related to the throne and can't inherit. End of the day, you're one of the pirates. Just like them. Disinherited. Disowned. A freed slave. Someone who has no use for the laws and traditions of any nation. *You*, the Universal Tavali Council will trust."

In that moment, Fain seriously hated the UTC.

"What about Chayden?" he asked Nykyrian. "Can't he do it?"

"Qillaq prince by blood whose full-blooded sister is the next queen of the Exeterian empire. Yeah . . . it's a no-go, too."

Nyk sat forward to pin him with an intense glare. "*You* have no real political ties to any throne and no blood loyalty to any single Tavali nation or group. You don't even run your own crew. Your only blood tie is to The Sentella and that, The Tavali trusts. Best of all, *we* trust you. Because you're an Andarion male with strong military ties, the Phrixians will follow you. There's no one else who can do this, Fain. You're in a unique position for it."

*Bloody effing awesome.*

The irony of it disgusted him. The very things that had ruined his life were now the very things that locked him into a position of power he'd never wanted.

"I can't work with her. She hates my guts, every individual one of them." He gestured to the blast mark on his battlesuit. "She shot me, Nyk. Point-blank. No warning. In the heart!"

"Well . . . we've all had the urge to shoot you, Fain. She just had the fun of it."

He mocked Nykyrian's misplaced humor. "And you want *her* to lead *your* army?"

Nykyrian nodded. "Besides, I'm told you're the only one she hates to this degree. Everyone else should be safe from her aim."

"You're not funny."

"I'm a little funny."

Fain growled at him. "You're an asshole."

"Is that the worst insult you can conceive for me? You're slipping in your old age."

Fain fanged him. But because they were such old friends, it didn't faze the bastard at all. "Is she willing to work with me? Or do I need to buy thicker armor?"

"I've been assured that she won't shoot you again."

"What about cutting my throat?"

"We didn't get that specific. Would you like me to draw up a contract, with her listing any and all possible ways she could end you and saying she won't?"

"I hate you." Fain sighed heavily. "Fine. I'll go get her and take them to the Posturnum. But if I die doing this, I plan to haunt you every day of eternity."

"Good. I won't miss you then."

Fain knocked on the door of Galene's condo. Only a block from the palace, it was one of the nicest buildings in the bustling metropolis of Eris—the Andarion capital city. The doorman had been a little skittish on his arrival, but since Fain had come in with an Andarion royal guard, he'd let Fain pass with nothing more than an irritated stare.

So what the hell was taking her so long to answer the door, anyway? Her condo couldn't be *that* big.

*She's doing it strictly to piss you off.*

Most likely.

He knocked again.

The door slid open to show her boytoy in nothing but a simple white towel. He had a blaster in one hand while he eyed them warily.

Anger boiled inside Fain at the sight. So she hadn't been lying. They really did live together.

*This day keeps getting better and better.*

Fain curled his lip. "I'm here for the commander."

Her boytoy sneered at him. "You should have called first."

"She was told to expect me."

"Not first thing in the morning." Grimacing at the group, the boytoy allowed Fain into the elegant condo, but not the others. He closed the door in their faces, and headed toward the kitchen, where he had a bowl of hot cereal set on the countertop. He placed his blaster beside it before he sat on a barstool and returned to eating.

"You have company, Commander."

At his disgruntled words, Galene leaned over the counter to see Fain. Dressed in a short lacy nightgown, she gaped, then pulled her robe closed and belted it. "What are you doing here?"

"I'm supposed to escort you to the Posturnum's HQ. Remember?"

"In an hour," she growled.

"What can I say? I couldn't wait to see you again."

She rolled her eyes at his sarcasm.

Her boytoy stood up and leaned over the counter to place his bowl in the sink. He met her gaze and arched a quizzical brow. "You want *me* to shoot him this time?"

She had the nerve to smile. "Don't tempt me, scamp." She moved his blaster away from his hand. "You should finish dressing."

"Yes, ma'am." He headed for the hallway.

"And don't leave your damp towel on the floor again. Hang it up."

Without a word, he jerked the towel off his hips and

tossed it at her. Completely naked, he passed a smug, taunting grin at Fain before he headed to the back of the condo.

Disgusted by his flagrant display, Fain wanted blood. It took everything he had not to go after the punk and teach him a valuable lesson in manners.

Laughing at they boy's actions, Galene took the towel into what must be the laundry room. She came out to add her own glare at Fain. "I wish you wouldn't antagonize him."

"*I* antagonize *him*? Are you serious?"

"Yes. I would think you're old enough to know better."

"But not him, huh?" Fain curled his lip. "Maybe you should sleep with someone closer to your own age."

She didn't respond as she headed for the hallway. "We'll be out in a minute."

Biting his lip, Fain had never been so furious in his entire life. It was actually painful.

As he waited and contemplated murdering them both, he drifted into the spacious living room that held an incredible view of the city. Something he would have appreciated more if he'd been in a better mood.

But right then, only bloodshed would placate him.

Trying to put it out of his mind, he swept his gaze over the contemporary furniture and noted the number of pictures in the place. More than that, he realized that the photos were *all* of her pet.

*Little effing bastard . . .*

He paused at one of her with the boytoy when the kid was a lot younger . . .

A *lot* younger. Like around six or seven, and dressed in a lorina costume for a play.

Scowling, Fain stepped closer to the frames that held the boy's graduation certificate, and an article from a sports magazine about him.

Talyn *Batur.*

*Oh dear gods, he's her son.*

*Shit! Talyn Batur.*

Talyn B-a-t-u-r, *the* Ring fighter of the century, was her only son. Her kid was an Andarion legend. That little bastard had also beaten every record Fain had set in the Ring. *Every* one of them. Records that no one had ever thought would be beaten by another fighter.

*And* that *is her son. Figures.*

He rubbed at his sore jaw. No wonder they called the kid the Iron Hammer. He definitely hit like one.

Disgusted with himself for how he'd behaved toward them, he sighed. *I'm such an idiot.* How could he have been so stupid?

But that thought ended as he noticed the date on the boy's graduation certificate.

If that was correct . . .

He scanned the certificate more closely. It was only a partial certificate because it was missing Talyn's paternal lineage.

*All* of his father's lineage.

Batur was *her* family name. And now that he looked closer at the photos of Talyn as a boy, Fain realized how much Talyn favored his nephew Darice. How much Talyn looked like him and Dancer.

*Ah shit.*

He tensed as he sensed a presence behind him. Turning, he saw Talyn there. Talyn, who was the same exact height and build he was.

The boy's gaze went past Fain to the certificate before he called out. "Hey, Ma! Dad just figured out how to do the math to calculate my age and date of conception. He's having some kind of apoplexy over it. I think you need to come in here before he pisses on your floor. And if he does, I did not do it, so don't yell at me for it."

Fain couldn't breathe as those words slammed into him like a hurricane.

*I have a son.*

He reached to touch the bruise he'd given Talyn yesterday during their fight.

His white eyes filled with hatred, Talyn pulled back and licked at the scab on his lip. "Don't touch me."

Galene hesitated in the doorway.

Completely aghast, Fain stared at her. "Why didn't you tell me?"

"I tried and you told me to shush, that you had much more pressing news."

Fain winced at the memory of her hurt expression that day in the dressing room. "That was what you wanted to tell me?"

"Yeah. Congratulations, Fain. You're a father."

And he'd told her that he was in love with another female. "No wonder you shoved me into that auditorium." He shook his head. "You still should have told me."

"Why? So that I'd be forced to marry a male in love with someone else? A human, no less. Call me provincial, but I wanted better than that."

Fain twisted the ring on his pinkie around with his thumb. Fate had seriously fucked him over.

No, fate had fucked all of them over.

"I'm so sorry, Galene."

"I'm not the one you need to apologize to." Her gaze went to Talyn.

His features were absolute stone.

Fain wanted to embrace him. It was a physical ache inside him to touch a son he'd never thought to have, but it was painfully obvious that Talyn wanted him to die on the spot. "I'm sorry, Talyn."

"There are some things sorry doesn't fix, old man. This is definitely one of them."

"I know. Believe me, I know." His heart shattering, Fain blinked against the tears that choked him as he thought about everything they'd all been deprived of.

Talyn met his mother's gaze. "I'll give you two the room."

As he started past her, Galene touched his arm. "Are you okay, baby?"

"I'm always fine, Matarra."

Galene winced. That wasn't true and she knew it. But it was the best she'd get out of him. Talyn never showed anyone his emotions. His childhood had been too brutal for that.

Without another word, her son headed for his room.

Her heart hammering, she watched as Fain scanned the other photos of Talyn over the years.

He met her gaze again. "I don't know what upsets me more. The number of times I made money off Talyn's wins, or the times I lost money betting someone would kill him in the Ring."

"Don't even talk to me about that, Fain. Or I *will* kill you where you stand. You've no idea how much I hated him fighting for a prestige that should have been his at birth. How many times I've paced a waiting room floor, praying he'd live through the injuries he'd sustained because he had no future without battling for it. And even then, he was never given his due, because he never had a real lineage to brag about." She clenched her teeth and glared at him. "Damn you for that."

Fain choked on the pain inside his heart. As a boy, he'd thought to trade his own life and future to save Dancer's. Instead, that "noble" action had cost his son his.

Galene's and Talyn's futures were not supposed to have been part of the bargain he'd made. Nothing had turned out the way it should have.

And never had he hated himself more.

"I can imagine what you've been through."

"No, Fain. You can't. Not really. You were always so popular. Everyone loved and adored you. Worshiped the ground the mighty War Hauk tread upon . . . Our son has never known that. No decent, self-respecting Andarion will socialize with him. At all. And the only female who will have anything to do with him is a paid companion he has set up in his condo, across town. I had to send him to school with Hyshians because they wouldn't let him attend an Andarion school with a broken lineage. Every door he reached for was brutally slammed, not in his face, but on his little hands."

He winced in response, and well he should.

"The Hyshian and human children weren't allowed to play with him because he was Andarion. And the Andarion children weren't allowed to talk to him because he was the bastard of a disinherited father. Do you know, he was even too humiliated to tell me that he'd finally broken down and paid for a mistress? Had he not been coldly shot down by his own commander—who hated *you*—and almost killed, I'd have never known he had *that* much in his life. And even then, because of his standing, her agency had refused to allow them to take anything more than a five-year, limited contract."

Fain ground his teeth. Every Andarion mistress he'd ever heard of or known would have sold her soul to make a life-long pact with a military officer. Especially one who held the second-highest rank in their armada, and wasn't fifty years old with it. Not to mention the fact that Talyn Batur was an intergalactic champion regaled by every known world who followed the Andarion Ring sport.

It sickened him to think of what his child had gone through because of him.

"If I'd had any inkling, Gay, I would have busted hell wide open to provide for both of you."

She let out a weary sigh. "It doesn't matter now, does it? We can't go back. We both have a hand in ruining our son's life."

"I don't know." He gestured at the trophies and awards on the shelves and wall. "You look like you've done an amazing job with him."

Galene looked away. Tears filled her eyes as she tried not to remember the past. "Every day, I ask myself if I could have done more."

Fain gave her a hard, harsh stare. "You're a much better mother than I ever had. At least you loved him. Protected him. You didn't eject him from your house and make him an Outcast who didn't dare step foot in any Andarion territory without a death sentence hanging over his head."

She swallowed at those words. Funny, she'd never thought of Fain that way. For all these years, he'd been a target for her hatred. She had never really considered how hard it'd been for him to be alone, without lineage.

Mostly because she hadn't cared. She'd wanted his life to be lived in total misery. Wanted him to pay for leaving her.

For leaving Talyn, and causing her baby harm.

Now that she knew he had, it didn't make her feel better as she'd thought it would.

It, too, made her sad.

"Having raised Talyn, I will never understand how my parents did me the way they did. Or what yours did to you. There's no way I could ever hurt him. Not intentionally."

"As I said, you're a much better mother than any I know. He was lucky to have you, Gay. The only thing he got shafted in was the father department, and for that I am *so* incredibly sorry."

"Commander?"

They both turned as Talyn rejoined them.

He handed a link to his mother. "There's been another attack."

Flinching, she took the link from him and left the room to answer the call.

Awkward silence filled the air between them as Talyn stared a brittle hole through him.

What did someone say to a grown child they'd never known they had?

All of a sudden, Fain had a whole new respect for Nykyrian, who'd been faced with this when his ex had dropped Thia on him out of the blue.

Uncomfortable, he cleared his throat. "Your mom said that you have a female?"

Talyn continued to stare at him.

"Does she have a name?"

A full and very slow minute went by before he answered. "Felicia."

"It's a beautiful name."

And still he glared at him. Damn. Forget Talyn's martial skills. That stare could let blood.

"How long have the two of you—"

"I don't talk about my personal life."

Fain nodded as he remembered reading that in a few different articles, over the years. It was something the media had beaten Talyn up over. The Iron Hammer didn't show his face in the Ring, or out of it. Nor did he speak of anything, other than his matches. The most the media had dragged out of him was that he liked to rock climb and camp on weekends. And that was *if* they could ever get an interview with him at all.

"Is there anything I can say to you that would end with us at least on friendly terms?"

Talyn shook his head. "Nothing comes to mind."

"Aren't you at least curious about me?"

Talyn snorted. "Not really."

"You've no questions whatsoever?"

"He's never asked any questions about you or your family," Galene said as she rejoined them. "Not even your name."

Fain didn't know why, but that hurt more than anything. "I see. We'll keep this strictly military, then. I'll stay out of both your ways, and you can contact me whenever you need me to relay orders to the Phrixians. Darling Cruel you can deal with directly. He has no problem taking orders from a female, as Jayne has bossed him around for years, and broke him in when he was young. If you need to contact one of his commanders, you can text me and I'll forward the orders. Most of The Tavali shouldn't have any problem with you. If they do give you any trouble, forward their names and I'll tell you who they answer to. You can easily deal with their four primary commanders, and if it helps, Ryn Cruel—Darling's older brother—is the son of Hermione Dane. She's the leader of the Wasternum, and she sits at the head of the UTC."

"UTC?"

"Universal Tavali Council. She goes by Kirren and you will need that name to get through to her. It's her code name, reserved only for those closest to her. All The Tavali operate that way. It's how we keep outsiders and spies from knowing anything about us."

Talyn narrowed his gaze on him. "What name do you use? Faithless?"

Fain let the insult go. "I don't. I'm what's called a rogue."

"And that is?"

He returned Talyn's glare with an equally cold look. "Someone with no family or country allegiance. What Andarions affectionately call an Outcast, only The Tavali don't try to kill us on sight."

Galene glanced away as she caught the pain that flashed into Fain's eyes. She shouldn't care.

At all. And yet she did.

*Because I used to love him.*

Maybe. And maybe it was because Talyn favored him so much that it was her love of her son that made her more sympathetic to the man he took after.

Yeah, she'd go with that, for now.

Fain tapped at his ear. "Yeah?" he said to whomever was calling. He waited several seconds before he spoke again. "We'll be right there." He met her gaze. "Your guard is on board and waiting with my crew. If you two are ready, we can be on our way."

As they started for the door, Talyn tapped his ear. "Hey, is something wrong?" He placed his finger against the link and frowned as he listened intently. He led them out to the hallway. "You need me to call for you?"

Fain duplicated Talyn's frown in a disturbingly similar manner. "Is he okay?"

Galene nodded as they headed for the lifts. "He's talking to Felicia."

"How do you know?"

"The warm concern in his voice and the amount of concentration he's giving the caller. The gentleness of his tone. He only talks to her like that." She led them into the lift.

"Honey, listen, if you need me to, I don't mind. I've still got a few before we're at the bay." Talyn completely ignored everyone else as he followed them in. "Yeah, okay. But if they give you any problem at all, let me know and I'll deal with them. I mean it. No one disregards you like that. Ever. I will totally bust their asses for it."

His features softened and he closed his eyes as if he was savoring whatever she was saying to him. "Yeah, me, too. I'll check in when I can. Stay safe." He lowered his hand and turned instantly stern again.

"Is everything all right?" Galene asked.

He gave a curt military nod before he elaborated. "The pool monitors went out and the company was harassing Lish because her name isn't on the account. She wanted to make sure it was okay to add herself to it." A fierce tic started in his jaw.

Fain pulled Galene aside in the lobby while the others went to the transports. "Why's he so angry about a pool company?"

She gave him a dry stare. "Why do you think, Fain? He can't pledge marriage or legally contract a mistress. So he, who is the second-highest-ranking member of the Andarion military, is forced to be bound by curfew and barracks restrictions. The only way to keep him out of a barracks is if he lives with the commander he serves . . . his own mother. Meanwhile, the mistress he has an unofficial contract with is left to tend his home with companies that don't want to deal with either of them because they both lack paternal lineage."

"Why doesn't he get out of the military, then?"

"And do what? He's the bastard son of a disinherited War Hauk. Who would hire him or deal with him in the private sector? The fighting schools wouldn't even allow him, the Iron Hammer, to train other fighters."

"Then allow me to adopt him. As his father, I can give him full protection of the royal house. He'd be an eton Anatole then, and no one would dare to look him in the eye, never mind say anything unkind to him."

"I will gladly allow it. But it's not up to me, is it? And it won't undo all the humiliation he's been put through since birth. You were raised with two of the most prestigious bloodlines on all of Andaria flowing through your veins. Andarions gravitated toward you in school. Everyone wanted to be *your* friend."

She jerked her chin toward Talyn, who was waiting for them on the curb. "With my noble family lineage and yours in his veins, he should have been a higher caste than even you were growing up. Instead, he was spat on and laughed at. Denied and degraded by those who aren't even fit to be speaking directly to him. I'm not the one you need to win over, Fain. He is."

Fain ground his teeth as Galene left him to join their son. She was right. He could see the way the other Andarions looked at Talyn. Even though he was a titled champion and their commander, they still showed their contempt for him. Something they would have never dared to do to a War Hauk.

"You okay?"

He nodded as Dancer joined him. Then he shook his head. "I can't believe I screwed over my own son."

"You didn't know."

"It doesn't change anything, does it?"

Dancer sighed. "I'm sorry, Fain."

So was he. "Can you do me a favor?"

"Anything."

"Find out who this Felicia is that he's contracted with." Maybe she could give him some insight into Talyn.

The one thing he'd learned over the years was that any male's weakness was always the female he loved. Talyn might hate him, but he would listen to her.

If Fain could win her over, he might be able to start building a relationship with Talyn. It was at least worth a try.

"Do you have her full name?" Dancer asked.

"No. She's living in Talyn's condo. That's all I know about her."

"Oh well, by all means, make it easy on me, why don't you?"

He gave his brother an irritated smirk. "If I knew more about her, I wouldn't be asking you for information. I'd find it myself."

Dancer fanged him. "You really suck as a brother."

"Yeah, well, you should have to deal with mine."

Rolling his eyes, Dancer got in behind Talyn, who sat beside his mother.

Fain sat across from them.

While they rode, he noted the way Talyn kept checking his link and biting back a smile while he covertly texted with his female.

Yeah, his son loved her. Dearly. She was the key to his heart.

And sadly, both Galene and Talyn, the two beings who hated him most, were the keys to his.

While he'd regretted much of his life, there was nothing he regretted more than having walked away from them. But he'd had no choice. Had he stayed, Dancer would have been killed.

His brother still bore those scars that had forced his hand. Now . . .

*I* will *make this right.* He had no idea how, but he would find a way. Even if it killed him.